The Deepest Night

The Deepest Night

Shana Abé

BANTAM BOOKS   NEW YORK

Copyright © 2013 by Five Rabbits, Inc.

Published in the United States by Bantam Books, an imprint of The Random House Publishing Group, a division of Random House, Inc., New York.

BANTAM BOOKS and the HOUSE colophon are registered trademarks of Random House, Inc.

Library of Congress Cataloging-in-Publication Data
Abé, Shana.
   The deepest night : a novel / Shana Abé
      pages cm
   ISBN 978-0-345-53173-5 (acid-free paper)—ISBN 978-0-345-53174-2 (ebook) [1. Supernatural—Fiction. 2. Magic—Fiction.
3. Hospitals—Fiction. 4. Prisoners of war—Germany—Fiction.
5. Rescues—Fiction. 6. Great Britain—History—George V,
1910–1936—Fiction.] I. Title.
   PZ7.A158935Dee 2013
   [Fic]—dc23   2013000810

Printed in the United States of America on acid-free paper

www.bantamdell.com

1 2 3 4 5 6 7 8 9

First Edition

Book design by Elizabeth Cosgrove

To you, again

Prologue

I'm not a ghost. I am dead, though.

My body lies in its casket underneath the pale sandy sod and wind-scrubbed grass of southern England, not far from where I was born. The marker for my grave looks much like all the others in the cemetery, plain gray stone, chiseled edges. Chiseled letters spelling out my name and significant dates, and a single phrase beneath all that about the salvation of hope.

Most visitors to the cemetery walk by it without a second glance; they have memories of their own dead clouding their minds. If anything, they might make note of my age when I perished—seventeen— and feel a hint of fresh sadness whisper by, thinking something like *Poor lad*, or *Tsk! His poor mum.*

Seventeen is young to most of them. Seventeen is a short sigh of years, barely time enough to taste the bitter joy of life, the ashen loss of death. Seventeen reminds them uncomfortably of how their own years are ticking down to a final, finite number.

But again, most people don't bother to look or figure the math. And with the Great War still raging on, the death of a young man isn't nearly as notable as it used to be, even in the countryside. It's an old cemetery laid out along a hill above an even older fishing village, and mine is just one more grave amid all the generations of others.

On the surface, that is.

Three feet straight out from the front of my marker and seven inches more straight down into the dirt—curiously enough, directly above my face, although I'm fairly certain that was coincidence—is buried a flower.

It's a buttercup, and it's made of solid gold.

I should know. I'm the one who made it, back in my mortal life. I used my earthly magic to transform it from a living thing into a golden dead one, and I gave it to the girl I loved, who has now given it back to me. In her own way.

I'm not a ghost. I am a star. I spin a celestial magic now high, high above her, waiting for her to take notice and hear me.

Because she's not a girl, really.

Actually, not at all.

She's a dragon.

Poor lass. She only just found that out.

The Deepest Night

Chapter 1

From: Mrs. Charles Westcliffe, headmistress, Iverson School for Girls
To: Mr. H. W. Forrester, former director, Blisshaven Foundling Home

May 18, 1915

Sir,

I hope this letter finds you in fine health and your new state of affairs satisfactory. I wish to express again my condolences for the loss of the Blisshaven Foundling Home. No doubt it was an excellent institution, and the orphaned children of the British Empire were privileged indeed to have found shelter there during its eighty-four years of existence. It was with great dismay that I learned of its destruction in a German air raid. Thank goodness for the government's decision to evacuate London's vulnerable young residents months before.

Perhaps you've heard that we also have had a brush with the

*kaiser's dreadful zeppelins! Happily, the school remains unscathed
and my charges unharmed.*

*However, I am writing once again to inquire as to the summer
circumstances of the pupil you sent me, Miss Eleanore Jones. I fear
I must point out that this is my third letter to you regarding her, and
I still await your response. Her schedule simply must be sorted soon.
The summer holiday is approaching and she absolutely cannot remain at the school during this time, as it will be closed but for a
small skeleton staff.*

*There is also, frankly, the question of whether it will be suitable
for Miss Jones to return for her final academic year with us at all.
Although her marks have proven adequate and her unexpected
musical gifts were a welcome surprise, she is, if you'll forgive the expression, rather a fish out of water here.*

*I realize this news will cause you no undue astonishment. Her
history as an orphan of unknown origins was certain to set her apart
from the other young women in attendance, all of whom descend
from the most prominent families of the empire. Her year spent in-
voluntarily confined to the Moor Gate Institute for Socially Af-
flicted Youth [although maintained as a strict secret between me
and select members of my staff, I assure you!] has indubitably only
enhanced these differences.*

*Miss Jones has made few friends and garnered what I might
charitably call the unlikely attention of a particular young man of
noble blood. It is a relationship that is entirely inappropriate and
rife with unfortunate possibilities. I'm sure you understand.*

*To be very blunt, our patron, the Duke of Idylling, is no longer in
residence at his manor nearby. His situation remains delicate, and
thus far I have been unable to ascertain if he wishes to continue the
scholarship for Miss Jones. I do not believe that his son, the Mar-*

quess of Sherborne, has the proper authority to decide her case, despite what he claims.

Kindly inform me of where to send this child come June. Most sincerely,

Mrs. C. Westcliffe
Headmistress, Iverson

Once there were dragons everywhere. Knit from the bones of the earth and the glory of the heavens, they hovered in the Divide, that thin wedge of existence that separates feral, untamed magic from safe, tamed lives.

They glistened metallic bright, thin as whips and swift as lightning. They scored the skies with wings and claws but walked on land as well, able to assume the shape of their mortal enemies—humans—when they wished. To live among them in human disguise.

They called themselves the *drákon.*

They hunted and fed. They wed and bred. Throughout history, human and *drákon* destinies entwined, but it was only humans who scribbled down the tales: about how dragons devoured crops or babies or virgins (one French anecdote I read swore they preferred truffles) and apparently were never quite smart enough to avoid being hacked to death by blokes in shining armor.

Then the *drákon* vanished. Just like that. Extinction came and ate them up like they were even more delicious than a virgin carrying a baby carrying a truffle through a wheat field.

Or so I surmised. Because as far as I could tell, there were only two of us left in this great and awful year of 1915, and ruddy little information to be found about even us two. Up until a short while ago, we both thought we were as human as anyone else.

But no.

There was me: Eleanore Jones, orphaned, impoverished, a slum girl scholarship student from the ghettos of London somehow improbably attending the prestigious Iverson School for Girls.

And the other, a boy as opposite my guttersnipe background as could be: Lord Armand Louis, the Most Honourable Marquess of Sherborne.

For a few short days and nights of my life, there had been Jesse, too. He wasn't a dragon. He was much, much more dazzling than that.

But I couldn't think about him yet.

Not yet.

So this is what you need to know first:

Ages ago, off the wild and jagged coast of Wessex, England, a stubborn fist of limestone and forest eroded from the mainland to become an island with no name. An island that sometimes wasn't even an island.

When the moon pulled just so, the island would shrink, surrounded by the blue salty waters of the Channel.

When the moon let go, the isle grew dry again, a mountain sitting on golden sand.

Ages after that, someone thought to build a castle upon it. The warlords then needed constant eyes to keep watch over the boats and tides, to stave off invasion by the barbarians who dwelled just across the sea.

The island had no name, but the castle had always been called

Iverson. It was vast and eerie and composed of things like turrets and battlements and Gothic buttresses. It had a domed glass conservatory, a haunted grotto, and secret tunnels hollowed through its walls. Most significant, it had me and about a hundred other girls within it, plus a scattering of stern-faced teachers and staff. Iverson had been my home for approximately two months, ever since I'd been sent there from the orphanage in London because the Germans were bombing everything in sight.

(The orphanage, by the way, had been called Blisshaven, and you can imagine how appropriate *that* name was. Iverson's headmistress informed me that it'd been blown to bits four weeks after I'd left. I'd stolen a bottle of fine Riesling from her cellar that very night to celebrate its demise.)

My world of late had become a tumbling kaleidoscope of color and change. For the first time in my memory, I had a home of sorts. I had a room of my own. I had enough to eat. I had fellow students who nearly tolerated me, and one in particular who loathed me. I had the zealous attention of a handsome lord, whether I wished it or not—which had everything to do with the tolerating and the loathing.

And I had known true love. Then lost it.

"*Dear* Eleanore, blue-deviled *again*! How absolutely refreshing."

Lady Sophia Pemington, the only girl at Iverson who would voluntarily be seen with me, plopped down in the chair next to mine at the library table and regarded me with her icy pale eyes. She was something of a mystery to me, a queen-of-the-class-at-any-cost type who still showed flashes of occasional generosity. She was also ruthlessly cunning—a trait I couldn't help but admire, since we shared it. In another life, we might have been genuine friends.

"You know, my nanny would say that if you aren't careful, your face will freeze like that."

"Like what?" I asked.

Sophia screwed her features into an expression that could only be described as tragic, with sad pouty lips and woefully wrinkled eyebrows. She rubbed a hand across her hair, freeing flaxen strands from her normally tidy chignon.

I closed the French grammar text I'd been pretending to study and leaned back in my chair. The library at Iverson was properly tall and stately, trimmed in mahogany and polished brass and drowsy, post-luncheon students. Afternoon sunlight streaked through the stained-glass windows behind me, painting the table and my hands and Sophia, blue and amber and red.

"Is that supposed to be me?"

The lips grew poutier.

"My hair isn't that messy," I pointed out.

"Now," she emphasized, dropping the face. "You should have seen yourself after—"

And Lady Sophia, who normally had all the tender instincts of a barracuda, stopped herself short. Even she knew some subjects were forbidden.

"I'm sorry," she said. "I didn't mean—"

"Of course not." I pushed to my feet. "Excuse me."

But I'd stood up too quickly, and had to sway there a moment with my hands gripping the chair until the gray spinning fog cleared from my vision.

I'd been shot not long ago, you see. Shot more than once. It turned out that even dragons masquerading as girls needed time to recuperate from serious blood loss.

Sophia had a hand on my arm; she actually looked concerned. "Don't be a ninny. I wasn't trying to chase you off."

"No," murmured a new someone, just to our right. "You haven't sense enough for that."

Lady Chloe Pemington, brunette and gorgeous and a year older than her stepsister and I, had paused in a particularly brilliant patch of painted light. She granted us both a bloodred smile.

"Do have a care, darling sister. I've heard that once one touches true filth, it's *ever* so hard to get clean again."

"Well, that certainly explains your mouth," I said. "Although it does make one wonder what you've been putting in it."

"Not Lord Armand," Sophia noted, which was really the best possible blow, because everyone knew that Chloe loved Armand, and had for years. She loved his enormous manor house and his family connections and his automobiles and his servants and most especially his glamorous future as a rich-rich-rich duke.

But Armand, it seemed, had finally noticed the tin beneath her gilt. Most of the other students were of the opinion that he was falling in love with me.

They had no idea we shared a bond far stranger and darker than that.

Chloe's eyes had gone to slits. "How dare—"

I flicked a hand at her, cutting her off. "Oh, marvelous. Are you about to go on about me daring things again? Truly? I'd think you'd have a new diatribe by now."

Mrs. Westcliffe, the school's headmistress, entered the library with a staccato clicking of heels and a rustling of black organdy skirts. She spotted us at once and paused, her gaze keen and her shoulders stiff; the three of us together could only mean trouble.

Chloe drew in a long breath through her nose. She exhaled, took a step closer to Sophia and me, and brought back the red smile.

"Soon *we* shall be off enjoying the summer, holidaying with all the very *best* people, attending dances and dinner parties and living the kind of life you will only ever read about in the rag sheets. And where shall *you* be, Eleanore? Which lice-ridden dosshouse shall be taking *you* in?"

"One with only the very *best* lice," I whispered back to her, but she was already swishing away.

Nightfall on the island nearly always meant velvet skies swept with stars, and the Channel filling the air with the tang of salt, and the slow, rhythmic drumbeat of waves crashing against the rocky shore.

As a child in London, I'd never smelled the sea, nor seen the heavens so spangled. I'd never known nights any hue other than black or brown or sooty gray, but here they came saturated in color. Navy, sapphire, indigo. And, very rarely: deep, pure amethyst.

An amethyst sky had welcomed me the first night I'd set foot upon the isle. It had reappeared for my first visit to Jesse in his cottage in the woods, and again for the night I'd been shot and Jesse had died.

It shone past my window on this night as well. It was a purple so thick and luminous I might well believe something Other than nature had created it. Something magical.

Less than a year ago I would have laughed at the thought. Tonight, though . . . tonight I wondered.

I leaned out past the sill of my room's sole window, surveying the stars. My hair was unpinned, draping over my shoulders to tickle my crossed arms. In direct sunlight it looked an ordinary pale mousy brown, but when I glanced down at it now, I was unsurprised to see it had gone almost as purple as the heavens. It did that, taking on other tints, reflecting back whatever color was near, especially pink. I'd thought perhaps it was a dragon trait, but since Armand's hair always seemed to be the same glossy chestnut, I couldn't be sure.

My eyes were like that, too. Changeable. Lavender gray most of the time . . . except, apparently, when they flashed incandescent. I'd never seen it happen—I guess I'd have to be looking in a mirror—but Armand and Jesse had told me about it.

I was sixteen years old, more or less. It was peculiar to think of my own body as a stranger, but it was. I was learning new things about it nearly every day.

The room assigned to me at Iverson encompassed the top floor of one of the smaller stone turrets. It was round and crammed wall to wall with just a bed, an armoire, and a bureau. The other girls at the school all shared lavish suites bedecked in jeweled glass and rosewood and lace, but I didn't think any of that compared to what I had been given: Privacy. Solitude. A window glazed in a thousand diamond pieces, with hinges that worked and a view to the sea and the mainland bridge beyond.

And the stars.

Oh, the stars, twinkling and winking at me.

come out, they sang, a celestial chorus only I could hear. *come out, beast. come fly to us.*

Somewhere belowstairs, from one of the parlors perhaps, a clock began to chime, followed by a cascade of others.

Midnight. Perfect.

I stepped back from the window so my nightshirt wouldn't blow away, took a deep breath, and Turned to smoke.

I'm not sure how best to describe what it's like. Imagine all the weight of your body, all those heavy pounds of muscle and bone and fat, abruptly melted away. *You* still exist, but you're vapor. Diaphanous coils, elegant and twisting, lighter than air. You can see and hear, even control your direction. You're not cold or warm. You feel no physical pain.

Only the hunger to fly.

This is the first step to Becoming a dragon.

As smoke, you can sift through an open window, float out past the walls of a castle. You can spread yourself as thin as sea spray or bunch up thick like a cloud. You can rise and rise and hear the stars more clearly than ever before, pulling at you, celebrating you. Humming and praising.

You belong to them; they belong to you. And there will always be an aching, festering fragment of you that yearns to just keep going up, forever and ever. To never touch the earth again.

I glided over the smooth manicured lawn fronting the castle, the tidy rose gardens and the sinister huge hedges that had all been pruned into animal shapes, wolves and lions and unicorns. I might well have been an odd sliver of mist, or the creeping fog that uncurled from the woods to slink along the grounds. Except I moved as nothing else did.

I left Iverson behind me, soaring farther into the forested center of the island. Black spiky crowns of birch and beech skipped past, their leaves flashing purple. Meadows opened up and closed again. If I dipped too low, the forest's branches would tear me into pieces. It wouldn't hurt, but it wouldn't be especially pleasant, either. I made certain to remain above the trees.

As compelling as the stars' songs were, I had a different goal in mind tonight besides just flight.

I knew the way to the cottage by heart. It sat alone and empty in an uncivilized portion of the woods, a place none of the other students would dream to venture. As far as I could tell, none of the staff came out here, either. The windows were shuttered. The door was locked, but it was wooden and old and no longer quite fit the jamb. The gaps were easily wide enough for smoke to slide through.

I Turned back to girl on its other side. Nude. Chilled.

I didn't like to linger here. It might have been my imagination or just a depressing truth, but the air inside Jesse's cottage was still scented of him, and I didn't like to breathe it. I think deep down I was worried that one day I'd breathe it all gone, and that would be the last of him. The last time I remembered his fragrance.

I removed a shirt and trousers from his closet, got dressed, and left by the door—then doubled back when I realized I'd forgotten the shovel stored by the woodshed. None of Jesse's boots fit me, so I went barefoot along the trail that wrapped around the cottage and vanished into the trees.

Leaves and grass folded soft beneath my soles. The tip of the shovel made a soft *chuck* into the ground with my every other step. A breeze slipped by in fits and starts, ringing me in the perfume of wildflowers and bracken and mossy logs.

It was bloody dark. But I was able to find my way by memory . . . and by following the subtle, lilting music that was gradually growing louder ahead.

Dragons hear all manner of music that humans don't. It was one of the reasons I'd spent a year of my life imprisoned in the hell of Moor Gate, because I kept asking the adults around me to explain all the unending songs. Songs from the stars, of course. But also from metals. From stones. Songs from stickpins or emeralds or iron bars, each one unique, strident or gentle, a ballad or a symphony—the music never ceased.

Not even when I was given the electrical shock treatments.

Not even when they submerged me in the ice baths.

Not even the morning they'd killed me because they could, and then forced my dead heart to beat again.

The music I followed tonight was muffled, because it emanated from several feet underground. I stopped finally at a tall rowan tree, leaned the shovel against it, and sat down at its base. I eased back against the trunk, dug my toes into the peat, and waited.

It wasn't too much longer before footsteps approached.

Chapter 2

"Miss Jones," Armand greeted me, winding his way through a strand of whispering beeches.

"Your Grace," I answered.

"Not quite. That's still my father."

My eyes had adjusted to the night by then, and I was able to make out the pale folds of his scarf, the ghostly outlines of his face and hands against his linen duster.

He would have driven from his mansion on the mainland to as far as the island bridge, then walked the rest for stealth. I wondered that he hadn't gotten hot in that coat.

"Your . . . lordiness. Whatever you are now. I don't know the proper address for a marquess, I suppose."

"Lord Sherborne," he supplied smoothly, coming close to the rowan. "Or simply *my lord*. But you can call me *sweetheart*."

"I don't believe I will."

His teeth flashed in the gloom; I'd made him smile. "We'll see."

Armand had nearly everything in the world he could possibly want. He had money, social status, and inhumanly good looks. His family owned the castle and the island the castle sat upon, along with most of the mainland nearby. He lived in a monstrosity of a manor house perversely named Tranquility, a few miles inland. He was intelligent, brooding, and dangerously magnetic in that way somehow unique to young men born to power. He'd been booted out of Eton twice and I still couldn't think of a single girl at Iverson who wouldn't give her right arm—or, more specifically, her left-hand ring finger—to him at the drop of one of his expensive hats.

Especially since his older brother, the previous Marquess of Sherborne, had been so accommodating as to go and get himself killed in the war. So the future Mrs. Armand was guaranteed a duchess's coronet.

I used to think it was selfishness or just boredom that had him constantly showing up at Iverson to seek me out. The desire to rebel against his father and Westcliffe and all the sticky spiderwebs of rules that entangled us both. I was hardly a seemly companion for the son of a duke, and everyone knew it, especially me.

Then we'd found out. About being dragons, I mean. And about how it would be in his nature to hunt me like this till the end of time.

I don't know which of us was more appalled.

But Armand's *drákon* blood was thinner than mine, and his powers were only just emerging. He couldn't Turn to smoke or dragon yet, so at least I had the advantage over him there. He knew if he pushed too far, I'd Turn and leave.

"Bloody dark," he commented, settling down beside me. He was holding something bulky in his hands.

"I hadn't noticed."

"Really?" He stilled. "Is that a dragon trait? You can see in the dark?"

Now I was the one smiling, though I was glad he couldn't tell. "No, my lord. It *is* bloody dark."

"In that case . . ." He rummaged through the bulky thing, and suddenly I smelled cheese and salty olives and bread and smoked fish.

"Good God," I said, my mouth beginning to water. "Did you bring a picnic?"

"A small something, perhaps. And . . ."

And a lantern, as it happened. He struck a match; the delicious food scent was briefly overwhelmed by sulphur, and then the amethyst shadows retreated against a small yellow glow.

"That's better," he said.

I drew my knees up to my chest. "Someone might see."

"Who the devil," Armand responded cordially, replacing the lantern's glass, "is going to *see* all the way out here in the middle of nowhere in the middle of the night? I'm not going to attempt to eat Russian caviar in the dark, Eleanore. It stains. And this is a new coat."

"Very well."

He sent me a glance from beneath his lashes. With the light cast up from below, he was all stark jawline and cheekbones and diabolical dark brows. I saw the dragon in him then as clear as could be. Only his eyes were reassuringly familiar: rich cobalt blue, the color of oceans, of heaven's heart.

"Hungry?" he asked, soft.

There was an implication in his tone that he meant for something other than food.

"I've never had caviar," I said deliberately.

His gaze fell from mine. "Then I'm honored to be the one to offer it to you now."

And that is how I discovered that caviar is one of the most purely revolting substances ever to exist. I actually had to spit it out and wipe my tongue clean with a fresh piece of bread to get the disgusting fish-jelly flavor out of my mouth.

"Charming." Armand was smearing more onto his own bread with a delicate silver knife. "Glad to know all those lessons in deportment aren't being wasted."

"What josser was the first person to slit open a sturgeon and see a slimy blob of eggs and think, *Right, I'm going to eat that*?" I swiped again at my tongue. "I never thought there existed a food I wouldn't like, but you, my lord, have proven me wrong."

"A first!"

"And last. What else did you bring?"

Ten minutes later, I realized I was the only one still eating. Crickets had begun to chirp sleepily from the bracken, filling the silence. I glanced up to discover Armand watching me, his face shadow-sharp and inscrutable. The last of the bread and olives lay untouched by his feet.

"Westcliffe doesn't want you coming back next year," he said abruptly.

I brushed some crumbs from my shirt. "That's hardly a revelation. She thinks I'm your doxy."

"She's sent letter after letter to Reginald, implying it's time to find a new scholarship girl. To cut you loose."

Reginald was the duke, and my sponsor at the school. I'd only ever heard Armand refer to him as "dad" once. Right after His Grace had tried to murder me.

"What does he write back?" I asked.

"Nothing, so far. I'm afraid all her letters have been regretfully mislaid."

I smiled, shaking my head. "You can't keep that up."

"No, I know. Eleanore—Lora—listen."

But he didn't say anything else, just kept staring at me, fierce. The flame of the lantern maintained its small, steady burn between us.

Crickets. Leaves rustling. Very dimly: the surging pulse of the sea.

"Don't worry." I tried to sound confident; I was an excellent liar, but Armand had a hardness to him that wasn't easily fooled. "They'll probably send me to another orphanage, but just for the summer. It won't be for long, and I'll be fine. You know I'm not nearly as helpless as I seem. I'll land on my feet, no matter where I end up."

"Another orphanage—or worse."

"No." I was pleased my voice didn't crack. "That won't happen, I assure you."

Hell would freeze over first. The moon would plunge from the sky, cats would bark, and dogs would weep tears of rubies and pearls. I would never, ever return to Moor Gate, or any place like it. I would never let demented people like that have control over me again.

Armand ran a hand through his hair, leaving a muss. "There is another option. We get married. You stay with me."

My attention zagged back to him; I'm sure my mouth had fallen open. "Married."

"Yes. Kindly try not to sound so horrified."

I covered my lips with both hands, then forced myself to drop them to my lap. "You—you're not of age yet."

"I will be in a month."

"Well, *I'm* not of age yet. I haven't the faintest idea when I'll be eighteen."

He frowned. "You don't know how old you are?"

"No. I don't even know my birthday."

"How could you celebrate it if you don't . . . ?"

I only looked at him.

"Oh. Right. Orphanage."

"And the fact that I have no memory of my life before 1909. The only thing I know about myself at all is that I was born on a steamship. And only because Jesse told me that, and the stars told *him*."

Armand picked up a fat green olive and held it between his finger and thumb, glaring down at it. "The stars, of course. Always the bloody damned stars." He flicked the olive to the trees, and all the crickets went quiet.

Jesse had been a star. *Of* the stars, human-born but with all the sorcery of the firmament rushing through his veins. He'd been a creature caught between realms, like us, and had recognized what Armand and I were long before we two did.

Everyone at Iverson assumed Jesse Holms to have been nothing more than the simple hired hand he'd pretended to be. But he'd become my light and my guide into my *drákon* Gifts. It was because of him that the stars now spoke to me, instead of just singing their wordless songs.

"Don't you hear them yet?" I asked gently.

"Yes, I hear them. I just don't like what I hear." Armand climbed to his feet, slapping noisily at the folds of his coat. "Look, waif, I haven't got all night. I have to wake up early for another excruciatingly instructive meeting with my farms manager about some cows or something, so let's get this over with. Did you bring the shovel?"

I rose to my own feet, lifting a hand to indicate the shovel, obviously just beside me.

He grabbed it, said, "Let's go," and moved off without another look.

I collected the lantern and the picnic basket and followed him. Neither of us really needed illumination to find the place where I'd buried my chest of gold a few weeks before, but I didn't want to leave any evidence of our meeting behind.

Like me, Armand heard the music of the metal and strode straight to it.

I'd chosen an area that looked like any other in the woods, littered with decomposing leaves and pine needles, a few handy ferns growing lush and random around it. Oak roots pushed through ivy and peat, sinking gnarled tendrils all the way down into the bedrock.

There was a gap in the root system exactly wide enough for the chest. A little too far in any direction, and a treasure seeker would end up just slashing at wood.

Armand sank the shovel into the perfect center of the proper spot.

I would have done the digging myself, but he'd insisted. I hadn't told him, but the truth was that burying the chest in the first place had made me so ill I'd actually passed out. I kept forgetting I was supposed to be on the mend.

"I've counted every piece," I warned him, watching the shovel jab in, lift out, great mounds of moss and dirt piled to the side.

He didn't glance up. "You think I'd steal from you?"

"Only once."

"Your faith in me is gratifying."

"Not especially wifelike, I presume?"

The shovel stabbed extra deep; his voice came ironic. "No. Not especially."

Minutes later the blade thunked into the lid of the chest, and all the gold song within went sharp in response. Armand straightened, tossed the shovel aside, and clambered out of the shallow hole.

"All yours," he said with a sweep of his hand.

I lay flat on my stomach at the edge and reached down. The chest had no lock—I hadn't thought there'd be a point to locking it, and anyway, I'd nicked it from Jesse's cottage and didn't have the key—so all I had to do was lift the iron tongue of the latch to raise the lid.

It was hard not to gasp. My treasure was *beautiful*, it really was. Gold glimmered and sang and gleamed up at me, magnificent even in the feeble light. But since it had come from Jesse, not pirates, it wasn't anything ordinary like ingots or doubloons.

It was a jumble of solid gold branches and acorns and leaves, pinecones and flowers. It was the work of a naturalist, of an alchemist who had lived amid nature, who had appreciated the unspoken splendor of the wild.

Jesse'd been able to transform any living thing into gold, another secret he'd taken to his grave. The contents of this chest had been his final gift to me.

So technically I wasn't impoverished any longer. I had all this. And I had it out here in the forest because there were maids and enemies and no locks on any of the doors at Iverson, and no reason on earth for an urchin like me to possess anything of value, much less a collection of sculpted golden objects.

Armand kept his distance. I could hear his heartbeat, though, how it had quickened at the sight of the treasure, a cadence that matched my own and the precise tempo of the music that lifted from the chest.

"Hurry," he urged, low.

I picked up one of the pinecones. It was on top of the tangle, a cool and heavy weight in my hand. I scrambled back from the edge and held it out for Armand to see.

"Will this do?"

He nodded, not even looking at it. "Done?"

"Yes."

He bent down and grabbed the shovel again.

It wasn't until the hole was filled once more, the music muted, and we were on our knees carefully rescattering the old leaves and needles that Armand sat back on his heels and spoke.

"Jesse's gone, Lora. Gone forever. Nothing can change that."

"I know." I crumbled a clod of dirt between my fingers, watching it dissolve into dust. "But we can't help whom we love."

Armand sighed, bitter. "No. We can't."

I awoke the next morning in time for breakfast, which was a relief. I was always hungry, and oversleeping meant I'd have to wait until luncheon for food. By then I'd be seeing spots from lack of nourishment.

Apparently my *drákon* metabolism wasn't quite as ladylike as might be hoped. Respectable young Englishwomen barely bothered to eat; the other girls at Iverson only nibbled at their meals and whined about their too-tight corsets. I, on the other hand, ate so much I had to hide it from Mrs. Westcliffe, and half the time I snuck about with no corset at all.

That fact alone was probably enough to get me booted from the school.

Did you hear about that tramp Eleanore? It turns out she was running around stark naked *beneath her clothes!*

Well, not entirely. I did usually bother with a chemise, because otherwise I got cold.

I rolled from my bed. My feet hit the stone chill of the floor and I hastened to the wardrobe, pulling open the doors to survey what I had to wear today.

Five white long-sleeved shirtwaists, all identical. Five dark plum slender skirts, also identical. Five sets of plain black stockings; ten garters. One pair of black buttoned shoes.

We all wore the same uniform at Iverson, society girls and slum girls alike. To be frank, it was a relief not to have to don my shabby Blisshaven clothes for class, even though I did still have to resort to them for the weekends. Sometimes it was just easier to mix with the herd.

A hard rap sounded on my door. It opened before I could respond, and Gladys, the maid appointed to my room, walked in with a pitcher of fresh water.

"Oh," she said, unenthusiastic. "You're up, then."

I smiled at her. She brought the pitcher to the bureau and plunked it down hard, sloshing water across the wood.

"What time is it?" I asked sweetly.

"Sorry, miss." She dried her hands on her apron, avoiding my eyes. "Been so busy, I forgot to look at the clock."

One of Gladys's tasks was to ensure that I was awake before breakfast was served. So far, she'd not managed it once, and that was not an accident.

Scholarship students were never local girls. I could have tried to explain to her that it wouldn't have mattered even if the duke hadn't set that rule; that a slippery combination of destiny and magic had brought me here to the castle, not just dumb luck.

But Gladys was skinny and hostile and too old inside for someone who was only about twenty. I'd wager she'd lost any last faith in magic the day she'd needed money badly enough to take this job.

Should she and Chloe ever join evil forces, I might be in real trouble. Fortunately, Lady Chloe stooping to converse with a common housemaid was about as likely as Kaiser Wilhelm showing up bearing roses at our door.

"Thank you," I said brightly to Gladys's back as she stomped out of the room.

I tried to be nice to her. Usually. I'd hate working here, too.

What Iverson lacked in electricity, enough water closets, and proper heating, it made up for in grandeur. The chambers were all done up in burnished fixtures and sinuous furniture. The staircases were of carved marble, the rugs were plush, the paintings massive and ornate.

Our dining hall was the original great room of the castle, a space so huge that the sunbeams slanting in from the windows barely reached its center, thick slices of light that blinded you on and off as you passed through them and struck rainbows from the crystal pendants of the chandeliers. Table after table was laid out in orderly rows, one for each year of students. The teachers' dais had been placed against the southern wall, where they could critique our manipulation of forks and knives without the light in their eyes.

I made my way to the tenth-year table—blinded, not; blinded, not—sailing past the usual giggles and gossip of the other students as though I couldn't hear any of it. Seating was assigned, so I wasn't stuck at the end of our table because I was the last to arrive, which I was. I was stuck there because that's where Westcliffe had put me.

I took my chair next to Malinda Ashland's. She lifted her nose in the air and reached for the teapot between us before I could, just barely managing not to whack me with her elbow.

Pretty, snooty Malinda. No doubt she secretly wondered if Westcliffe bore her some grudge, fixing me next to her.

The rest of the girls of my class were hardly more pleasant. Beatrice, Caroline, Lillian, Stella, Mittie. I'd describe them to you, but to be honest, all you truly need to know is that they were the pampered, drawling daughters of the empire's so-called best families. On weekends they wore cashmere and chiffon and gemstones. They knew all the rules of lawn tennis and polo and would sooner curse out loud in front of their mothers than sip champagne from a sherry glass. I existed as a boundless source of scandal for them, and that was about all.

Except for Sophia, their leader. Ever since she'd started speaking to me, they'd backed off a bit.

A bit.

"Pass the bacon, please," I said to Malinda, who ignored me.

I leaned past her for the platter. I didn't bother to stop *my* elbow from knocking into her hand just as she was lifting her cup.

She let out a hiss, shaking the tea from her fingers. "*El*eanore, *real*ly! Were you raised by *wolves*?"

"Worse," snickered Lillian, on her other side. "Plebeians."

"Wolves have better manners than certain humans I know." I

scraped the last few pieces of bacon onto my plate, then moved on to the scrambled eggs. "At least they share."

"Only after the alpha has had his fill," chimed in Sophia, at the far end of the table.

"Or *hers*," I added pointedly, with a glance at her nearly empty plate.

She sent me a lazy smile. "True enough. But then, leading a pack of lesser minds can be such exhausting work. Still, *someone's* got to be in charge."

"Someone," echoed Beatrice, pausing over her grapefruit. "Rather odd thing to say. They're just wolves."

Sophia never took her eyes from mine. "Pour me another cup, Bea, won't you?"

"Of course!"

The hardest part of meals for me was figuring out how to eat as much as I wanted without attracting adult attention. In Blisshaven there had been no assigned seats, no snowy crisp tablecloths, no chinaware, no fine silver. There had been minders instead of professors, and they'd all carried wooden batons. Breakfast had been nonexistent, tea was nothing but day-old bread, and dinner was usually a thin fish stew or veggie soup or—only on Sundays— gristly bangers and mash. About once a year someone from the government would show up for a tour, I suppose to ensure we orphans weren't wasting any of their enormous goodwill, and suddenly our boots would be patched and our clothes mended and there were apple slices to share, or crumpets, or even gingerbread.

Imagine going from that to this: Huge salvers of roasted meats, steaming in their juices. Seafood lapped in creamy rich sauces. Vegetables no longer dissolved into soup but sautéed or baked or boiled, so you could tell what they were. Fresh rolls, so fresh the insides were still warm when you tore into them. Butter and jam, white sugar and chilled milk. Whole apples, pears, persimmons. Bread pudding, iced cakes, sweet biscuits for dessert.

Every day. Every single day.

It isn't sloth or even birth that pins the poor in their place. It's hunger. Hunger kinks you up. Keeps your mind obsessed and your body cramped and shivering, and you dream of how lovely dying is going to be because no one ever goes to bed starving in heaven.

I added more eggs to my plate. Malinda rolled her eyes and gave a sniff.

"Look at her," fake-whispered Lillian to Caroline, loud enough for all the table to hear. "Speaking of wolves! She bolts down her food as if it's the very end of the world, doesn't she?"

"As if she's doomed never to dine again!" Caroline fake-whispered back, stirring sugar into her tea, *clink-clink-clink*.

I didn't bother to respond. As far as my stomach was concerned, it might well have been my last meal. You never knew.

I was nearly a third of the way through when I heard the ominous, unmistakable rustling of organdy and the snap of high heels against stone.

Blast.

I slowed my chewing, swallowed, and lifted my gaze to find Mrs. Westcliffe standing beside my chair. I hoped like hell there weren't any egg bits on my face.

"Miss Jones," she said, pinch-lipped.

"Yes, ma'am?"

"You will join me in my office, if you please."

"Yes, ma'am."

I cast a longing look at my unfinished breakfast.

"*Now*, Miss Jones."

"Yes, ma'am."

I pushed back from the table. Westcliffe was already pacing away, so I don't think she noticed the giggles that whipped up anew, my classmates with their hands pressed over their mouths, their eyes sparkling with malice, and Sophia real-whispering *"Doooooooom"* under her breath as I walked past her.

Chapter 3

When you find yourself really, truly in the thick of trouble, there's one very important rule to remember: Never volunteer information. Just keep your mouth shut and let the others do the talking, and maybe they don't really know anything much and you'll get to walk away.

I'd learned that rule, and learned it well. But as I followed the ebony-clad figure of the headmistress out of the great room and down Iverson's hallways, my thoughts were already babbling.

Oh, was I eating too quickly, ma'am? I beg your pardon! I'm ever so anxious not to be tardy to class!

Oh, did I use the fish knife to slice the butter? How careless of me! Of course I know the difference between a fish knife and a butter knife and a tea knife and a fruit knife!

Oh, did it seem I struck Malinda on purpose? Honestly, that was an accident! I had no idea she'd be thrusting her hand in front of me then, and in her defense, I don't think she saw me at all, since her head was turned and she was talking with her mouth full to Caroline. . . .

The office of the headmistress was a place no student normally wished to go, nor—if she was well-mannered enough or at least clever enough—would she have reason to.

I, however, was already dismally familiar with the chamber, from the lace panel curtains patterned with pansies and pearls to the vases of lilies discreetly scattered about, freshened every three days. Even the porcelain angels framing the clock on the mantelpiece smirked at me with their same familiar smirks.

You again, eh? What a shock.

I was most especially familiar with Mrs. Westcliffe's imposing cherrywood desk (always smelling of beeswax) and the pair of baroque leather wing chairs set at precise angles before it.

Westcliffe took her seat behind the desk. I waited until she gestured at me before sinking into mine.

They were huge wing chairs. I fancied I looked like a cornered elf whenever I was perched in one.

The headmistress stared down at me with narrowed eyes. I pressed my lips into a line and stared back until I realized I shouldn't. Then I stared at my knees.

"How are you feeling these days, Eleanore?"

I lifted my head, wary. Whatever else I'd been expecting, it wasn't this.

"Very well, ma'am."

"And how is your—ah—arm?"

I'd been shot in the arm. I'd been shot in the wing, too, but she couldn't know about that.

"Doing better, ma'am."

"The village physician has informed me that your physical recovery appears to be properly on course."

At least something about me was proper. "Yes, ma'am."

"It is unfortunate about the scar, but—well! What can one do?"

One can avoid being in the path of a spray of bullets, that's what.

Mrs. Westcliffe looked away and cleared her throat. She lifted a hand to her immaculate black coif and patted at it fretfully, and I thought, incredulous, *Crikey, she's going to do it. She's going to boot me out of the school.*

Despite what I'd said to Armand, I hadn't really thought about not coming back next year, and sitting in that overstuffed chair right then, I realized how very much I *did* want to come back. That however difficult my life had been at Iverson, it was still the closest thing I'd ever had to a home. I wasn't ready to give that up yet. I'd just thought . . . somehow it'd all work out. Somehow the magic would keep me here, even with Jesse gone.

The angel clock began to chime.

"I'll be late to literature, ma'am," I said hopefully.

"You will be excused," she replied, curt. "In fact, you will be excused for the remainder of the day. I've received a cable from the Duke of Idylling's personal physician in Bath. It seems His Grace has requested a visit from you."

Now I was the one who had to clear her throat, because when I'd sucked in my breath I'd inhaled my spit. "Uh—from *me*?"

"Yes. In addition, it was specified that for the sake of the duke's continued . . . peace of mind, the visit is to take place at once. There are tickets already reserved for us at the train station in Bournemouth. We must leave immediately." Westcliffe drummed her nails atop the desk, frowning. "I have struggled to maintain contact with His Grace, I admit. It seems the communication policy of his new . . . place of residence is rather restrictive. Still, I find the haste of this plan very nearly mysterious, especially since not even one of my letters . . ."

She trailed off, glanced up, and noticed I was still there. The frown deepened.

"You may cease looking so stupefied, Miss Jones. Did you imagine I'd allow you to see His Grace alone?"

No, actually, I didn't. Because Reginald, the Duke of Idylling, was locked away in a madhouse, and what I'd imagined was that I'd never have to see him ever again.

Bugger it.

I had been on a train only once before in my life. Once that I recalled, that is. Earlier this year I had traveled third class from London to the town of Bournemouth, which had the station nearest to Iverson, and it had been cramped and stinky and slow and absolutely fantastic, because every hour that passed had put more distance between me and my life at the orphanage. I hadn't even minded the torturously upright wooden pews they'd called seats.

But I wasn't traveling third class now. Mrs. Westcliffe and I made our way down the station platform to the first-class compartments, and strange men touched the brims of their hats to us, and a porter took my hand to help me up the steps—which I appreciated, since my skirt hobbled me so severely I had to hitch it to my shins just to climb the first rung. Good thing Westcliffe had gone aboard first.

The first-class seats weren't merely padded, but padded in real burgundy velveteen. More porters moved up and down the aisle, offering glasses of cold water or ale and doily-lined trays of chocolates and nuts. The handful of other passengers already seated glanced up idly at the headmistress (clearly I was only a schoolgirl, and thus insignificant) but then just continued on with whatever they were doing, chatting or reading or staring out the windows as they (probably) pondered their great gobs of money.

We found our seats. I sat back and closed my eyes, hoping West-cliffe would take it as a sign I was far too weary and delicate for con-versation.

No such luck.

The train gave a hard whistle to signal our start, and everything lurched and gradually settled again.

"I do not wish for you to feel apprehension at our upcoming appointment with the duke," Mrs. Westcliffe said over the rising whine of the wheels.

I opened my eyes. She was gazing not at me but at the wall ahead of us, walnut paneling heavily varnished and a brass plaque that read *Mind the Cinders*. Beyond our window, the world was slip-ping by, faster and faster.

"No, ma'am," I said.

"I realize that on the last occasion you saw him, matters were . . . extraordinary. His rational mind had retreated beneath the unbearable grief of his eldest son's demise." Now she did shoot me a look, sharp and pained. "His Grace is a good man, Eleanore. One who, under ordinary circumstances, would never harm a soul."

"Yes, ma'am."

"Do not be afraid of him."

"No, ma'am," I said, looking her square in the eyes. "I'm not afraid."

She returned her gaze to the wall. "I also wish for you to know that I have appreciated your discretion in the matter. Prudence and kindness are the hallmarks of a lady, ones we foster at Iverson with great diligence."

"Of course," I agreed, without even a trace of sarcasm.

England past the window glass was green and blue, smeared up close, crystalline in the distance, all trees and cloudless sky.

"A good man," Westcliffe repeated to herself, very softly, as the train rocked along the tracks.

I couldn't help but feel for her. She loved the duke, I knew she did. And both of us knew that him loving her back was as impossible as a slum girl turning into a duchess.

Richardson Home. That was the name of the duke's madhouse. My own had had an equally oblique title, but names are dismal hiding places, really, and there was no getting around what either building actually was.

Richardson turned out to be a peachy-stoned, Georgian sort of prison, with a good long lawn opening up behind its iron gates and a few spindly trees peppering the grounds, but no hedges or ditches or anything but flat grass from here to there.

Again: no place to hide.

We were escorted inside by a burly, broken-nosed man who was obviously not a butler, although he was dressed as one. I noticed Mrs. Westcliffe delivering him a sidelong glance as he accepted our wraps, but all he did was ask our names and then disappear behind a door—also burly, composed of wide oaken planks and steel studs—leaving us standing alone like almswomen in the foyer.

"My!" said Mrs. Westcliffe, but not too loudly.

The foyer was plain stone, unfurnished and chilly; I'd bet those walls were ruddy thick. I hugged my arms over my chest, then rubbed at my cold nose. Westcliffe drew her spine straighter and stared fixedly at the oaken door.

If she was willing it to open, it worked. The man who came out now was nothing at all like the make-believe butler who'd gone in.

"Ladies," the new man greeted us. He was short and pudgy and nervously blinking, rather like a mouse spotting a pair of cats before him at the last second. But he kept coming forward, and with his very next step the stench of rancid grease from his hair pomade nearly flattened me.

Westcliffe was shaking his hand, introducing us both. I nodded at the right moment, then eased behind the headmistress and tried to breathe shallow breaths.

This, then, was the duke's personal physician. This fidgety, fat, smelly man.

For the first time ever, I think, I felt a thread of sympathy for His Grace.

The doctor led us through the doorway, talking all the while.

" . . . that you made it here in all haste. It will please the duke mightily. He's been adamant that he speak with you—that is, with the young lady—as soon as possible. We've been utterly unable to reason with him about it."

"I see," said Westcliffe faintly.

Richardson Home on the inside was nothing whatsoever like a real home. We were walking down a corridor lined with sulphur-glass sconces, passing no parlors, no drawing rooms, only closed doors, most inset with small, barred windows. The reek of pomade had become overwhelmed by that of bleach and morphine and sour human waste.

Faces popped into view from behind the bars. Hands reaching up, fingers clawing, palms slapping at the doors. Voices keening, moaning—one man actually barking—all the prisoners feeding on the noise, an awful chorus of desperation bouncing against the barren walls.

Westcliffe's feet began to drag. Her skin had blanched, but I . . .

Oh, I had seen all this before. I had lived this before.

I bit down hard on the inside of my cheek, tasting blood. There was a sound building up inside me, a hot hopeless pressure inside my throat, but I wasn't going to moan back to these people. I wasn't.

A woman's hand with dirty, chipped fingernails poked out from a window as my head went by. I ducked out of the way just in time, leaving her fingers to scratch at empty air.

"Jeannie," the woman shrieked, now her cheek pressed against the bars, one rolling eye. "At last! Come visit! Jeannie, Jeannie, where have you been all this while? Come visit your mother!"

"Pay them no mind," the doctor called from over his shoulder. "Pitiable, of course, but one does grow accustomed to the everyday sights and sounds of their sickness. They'll quiet after we pass. Er— avoid the cell windows, please. Some of the younger children have a fair reach."

"Children," repeated Westcliffe, still faint, but the good doctor had heard her.

"Oh, yes," he enthused. "At Richardson we utilize the most modern medicines and methods for every manner of patient. Weakness of the mind acknowledges no boundaries of age, and I'm pleased to say that neither do we. All who are in need are welcome here."

For the right price, I finished silently for him.

Moor Gate, asylum of the indigent, hadn't used nearly this much bleach.

And that wasn't the only difference, I soon saw. When the doctor unlocked the door to the duke's cell, I had to stop in place and stare.

Here, then, was the *home* part of Richardson Home. Here was the gracious space, the luxurious surroundings, a peer of the realm would expect. There were rugs and tables and chairs, a writing desk, a silk folding screen, and a hulking canopied bed done up in royal blue damask. There were even windows set up high along two walls, letting in the sun past the bars, something I'd never glimpsed once in my year spent in the bowels of Moor Gate.

A fireplace held a crackling fire—no chill in here—and Reginald, Armand's father, was seated before it in a smoking jacket with a blanket over his lap and a cup of something in his hands.

His Grace took in the three of us at his door with an air of mild astonishment. Then he set the cup aside and rose to his feet.

"Look, my lord," said the doctor in a chipper tone. "Only look and see who has come to call on you."

"Yes," said the duke. "How kind."

Mrs. Westcliffe slid an uncertain step toward him. "Your Grace."

"Irene." A brief smile lifted his lips. For a heartbreaking instant he looked so like his handsome son. "Lovely to see you."

She sank into her curtsy, and I copied it. Reginald's gaze jumped to mine.

"Miss Jones. I am glad you've come."

I couldn't think of a polite response to that—*Blimey, I'm not!*—so I only nodded.

"Timothy," said the duke, sounding abruptly like his old, imperious self, "we'll need tea. Some of those scones with the currants in them, fresh ones. See to it, old boy."

"My lord, I don't think—"

"The ladies shall be perfectly fine in my care," Reginald interrupted. "I can assure you of that."

"Yes," agreed Westcliffe, forceful. "We shall be."

"Indubitably true, my dear woman! The Duke of Idylling is a model patient, a paragon of a patient. But I cannot—"

"Do go," I said, stepping in front of him, drawing his eyes to me. My voice slipped soft and smooth. "Go and see to the tea in the kitchens yourself."

There is another *drákon* Gift I've not mentioned yet, and like all the others, it's one I hadn't mastered in the least. Occasionally—rarely—I was able to induce people to do what I wanted simply by darkening the tenor of my voice. There were times I tried it and failed miserably; I ended up sounding like nothing more than a cheap fortune-teller at a carnival sideshow.

But this time it worked. I hadn't even meant to attempt it, but it had happened, and it worked.

The duke's physician offered me a few more squinty blinks, but they were slower now. Baffled.

"Yes. I'll . . . go to the kitchens. . . ."

"Splendid," said His Grace.

I let them reunite with my back to them, hands clasped before me, studying the curtains that draped so stylishly from the canopy of the bed.

I pretended I didn't hear them at all.

I pretended I didn't hear the moans that still ricocheted down the hallway past the open door, and the woman weeping, "Jeannie, my Jeannie," from behind the walls of her cell.

"And now, Irene, if you don't mind, I'd like to speak to Miss Jones."

I turned around. They were seated a nice proper distance from each other, the fire glowing between them.

Westcliffe pursed her mouth.

"Privately," added the duke.

"Well . . . I . . ."

I looked at her. I said nothing.

"Certainly." She stood and went to the door. "I'll wait here for the doctor to return, shall I?"

I approached the empty chair. The duke lifted a hand to it—and there was Armand in him again, sweeping a hand at me in the forest to inspect the hole he'd dug.

I settled gingerly against the cushions. The heat from the fire caressed the left side of my face and lit the right side of his, highlighting the deep hollow of his cheek, the sallow skin. Reddish glints danced in his lank brown hair.

"I know what you are," Reginald said quietly.

I froze, then made myself relax back and cross my ankles.

His Grace had never seen me as a dragon. Not only that, but Armand's *drákon* blood had come from his mother's side, and even *she* hadn't known what she was. She'd died not knowing, so I didn't see how Reginald suddenly could.

"Oh?" I murmured.

"Yes, Miss Jones. I do."

"If you mean that I am the very grateful recipient of your scholarship to Iverson, Your Grace, you are absolutely correct."

"Oh, you're *that* as well. Indeed you are. But you're far more than meets the eye, Miss Jones. Armand sees it, too, though he won't speak of it. You are something . . . dangerous."

"Hardly." I forced a stiff smile. "Just an ordinary girl."

"No, Eleanore. No. You've been sent here. Sent to me, sent to Armand. And now *I* am going to send you to Aubrey."

I let out a huff of surprise, but he wasn't smiling back or even looking especially barmy. The lines of his face were drawn serious, his brown eyes glittering.

I leaned in close so Westcliffe wouldn't overhear.

"Reginald, Aubrey is dead. Your eldest son is dead. His plane was shot down by the Germans this spring. Remember?"

"That's what we were told. That's what the telegrams said."

"Yes."

"But the telegrams were wrong. They were all wrong, because Aubrey is alive. And you're the beast that's going to bring him back to me."

The beast.

A chill prickled my skin, creeping over me despite the fire. Reginald never released me from his dreadful gaze.

"That's what he told me. That it will be up to you. Smoke-thing, winged-thing. Monster within."

"What?" I managed.

"The boy in the stars. He speaks to me in my dreams, you know. Tells me things. *You* will be the one to find Aubrey. You *must* find him!"

I'd risen from the chair. I hadn't meant to, but like my voice changing, it had just happened, and now Westcliffe was watching us and the duke's fragile grip on his composure was beginning to crumble.

"Tell me you will!"

I licked my dry lips. "Your Grace, I'm sorry, but I have no notion what—"

"Do not lie to me, miss!" he thundered, leaping to his feet to tower over me, because all at once he was very tall, and I was very much not. He clapped his hands on my upper arms and gave me a wicked shake. "Do not lie, *thing*! I'll not have it!"

"Reginald!" Westcliffe was moving toward us, her skirts black wings flapping. "Reginald!"

Everything seemed to slow. Westcliffe was slow, and the duke was slow, but one of his hands was clamped right on my injury and it *hurt*, so I cried out with my knees buckling and my own hand coming up to pry apart his fingers—

And then Armand was there. Right there behind Westcliffe. Past her, and Reginald was pushed off me and Armand stood between us nearly as tall as his father, his fists knotted into the duke's satin lapels.

I stumbled back, knocked into the chair. Westcliffe caught me up and released me at once, both of us panting.

"Don't you hurt her!" Armand snarled. "Ever! Do you hear me?"

"I—I had to tell her—"

"You *never* hurt her, never again!" He shoved his father back, and Reginald didn't fight it, didn't do anything but sort of deflate, all the heat and anger and glittery conviction vanished, leaving him empty as a sack. He sagged back into his chair.

"Good God." He lifted a hand to his face, hiding his eyes. "Good God, no. I—I—I'm . . ."

None of us moved. Beside me, Westcliffe stood brittle as glass.

Armand had his back to us both, broad and tensed, his fists still clenched. He radiated menace.

A random wild thought came to me, burrowed in: Here *is the beast. Here he is.*

My arm lifted. I touched my palm to his shoulder blade, and even with his shirt and jacket between us, I felt an electric, snapping shock.

"Armand. Mandy. I'm unharmed."

He rolled his shoulders to shuck me off, then threw me an unreadable glance.

"My lord," pleaded Westcliffe, her words trembling. "Lord Sherborne. He meant no ill."

"No," the duke was muttering. "No, no, no . . ."

Armand dropped to his knees before his father, bracing both hands against the arms of the chair to pin him in.

"Reg. Listen to me. Are you listening?"

"Yes . . ."

"I've received news. A wire from the prime minister. I drove straight here as soon as I got it. It's—it's tremendous, *wonderful* news." Armand's voice was rough with emotion; he let out a shaky breath. "Aubrey is alive. He didn't die. Dad, he's *alive*."

The duke lifted his head. His hair had fallen forward and his cheeks were mottled. He flicked back the hair, scowled at his son, and brushed both hands down his crushed lapels.

"That is *precisely* what I've been *saying*," he announced peevishly. "Aubrey is alive and captured. And this thing here, this beast named Eleanore, is going to be the one who flies there and brings him home."

Like a puppet yanked upright by a single jerk of its strings, Armand was standing, staggering a few steps toward me. Our eyes locked. I didn't know if my expression mirrored his, but I knew my insides did: disbelief, smothered guilt.

That cold, budding fear.

He looked from me to his father to Westcliffe, who had both hands knuckled against her mouth and really, truly appeared as if she might keel over.

Armand tipped back his head and pinched his fingers over his eyes—just like his father had done. "Where the deuce is that wretched doctor, anyway?"

"Kitchens," I whispered. "Sorry."

Chapter 4

There was no taking tea after that. There was a great deal of fussing from the doctor when he finally showed up, and Mrs. Westcliffe attempting valiantly to pull herself together, and Armand hanging back by me, ensuring that he stood between the duke and me no matter which of us moved.

More doctors arrived, some nurses, everyone exclaiming over the news about Aubrey and worrying over Reginald's "mild fit." The tea service His Grace's personal physician had carried into the cell sat forgotten on the side table by the door.

I edged closer to it. I snatched a biscuit from a plate when no one was watching and ate it in one bite.

Almost no one had been watching.

"Shortbread," noted Armand, and grabbed two more. "How reassuringly orthodox." He handed me one, broke the other absently into pieces in his hand. His face was still strained and white.

"Don't destroy it." I wiped at my lips. "Give it to me if you don't want it."

His palm opened. The biscuit had gone to crumbs.

"You're bleeding," he said quietly. "Your arm. The wound. I can smell the blood."

Of course he could. Dragon senses, supernaturally sharp. I could smell it, too, but my sleeve was loose enough that so far the blood didn't show.

I kept my voice as low as his. "It's fine. Don't say anything."

"Lora, it needs attention."

"Yes. Back at the school. First thing."

His mouth tightened. "Look—"

"I'm *not* going to let these people touch me," I whispered, vehement. "I'm not going to their medical chamber and I'm not letting them remove my blouse and I'm not letting them lay a finger on me, I don't care if my arm festers and falls *off,* so kindly *shut up.*"

Mrs. Westcliffe had recovered enough to notice us standing there, our heads together, my heated cheeks. She began to approach.

"Only if you come to me tonight," Armand said swiftly. "At Tranquility."

"Fine!"

"Lord Sherborne—" the headmistress began.

"No," he cut in at once, turning to her. "I'm merely Lord Armand again."

She stopped before us, blinking. "Oh—yes! Forgive me. Lord Sherborne is—that is, I'm so pleased that your brother has regained his—er . . ." She flattened a hand against the base of her throat, then tried again. "Lord Armand, I fear our visit has overtaxed your father. Miss Jones and I should leave."

He gave her a short bow. "Allow me to drive you back to the school, ma'am."

Westcliffe and I exchanged a look; whatever our differences, we both knew how Armand drove. "A most chivalrous offer, my lord, but we couldn't possibly—"

"I insist. It'll be faster than the train, and I could use the companionship."

"Oh," she said again, defeated, and summoned a smile. "Why, then, we accept. Naturally."

Outside the madhouse, back in the cool May air and a lemony, waning light, the lawn a sheared carpet spread before us, I waited for him to hand Westcliffe into the front seat of the auto before muttering, "The *train* has *chocolates*."

"Surely my company is sweet enough," he muttered in return, and helped me up into the high, uncomfortable backseat.

Armand's motorcars tended to be roofless and very, very fast. We weren't dressed for a drive in the open air, so his lordship had politely presented his duster to Mrs. Westcliffe, who had sense enough to accept it. I had her wrap and mine around me, but the wind was relentless, and the dust from passing horses and carriages even more so.

Armand needed the driving goggles to see; Westcliffe and I squinted at the land flying by, the outskirts of Bath swiftly unspooling into fields of grain and flocks of sheep, dogs and hedges and farmhouses.

It *was* quicker than the train. And it was noisy enough that I didn't have to endure any uncomfortable questions from Westcliffe (yet), or even worry about holding up my end of a conversation. We'd have to shout to be heard, me most of all, and I had no doubt about how the headmistress of the Iverson School for Girls would feel about that.

Automobiles clearly had not been designed with ladylike sensibilities in mind.

So I sat back and held on to the strap fixed to the door, trying not to slide around too much, studying the sunset to our right, the intense red and pink of the clouds, thin streaky lines drawn just above the horizon. The stars beginning to kindle against the fading blue.

Jesse, are you up there somewhere? Do you visit Reginald in his dreams, but not me?

I swiped at my eyes with my free hand, smearing tears and grit.

The auto slowed, slowed, then rolled to a halt at the side of the road. Armand pulled the brake, and Mrs. Westcliffe twisted to face him inquiringly. Her black hair looked frosted in dust.

"I think perhaps we'll pay a call on Dr. Hembry in the village before going all the way to the castle," he said to her.

"Oh?"

"I believe Miss Jones has reinjured her arm."

They both looked back at me, and I looked down. The seam of my fitted white cuff had a wet, growing stain, crimson as the clouds.

He waited for her in his bedroom.

He would have chosen another room, but this was the only place in all the mansion he could be certain a servant wouldn't enter without his express permission first. And it was the only place Eleanore had ever visited him before.

As smoke. As her true self.

Armand paced a circle from one end of the Turkish rug to the other, examining his surroundings for the hundredth time: the bed crisp and tidy, the cushions on the chairs straight, his dinner tray already taken away—minus the dessert he'd requested but kept for her. He'd already pulled all the curtains safely closed. A wineglass had been left on his desk, a gleam of Bordeaux at the bottom. He paused by it, uncertain. Should he have finished that? Should he have saved the bottle to offer her some? Did she even like wine?

It seemed incredibly, deeply stupid that he didn't know.

But then the fire in the hearth popped and the log fell apart in a splendor of sparks, and Mandy found his gaze tugged to that and his regrets about the wine falling and dying with the light.

He resumed pacing.

The room was large and sparsely furnished. Years ago, because it'd been easy and because he could, he'd picked what furniture he'd liked from Tranquility's other chambers and hauled them up, piece by piece, to his own. Aubrey'd thought it funny and Reginald had been too drunk to notice—all this time, and Mandy was fairly certain he still hadn't sobered up enough to notice—so nothing matched, but that was fine.

He didn't care about that. It wasn't as if he was going to host a soirée in here. Only Eleanore, and he doubted very much she gave a damn about matching furniture, either.

But where was she?

On his fifth pass by the big window he paused again, parting the curtains with the side of his hand. Country darkness loomed past the glass, unbroken but for the stars over the sea, glistering and humming, whispering their soft and silken secrets.

He dropped his hand, shutting them out.

Bugger them. He didn't want to hear them now.

He was just . . . waiting.

In the far, unlit corner of the room, buried in the drawer that held his ascots and a handful of formal scarves, was a ring, and if he was going to be perfectly honest with himself, that's what he was trying not to hear—that more than anything, more than even the stars.

It was a ruby ring, set in gold, and the ruby was big and round and clouded, and its song never, ever ended.

How he hated that sodding song.

He wasn't expected to wear the ring yet, thank God. He considered himself more the guardian of it, because it was the ring of the duke, and Armand wasn't the duke. Reginald was. Slipping it over his knuckle and wearing it outside this room would be the same as declaring to the world that Reginald was as good as dead, which he wasn't.

It was *like* he was dead, all right. Stuck in his madness, stuck in that godforsaken asylum: *like* it. But that wasn't the same.

Mandy's feet stopped; he was caught up short by a sharp, internal jerk of reality.

The ruby ring *wasn't* going to be his, and he'd *never* have to wear it. Aubrey would.

Aubrey.

He sank into a chair by the fire, scrubbing his hands over his face, feeling rough evening whiskers and the sullen heat of the flames.

He should have taken the time to shave for her. Why hadn't he done that?

Mandy tipped his head back, staring up at the ceiling. Seeing her.

Eleanore, pale and pinched, so almost-beautiful.

Reginald this afternoon trapped in his cage, calling her a *thing* to her face. Ranting.

she's coming, whispered the stars. That one particular, infuriating star, louder than all the rest. *she's here, louis, let her in.*

Mandy stood. He grabbed the blanket he'd set aside for her and went to the door. He had his hand on the knob before she even knocked.

The door opened just as my hand was lifting. I supposed he felt me there beyond the wood, maybe sensed my Turn from smoke into flesh. The door didn't open all the way; Armand's arm emerged through the crack to offer me a soft gray blanket. I caught it up to my chest, then shook it out and flung it over my shoulders like a cape.

The perils of Turning. It would have been convenient if my clothing somehow made the transformation with me, but it never did. Nothing ever stuck to me when I Turned, not even rain or blood or dirt. I'd spent a lot of time naked recently.

"You made it," Armand said, opening the door wider. He sounded relieved, as if he'd thought I wouldn't actually come.

"You seemed to require it."

I spoke softly. It was late and I didn't think there was anyone nearby, but Tranquility was a decaying mess of a maze, to put it kindly. It'd be easy to overlook a hidden servants' door. Armand gave a quick glance up and down the empty hallway before stepping back.

"Come in."

I did. I was glad to see he hadn't turned on the electric lights, so the shadows of the room danced strictly from the fire. I didn't like electric lights. I didn't like electricity in general, not after Moor Gate, but even the fashionable stained-glass chandeliers here made me feel ill when they were lit. Like bees in my head, buzzing and buzzing.

I was curious if it was the same for him, but I had never asked.

"How's your wound?"

I shrugged. "It'll heal. Again."

"Let me look."

I freed my upper arm from the blanket. His touch felt light against my skin, gentle. His fingers were cold and long, like mine.

"It's not as bad as I thought today in the auto. All that blood, I mean."

"Dr. Hembry put a stitch in it," I said.

"Did he?" He tipped his head, looking closer, and I smiled.

"The Turn," I said. "It's gone now."

"Oh."

He stood there, frowning, and I wondered if he noticed the bruising around the freshly broken scar. The unmistakable shape of his father's fingers imprinted on me.

I pulled the blanket back over my shoulder and surrendered to a giant yawn.

"Tired?" he asked.

I shrugged again. "New moon. You know."

"You're still keeping watch?"

"Is there someone else to do it?"

It came out sounding cruel, and I hadn't meant it to; I touched my hand to his sleeve. "Never mind. I know you'd help if you could."

His lips thinned. I spoke again quickly to stave off whatever he was about to say.

"Is that sugar in the air?"

"Yes. I saved you dessert."

"Cheers!"

Oh, pie! Blackberry pie, a nice fat wedge, the crust so buttery tender it flaked apart at the first touch of my fork. I sat before the fire and devoured it all in about a minute, then swiped the plate with my finger, eager for every last crumb.

Armand was seated cross-legged at my side. I sucked the mashed blackberry goo from my fingertip, sending him a glance.

"What? No comments about my charming manners?"

"Er . . ." He seemed dazed in the firelight, watching me. "No."

I placed the china plate on the floor. Gilt traced its rim, a ring of golden light, and the fire before us sighed and worked its way along the final orangey bit of log.

"You never told your father." I didn't make it a question. "About me. What I am."

Another frowning, thin-lipped look.

"He said there's a boy in the stars who speaks to him in his dreams. Who told him what I am."

"A boy in the stars," he repeated slowly.

"How could that be? Could Jesse . . . *do* that? Come to him like that?"

"You're asking *me* about Jesse?"

"Well," I said, and stopped, a little flustered. "Well, there's no one else to ask, is there?"

Armand lowered his gaze. After a moment, he began to tap the pie plate thoughtfully with one finger. "All right. I think . . . I suspect it must be true. You've never told Reg about any of it, and I haven't, so aside from Jesse, there really *is* no one else who knows the truth, right?"

I shook my head.

"There's your answer, then." He gave the plate an extra tap. "Unless he's a bloody good guesser."

"Or a bloody astute lunatic," I countered, unthinking.

The words hung between us. I winced and ventured a look back at him, but the lunatic's son was staring bleakly into the fire.

"I'm sorry, Mandy. I'm a moron."

"No harm done," he said, but he sounded just as bleak as he looked.

I tried to rally. "That means, then, that somehow Jesse really does talk to him. That everything that your father said that Jesse said is true. That Aubrey is alive and imprisoned somewhere. That I'm meant to fly to him."

"To rescue him," Armand finished.

I shook my head again. I didn't dare blurt out what I was thinking now: *That is truly, truly insane.*

I played with a fold of the blanket draped along my knee. I ran my hand over it, the center of my palm, thinking hard.

"No," I said finally. "It can't be done. I'm supposed to fly across the front? Across Europe, into the thick of the war, dodging zeppelins and bombs and aeroplanes and God knows what? I mean, we don't even know where Aubrey's being held."

"East Prussia," said Armand. "Schloss des Mondes. It's a medieval ruin. Apparently they converted it into a prison camp."

I stared at him, mute, and he lifted a shoulder.

"He's a nobleman and an officer, a prisoner of war. Rules of the game say they have to tell us, just as we have to tell them about our prisoners."

"They just—give you his address?"

"Something like that. So we can send him aid parcels. Extra

clothing, food. Sweets. Cigarettes. Things to trade. Since he's an officer, he's likely to have some enlisted bloke as a servant, so you send things for him, too."

I couldn't help it; I let out a laugh. "Does he even *need* rescuing?"

Armand lifted his head. "I think he must," he said, quiet. "If Jesse says so."

And that was the end of my laughter.

"You should get back to Iverson." He climbed to his feet. "Try to get some rest. We'll work out a plan soon."

Work out a plan. As if it was all going to be so, so simple.

Maybe it would be, for him. After all, Jesse hadn't told the duke anything about Armand coming along, had he?

"I didn't have a chance to sell your pinecone yet," he said, walking a few steps away from me. His voice had taken on a flat, businesslike tone. "I'd meant to go up to London today, but then the wire came."

"I understand. I couldn't take the money now, anyway. I can't carry it when I'm smoke."

"No. Of course not."

"Perhaps, if you've managed to sell it by graduation—"

"Fine."

He turned in place, looking at me from across the room. I clutched my blanket to my chest with both hands and gazed back. I was suddenly, acutely aware of how attractive he was, and how very expressionless, and how only twenty-four hours ago he had asked me to marry him and I'd never bothered to answer.

"I hope there's no trouble with it," I said awkwardly.

"Don't worry, Lora. No one ever gives me trouble about anything anymore."

Except you, he might as well have finished.

The air felt heavy and sad. Even the fire seemed sad, the last, diminished tongues of flame beginning to flicker out. I opened my mouth to add something else, something encouraging or cheerful or even just a polite goodbye . . . but instead I Turned and flowed away.

Armand watched me go. He didn't say goodbye, either.

Chapter 5

Before the war, I had never given a second thought to moonless nights.

But before the war, I'd never been given a reason to.

Now I had one.

For a few terrible nights a month, every month, England went dark. In London and Brighton and towns up and down the coast, windows were papered in black. Streetlights were extinguished. Carriages and automobiles combed the streets without the help of lanterns, and everyone hurried to get home before dusk. Just carrying a rushlight outside to check on the family dog was considered a foolish risk, not only for you but for all your neighbors as well.

Even at Iverson, we kept the oil lamps and chandeliers cold.

Because on the moonless nights, German airships slunk across the Channel. And they had bellies full of bombs.

With my dragon hearing I'd learned to recognize two new sounds since the war began:

Thup-thup-thup-thup.

That was the sound made by the propellers of the airships.

And: *shoom-shoom-shoom*.

The engines of a U-boat.

I listened for them every night before falling asleep, but, oh, on those damned dark nights when the moon went away, it seemed I was either awake in my bed or else smoke above the Channel, drifting. Waiting.

Even after the stars would whisper reassurances *(safe, beast, tonight you're safe)*, I kept my vigil. If I stopped paying attention, who would hear Death descending? Armand's hearing wasn't as keen as mine, not yet. So there was only me.

Smoke-thing, winged-thing. An injured monster who couldn't even hold her shape half the time.

But still.

After leaving Tranquility that night, I didn't return to my room. I floated with the wind out to sea, letting it thin me sheer, hoping it might ease the bittersweet ache that felt as real as anything solid above or below me.

Jesse was still here. Somehow, still here.

A boy in the stars.

Where are you? I wondered, mist beneath their shimmer. *I love you, where are you?*

safe, beast, was all I got in response. *tonight you are safe.*

Chapter 6

The school was awash in the news of Aubrey's survival, but even that could not usurp the bubbly, simmering excitement of this year's upcoming graduation. I was in the tenth-year class, the second-to-final year before we were unchained and loosed like primped and powdered lionesses upon society. So although I personally wasn't going to graduate from the esteemed Iverson School for Girls (or, as Sophia once put it, "this wretched pile of rocks") in about a week's time, I was still expected to contribute to the official celebration.

Every year but mine had a single, chosen girl perform some role at the ceremony to send off the graduating class. The younger pupils mostly presented bouquets or demonstrated their curtsies. But it was Iverson tradition for *all* the tenth-year students to do something showcasing their own particular talents. Even scholarship students.

I assumed that because the graduating girls had suffered through this the year before, all that was required of them now was to sit in the audience with their parents and make fun of us.

Lillian, Mittie, and Caroline were going to take turns reading a poem they had composed. Stella and Beatrice were going to sing a duet while Malinda accompanied them on the piano.

Sophia was going to recite a passage from one of the headmistress's favorite books, *A Young Woman's Guide to the Veneration of Modesty and Decorum*, a choice so ironical that even Mrs. Westcliffe raised a brow.

And I . . . well, it was clear to everyone that I had but one talent. It was also the piano. But no one could sing to any of my songs, because I made them up as I went.

Despite the best efforts of Monsieur Vachon, our music instructor, I wasn't any good at doing it any other way. I couldn't understand the pages and pages of music he compelled me to study. It all still looked like dots and dashes to me. I couldn't seem to remember which piano pedal did what; my wrists were never straight enough, my posture never regal enough. And I couldn't keep perfect time, no matter how hard he smacked me on the shoulder with his wand.

I could only invent songs, not copy them.

Or so they all thought.

The truth was, I was far from the creative idiot they all believed. I'd actually copied every single song I ever played . . . but only Armand knew about that.

One of the most interesting aspects of living in a real castle was that it had real castle parts to it—that is, an authentic dungeon and solar and great room, things like that. Music class always took place in the ballroom. With its high vaulted ceiling and limestone walls and bouncy wooden floors, Monsieur claimed the acoustics were superb, although to me it always seemed we were battered by echoes.

No matter.

Hanging from that distant ceiling was a series of rock crystal chandeliers, massive and covered in sheets. I'd never seen them lit before, and likely I never would. Perhaps they were nothing more than giant skeletons of pendants and beads, but in my imagination, they sparkled like snowflakes in the sun.

And they never stopped giving me songs. Not even when I wanted them to.

"Once again, Miss Jones," commanded Vachon, looming behind me in his usual spot as I sat facing the grand piano.

I set my teeth. I closed my eyes, opened them, and glared harder at the sheet music before me. "Bumblebee Garden" was the title of the piece he wanted me to perform. It might well have been "The Simplest Melody We Could Find for You" or "Just Play These Five Notes Over and Over," but it was no good. My head was filled with the concerto floating down from the chandeliers.

My fingers fumbled across the keys, getting them all wrong. I could've played the chandelier song without a second thought, but trying to plink out bloody "Bumblebee Garden" was like pushing a boulder up a mountain.

A boulder the size of this bloody island.

Up the side of bloody Mount Everest.

I began to break into a sweat. Monsieur's eyeballs burned an itchy hole in the center of my back.

"No, no, no! *Mon Dieu,* what was that? Do you not see the score before you, Miss Jones? Do you not see what is inscribed right there before you?"

"No," I mumbled. "I mean, yes, I see it."

"Seems her *garden* is scorched earth," jeered Beatrice in a whisper, but everyone heard her.

"Again!" barked Vachon.

Fumble. Fumble. I was awful at this, I really was.

My classmates began, one by one, to snicker.

Vachon moved to my side. I saw the wand in his fist and switched instantly to the ripple of sound falling down around me like droplets from a waterfall, lovely and soft and intricate. It made him pause, as I'd hoped. The hand holding his wand gradually lowered to his side.

Ah, this—*this* was easy for me. Easy to let the rock crystal music sink into me, lap through me like the ocean's tide, bones, blood, cells, my fingers dancing faster and faster now, everything beautiful, everything effortless. My soul lifting free.

It ended, though. I let it end, and before some new song could take me, I tucked my hands in my lap and gazed up at my professor, trying for Armand's trademark stoic expression.

Vachon removed his spectacles. He wiped the glass lenses on a corner of his coat and then carefully put them back on, wrapping the wires behind each ear before speaking.

"You have made your point, Miss Jones. I hardly wish to embarrass myself by presenting you to the faculty and parents of Iverson with your practical skills in such a state. You may play what you wish for the graduation."

"But, *sir*," protested Mittie, either because she hated me the most or loved whining the most (probably both), "is that *fair*? All the rest of us have to show what we've learned—"

"Do you desire to sit through a ten-minute cacophony of sharps and flats, Miss Bashier? I do not. I assume your parents do not. Let us accept with grace what we cannot change in a week, ladies."

"Or in a lifetime," muttered Caroline, provoking a fresh round of snickering.

After class, as everyone was crowding through the ballroom doors, Sophia swung into step beside me and sent me a slanting look.

"Are you really that poor a player? Or is it on purpose?"

"No," I answered grimly. "I really am that poor."

"That's too bad. I was rather hoping you were doing it deliberately. To put a tweak in Vachon's nose."

"Vachon carries a stick with him, in case you didn't notice, and he's very glad to use it. I have no interest in tweaking any part of him."

"How disappointing," she sighed. "And all this time, I thought you such the rebel."

I was surprised into a laugh, and her pale eyes grew just a tad too wide.

"Well, after all, there was that business of you getting shot. Certainly no other girl here would ever have done such a thing."

"Yes. It was so rebellious of me to have put myself in front of a bullet I never saw coming."

She went on as if I hadn't spoken. "And the fact that you've captured Armand's attention, if not his heart. The mudlark and the aristocrat! If that's not the out-and-out definition of rebellion, I don't know what is."

"Lord Armand and I are friends, Sophia. That's all."

"Oh, come! We've been chums for *weeks*! I thought we were beyond all these silly lies. He practically salivates whenever he sees you."

Ahead of us Stella and Mittie were strolling arm in arm, whispering and tittering.

"Friends," I said again, firm.

"Is that why he was driving you back from wherever you went yesterday? Just to be friendly?"

"He was driving me *and* Westcliffe," I pointed out.

"Hmm. Where *did* you go yesterday, by the way?"

To see the mad duke. To hear a mad idea.

"Nowhere," I said. "Just to the village, to see the doctor."

"I say, Eleanore." Mittie broke off the whispering to throw me a glance from over her shoulder. "Stella and I have had the most marvelous notion."

"Yes!" Stella gave me a big grin. "We're all so concerned about how you have nowhere to land soon. Summer and all that. So why not go stay with Sophia for the holiday? She could always use—" She paused, brimming with glee; I braced myself. "Another *maid*!"

This sent them both into peals of laughter. Lady Sophia shook her head. She walked up between them and put her arms around their waists.

"I have all the maids I need, thank you. But perhaps the scullery? I can check with the cook, I suppose."

More laughter, and I watched the three of them saunter away down the corridor, rich and happy and secure in their world.

I confess, sometimes I daydreamed about Turning into a dragon and biting their heads off.

But they were probably poisonous, anyway.

The conversation I'd been dreading came two days later.

Again, in Westcliffe's office.

"Miss Jones. You will be pleased to know I've received notification regarding your new residence for the summer."

"Oh?"

"I'll not draw out the suspense. You've been assigned to the Sisters of the Splintered Cross Orphanage. It is in Callander. In Scotland."

"Oh."

"Southern Scotland, I believe. Have you ever been?"

"No, ma'am."

"Ah. Well, I'm certain it's a fine place. Scotland is, by all accounts . . . quite interesting. I have your schedule here, your train tickets and such. You are to depart the day after graduation. A fortuitous bit of timing, I think! I suggest you begin packing soon. It's never wise to leave matters to the last minute, is it?"

"No, ma'am."

"I shall be candid with you, Miss Jones. It may not be practical to plan for your return to Iverson next fall. The war has forced many unfortunate changes upon us. Shipping you all the way back from Callander a few months from now might not be in anyone's best interest."

"But it will, of course, be up to the duke to decide my fate?"

"Er—of course. The scholarship is entirely in His Grace's control. In his current state, however . . ."

"Yes, ma'am."

"You are a sensible girl, Eleanore. I will not encourage you to cling to false hopes; they will not serve you well."

"No, ma'am."

"We understand each other. Excellent. I know I may count on you to make the most of your final days here at Iverson, the better to shape your years to come."

"Yes, ma'am."

"Good afternoon, then."

"Good afternoon, ma'am."

That night before dinner I visited the library. It was mostly deserted, only a trio of ninth-years at a table poring over a fashion magazine stuffed with drawings of coy, smiling debutants in viciously expensive gowns.

I sent them a look; they returned it. None of us spoke, and they all went back to cooing over the gowns.

I had no interest in magazines, at least not in any of the ones Mrs. Westcliffe deemed suitable for proper young ladies. I'd come for a book I'd noticed in passing not long ago, one of the few books here that wasn't about housekeeping or sewing or the care of husbands: *Charts of the Principal Cities of the World, Including Railroad and Telegraph Lines.*

It was large and heavy, with a jolly thick layer of dust along the top. I hefted it from the shelf and dropped it onto the nearest table, earning me another look from the trio, which I ignored.

I flipped through the pages. Buenos Aires, La Paz, Havana, New York. Cairo, Dakar, Cape Town, Riyadh, Angora, Budapest . . . Rome, Paris. London. Glasgow.

I squinted at the Glasgow page, which was indeed cobwebbed with lines representing every railroad and telegraph line imaginable. I turned to the previous page, which showed the city as a dot in the big, flat map that was Scotland.

Callander was inked in there, a speck on the page. It wasn't even in southern Scotland, as the headmistress had claimed. From what I could tell, it was much nearer to the middle. Far from Wessex. Far from the impeccable Iverson School for Girls and the eligible youngest son of a duke.

I studied it awhile longer, trying to measure the distance with my fingers, but all I could figure was that it was hundreds of miles north of where I was sitting.

Hundreds.

I riffled through the pages again until I found Prussia (principal cities: Berlin, Königsberg). I didn't know exactly where Aubrey's medieval prison-ruin would be, but honestly, it hardly mattered. Prussia was huge and impossibly remote. Past England and the Channel, past all of France and Belgium, too. It made the distance to Callander look like a jaunt to a neighbor's house.

I slapped the book shut, sending motes of dust aloft and forcing the trio to coo even louder over the absolutely dreamy smocking on a plaid taffeta dinner frock.

You're waiting for the moment I Turn into something more than just smoke. You're waiting for Lora the dragon.

Lora-of-the-moon, Jesse used to call me.

It's not yet. But soon.

Chapter 7

To my great astonishment, the graduation ceremony was to take place out-of-doors, upon the wide, open green of Iverson's front lawn. It was a picturesque enough setting, with the cerulean sky and trimmed grass, the rose gardens framing it all in pathways of flouncy bright blooms. Even the animal-shaped hedges looked nearly benign. But out-of-doors meant the sun, and the sun meant parasols, a bobbing sea of them above the audience in their wicker chairs, a handful more held by those of us stranded in our row upon the makeshift stage.

A patchy breeze tugged at the trim of our formal uniforms like a fussy toddler wanting attention.

The trim was black lace. Every inch of our formal uniforms, in fact, was black, because they'd been dyed that way about a month past to honor the death of our school patron's eldest son.

Which meant that I was clad in the most stifling outfit imaginable from neck to toe, perspiring and miserable in the heat of the day, for no good reason. The breeze wasn't strong enough to cool, and the parasol I'd been handed before being ushered up to the stage was also made of lace. I sat dappled in fiery sunlight.

"What a silly to-do," Malinda was grumbling. As ever, she'd been seated at my side. "When we'll be seeing all these same people at parties as soon as next week."

"*Some* of us will," Lillian corrected her, with a smug glance at me.

"Yes, I guess this *is* something for Eleanore to remember. You *will* remember it, won't you, darling Eleanore? When you're back with all the other sad, tatty orphans in your sad, tatty orphanage, mucking about in the Scottish slums?"

I gazed at the parasol sea before me, dark shade hiding porcelain faces, fans undulating, diamonds flashing. Silks and linens and hats and feathers. Servants weaving through with lemonade and champagne.

Not a single snatch of conversation I'd overheard had been about the war. It was all who had seen whom where, and when, and whom they'd been with, and what they'd been wearing.

"Oh, yes," I said softly. "It would be quite impossible to forget such a magnificent display of affectation."

It took Malinda a moment to untangle my sentence. Then she straightened, her cheeks going pink.

"Well! I like that! Here you are amid your betters, and you have the nerve to say something like that!"

"I have the nerve for rather a lot of things, actually." I turned my head to hold her eyes. "You've no idea."

"I don't doubt it!"

"You seem indisposed," I said, darkening my voice. "Indeed, darling Malinda, I fear you're horribly ill."

It wasn't nice of me. I know that. But sometimes the best way to fight nastiness is with a good, sharp dose of something even nastier.

I turned away again as she began panting, pulling at the collar of her shirtwaist.

The very first row of the audience held the most important people, I assumed, because Mrs. Westcliffe was there, and some old men in fine coats, and one young man in particular at the end of the row, dressed in black like me, but with a starched white shirt and a dove-gray waistcoat and tie, and a ruby ring that wasn't his on his right hand.

Like everyone else, Armand's face was obscured by the shade of his hat. Unlike everyone else, however, I felt him staring at me. I could always feel it when he stared.

Malinda began to make small mewling noises under her breath. She sounded distressingly like a sick kitten.

I leaned in close. "You're fine," I said, and went back to gazing out past the parasols.

I hadn't been able to tell Armand about Scotland. I'd smoked to his room twice since that night, but he'd never been there; I thought it likely he hadn't been at Tranquility at all. I'd hoped it meant he'd gone to London, as he'd said, and sold my pinecone.

I had no intention of mucking about in slums any longer, not in Scotland or anywhere else. If Westcliffe wasn't having me back next year anyway, there was no point in doing what the government or any of the adults ordered me to do.

I would take my money from Armand, purchase some decent traveling gear and a ticket to Someplace Else. I would empty my chest of gold into my suitcase, board a train, and not look back. Never mind Westcliffe and Armand and Jesse and the Splintered Sisters of the Holy Whatever. Not only was I magical, I now had means. If I desired to disappear, no one would ever find me.

After I was settled somewhere, I would think about—*think* about—rescuing Aubrey.

If Jesse truly expected me to risk my life for a stranger, he could damned well come to me in a dream and tell me so himself.

This is what I remember from the momentous 1915 Observance of Graduation at the Iverson School for Girls, Wessex, England:

Westcliffe taking the stage for her welcome speech, which was about—surprise!—the virtues of modesty and faith, and how this was unquestionably one of the most promising classes of young ladies she'd ever had the pleasure to host.

(Sophia, hiding her mouth behind her hand: "She says that every year.")

Malinda playing the upright piano that had been rolled into place beyond the podium; she'd recovered enough by then to destroy only a few bars of Stella and Beatrice's treacly duet.

My head beginning to ache.

Chloe Pemington walking up the stairs to the stage, enveloped in a cloud of overripe perfume. She'd won some sort of award from the professors for perfect deportment.

(Sophia, snorting.)

Chloe accepting her engraved silver chalice with a condescending nod, floating like a sylph across the stage. Men in the audience transfixed.

Sophia after that, reciting her book passage with a familiar crisp yet singsong elocution that had the headmistress beaming, because apparently she couldn't tell when she was being mocked.

My head, throbbing.

Another speech from one of the front-row gentlemen, who mumbled so severely I couldn't make out a single word besides *wives*. Although I suppose it might have been *knives*.

The hot broken bits of sunlight on my arms and lap, blinding.

Lillian, Mittie, and Caroline and their poem, entitled "An Ode to Good Old Iverson, My Home of Homes!"

Demons with machetes inside my skull, hacking to come out.

And then Lord Armand Louis, striding past me without a glance to take the podium, about to give the speech that would change everything.

"I hope you will forgive the Duke of Idylling's absence on this important day," he began, his voice smooth and commanding, the very opposite of Mr. Mumbler. "My father sends his best wishes to each of you, and most especially to each of the young women graduating from this fine school, of which he is quite justly proud. I realize I am not so eloquent nor so fluent in public discourse as His Grace, but I shall do my best to be an adequate speaker in his stead."

Armand paused to flash a smile at the audience. Four of my classmates released audible, smitten sighs.

"I believe I echo my father's sentiments when I state that it is imperative, even in turbulent times, to celebrate the importance of learning and perseverance. Indeed, in times such as these, recognition of such achievements becomes even more significant. What else do we truly fight for? We fight for the glory of our country, of course. For our king. But also for our way of life. Our way of thinking. Of being."

Was this some emerging *drákon* skill? I'd never heard him speak like this before. He was cool and calm and mesmerizing. He had all of us, including me, leaning forward in our seats, hanging on his words.

Armand removed his hat and let the sun illuminate him entirely. Shining dark hair, intense blue eyes. The harsh light along his white shirt and skin cast him almost aglow.

"Iverson is an ideal illustration of who and what we are. Of what we must defend. The welfare of your daughters is dear to every fighting man out there, I promise you. They risk their lives for them, for us. Such a sacrifice is overwhelming.

"I was reminded of this recently by a student from this very school. A tenderhearted girl who came to me with an idea, one I hope you will all embrace as fervently as I did. Miss Jones? Miss Eleanore Jones? Where are you?"

Oh, God. I shrank back in my chair. What was he doing?

Armand pretended to search the crowd for a few seconds before spotting me cowering under my parasol. He gestured emphatically in my direction.

"Ladies and gentlemen, it is due to this girl that a plan has been set into motion that I hope will benefit the lives of a good number of soldiers and their families. As many of you know, my home, Tranquility at Idylling, is large—and largely empty. With my father's blessing, I intend to fill those empty rooms with heartbeats, with souls. I am going to transform Tranquility into a convalescent hospital for our own wounded soldiers."

Another pause, and a gradual, rumbling, swelling resonance from the crowd that I read as part approval, part disbelief. Armand spoke again, louder, before the sound could grow beyond him.

"And I am delighted to inform you that this same kind girl, as true an example of the Iverson spirit of generosity and service as ever was, has volunteered to spend her summer there as our very first nurse!"

Armand took a half step back from the podium, smiling again, allowing the swell of sound to crest into happy applause. Then he walked straight to me, bowing before me and lifting a hand in an invitation to take mine.

What else could I do? I placed my fingers over his and he lowered his head to press a kiss upon my knuckles. The applause grew even louder.

"Voilà," he murmured, a word that only I could hear.

Well, forget about my piano performance. There was no way I was going to try to follow that.

One hour later, at the alfresco reception, beneath some anemic clouds and that unrelenting sun:

"A moment, Miss Jones."

"Yes, ma'am."

"You are certainly full of surprises. Why did you not mention to me your conversation with Lord Armand regarding the hospital?"

"Uh . . . I beg your pardon, ma'am. I assure you, I was as amazed as you when he spoke of it today."

"Had you bothered to tell me you'd volunteered as a nurse for the summer, you might have saved many of us a good deal of trouble. It is not an uncomplicated task to arrange a future, Eleanore. A good many people went to some effort on your behalf to secure your place at the Callander orphanage."

"I beg your pardon, ma'am."

"Indeed. Had I any inkling of your interest in *nursing,* I might have arranged to send you to one of the many worthy hospitals already in existence."

"It—it was a very sudden interest, ma'am."

"Plainly. Is that champagne I smell on your breath?"

"No, ma'am. I wouldn't dream of—"

"Good day to you, Miss Jones."

"Good day. Ma'am."

Chapter 8

The next day was Saturday. Technically, only Sundays were marked as Visitors' Day at Iverson, but since the school year had officially ended, it seemed that rule was done as well. The castle was filled with sounds of girls laughing and crying their goodbyes, of doors slamming and the heavy, plodding footsteps of the menservants carrying trunk after trunk down the main stairs to be loaded up in the line of automobiles along the drive.

Mrs. Westcliffe had arranged for tea service in the front parlor, and that's where most of the parents lingered, quenching their thirst and girding their loins for the coming months. Girls out of uniform—at last, out of uniform!—darted every which way, eager not to miss a single departure of a classmate they'd probably despised only yesterday.

I, too, walked the halls out of uniform. Which meant that instead of wearing black or white, I was in brown: plain brown blouse, brown twill skirt, scuffed brown boots. Every single child at Blisshaven had worn this color. I wondered sometimes if it was to make us even more invisible than we already were.

The ends of my sleeves cut short just above the bones of my wrist. Only three months ago, they'd been the right length. My boots pinched smaller, too, and the top buttons of my skirt strained to pop free. The only thing that fit well at all any longer was the cuff of golden flowers I wore.

The cuff that Jesse had made for me out of real, living flowers transformed into gold.

I might have sold it, instead of the pinecone. But I was as likely to do that as to chop off my arm.

I was approaching the open doorway of the parlor, trying to ignore the inviting aromas of spice cake and tea and cucumber sandwiches wafting through, when voices reached me. A cluster of people, stationed near the door.

"Mamá, I told you—she's a very little nobody from nowhere. She has no money, no family, and no friends."

Aha. Lady Chloe, sounding petulant.

"Excuse me," countered a new someone. "But *I* am her friend."

Sophia! My feet slowed.

"Very charitable of you, my pet, very charitable." A man this time. Lord Pemington, perhaps? "I have always admired your generous nature."

"Thank you, Papa."

"Yes, yes." A woman now, impatient. "But how did this scholarship girl manage to wrangle an invitation to Tranquility for the entire summer?"

"Armand is in love with her," said Sophia.

"He certainly is *not*," hissed Chloe. "She's connived her way in, that's all. She's a scheming little chit! Anyone can see that!"

"Anyone but Lord Armand, it would appear," said the woman.

"And no wonder, what with this unfortunate business about his fa-ther! The poor boy, his head must be muddled. This won't do. This won't do in the least."

I whipped past the open doorway, but no one was looking at me, anyway.

Invisible, remember?

The castle kept any number of secrets locked within its stony heart. Among my favorites—and the most useful—were the hidden pas-sageways that tunneled behind the walls, connecting different floors and chambers from the rooftop all the way down past the dungeons. Some of them had been sealed up or filled in with rub-ble; those that were left intact seemed to have been forgotten, lost to generations of memories gone to dust.

Certainly Westcliffe didn't know about the tunnels, nor did the other students or staff. But Jesse had. And now I did.

I stood alone on the cold, flat slab that was the floor of another fine secret: Iverson's grotto. It was a cavern, really, a natural bubble in the bedrock of the island that had been reinforced with man-made pillars and this smooth embankment of limestone. Seawater lapped at the edges of the embankment, making the softest, softest of sounds. It entered and exited through another significant hole in the rock at the far end of the cavern. The only way in or out of this place was through that hole—or else the secret tunnel that had led me here.

The grotto had been designed as a refuge for the medieval castle folk. As a place of escape should invaders come and Iverson fall. The tide came in, and rowboats could steal away out the hole. The tide went out, and all other boats would be stranded, unable to pursue.

It was a place of refuge for me, too. It was here that Jesse had first explained to me about who I was. What my Gifts would mean.

Where we had broken bread together and kissed, and wrapped ourselves in blankets and laughed at fate.

I crossed my arms over my chest, warding off the chill; it was always much cooler here than anywhere else. I gazed down at the seawater, a strange silvery radiance at my feet, dancing its subtle silvery dance.

His hair had been blond. His eyes had been green. If I closed my own I could still see them, the summer storms behind them when he looked at me, and I wondered how much longer they'd remain so clear in my memory. It was already getting harder to summon the exact pitch of his voice.

I squatted down and touched my fingertips to the water, then brought them to my lips. The salt water tasted like tears.

"I miss you," I said. The grotto took my words and bounced them back at me: *you-you-you* . . .

No one else answered.

"I have to go soon," I said.

. . . *soon-soon-soon* . . .

"And I don't know if I'll be back. I—I'll try, though. I'll try."

. . . *try-try-try* . . .

"Damn you," I whispered. "I hate you for leaving me behind."

. . . *hind-hind-hind* . . .

"Lora."

I stood and flicked the water from my hand, composed myself, then turned and faced the concealed door in the cavern wall behind me.

Armand, of course. Iverson Castle had been his home once upon a time. He knew about the tunnels, too.

"I thought I might find you here."

"Looks like you were right. Why aren't you upstairs bidding adieu to all the schoolgirls in love with you?"

"All those heaving bosoms and soggy pledges of eternal devotion," he said, reaching my side. "Who can bear it?"

The walls of the cavern were studded with minute crystals. They blinked in time with the shifting sea, framing him in sparkles.

I returned to regarding the seawater at my feet. This close to the end of the embankment, my boots were getting wet. "I was going to tell you that I'm being sent to Scotland. But it seems you're rather more crafty than the rest of us."

"One of my finer attributes, if I do say so myself."

I thought of the packet of never-to-be-redeemed train tickets upstairs on my dresser, and my threadbare Blisshaven clothing still tucked in its drawers. I thought of Mrs. Westcliffe's face in the audience after Armand's announcement, how she had looked as if she'd swallowed a toad.

"I wasn't actually going to go," I said.

Armand bent his head, lower, lower, until he invaded my line of vision and I had no choice but to meet his eyes. "You're welcome, waif."

"Thank you."

He straightened into a stretch, both arms out. "How about that? You uttered the words and lightning didn't strike you dead."

"Is it true, though? Are you really going to make Tranquility into a hospital?"

"Convalescent hospital, and yes, it's true. I've already been in contact with the minister of defense, who's assigned all the correct people to the project and assures me I'm a damned fine lad who's doing a damned fine thing."

A hint of something in his voice. Not irony, but something veiled and biting like it.

"Not just for me, then," I said.

"No."

"Aubrey," I realized.

He looked full at me again. "I can't join up. You know that. After Aubrey left for the Royal Flying Corps my father pulled every string possible to keep me out the fight and stuck in England, so sod him. I'll stay here—at least for now—but on my terms. Putting those wounded men in Tranquility will be the best thing that's ever happened to it. Perhaps it'll even give the place a soul."

"I'm glad," I said simply.

"Good."

. . . *ood-ood-ood* . . .

"Listen," he said. "You should learn how to swim."

"Why?"

"We'll have to cross the Channel on the way to East Prussia. It's not an insignificant distance. We don't know what might happen."

I raised my brows and cocked my head. " 'We'?"

"Yes, *we*," he replied, irritated. "Of course *we*. And I'd appreciate it if you refrained from looking at me like that all the time."

"Like what?" I snapped.

"Like I'm an irksome fly orbiting about your oh-so-marvelous self. Whether you like it or not, Miss Jones, this is a team endeavor, and you and I together make up the team. We can count Jesse in, too, if you like. If that makes it all so much *better* for you. Oh, and the mad duke as well, of course! Couldn't do any of this bloody nonsense without *him*."

He walked away from me before I could think of a response. He didn't just leave me alone there in the cavern, though. He placed his hand on the lever that would open the hidden door, but he didn't leave.

"You're not a fly," I muttered.

"A mosquito, then."

"Mandy, you're the only person in the world who's like me." I spoke quietly, to defeat the echo. "Perhaps a little too like me. And I—I don't care to learn how to swim. The sea is cold."

"Tranquility," he said, without turning around. "There's a heated swimming bath inside."

I paused, astonished. "There is?"

"Yes. And a bowling alley. And a gymnasium. Didn't you know? Nothing but the wildest extravagances for the mad duke."

"I never called him that." *Out loud.*

"You don't have to. Everyone else does."

"What do they know? He's the only one of us gifted with the future by the stars. The only one Jesse talks to."

"Yes," said Armand. "The only one." He sent me a look. "We should go back up."

"You first. We don't want to be caught alone together in some deserted dark hall. Westcliffe'll use any excuse to keep me from you."

"She can try," he said.

We weren't caught, though. Armand vanished into the warren of tunnels, and about five minutes later I did, too, and I didn't see him again.

The flood of families exiting the castle had slowed to a trickle. There would be a few girls like me who stayed on another night or so, but most of the student population was already gone. The air was choked with the pong of diesel and perfume and sweat, stale beer (from the servants?) underneath. I stepped outside to escape it, walking past the final few automobiles idling on the drive.

Bored chauffeurs puffing on cigarettes looked me up and down. A seagull slung a high, leisurely loop overhead, wings open wide, a hard white chip against the blue.

The motorcar at the front of the line was bright yellow and huge. It needed to be, I presumed, to hold all the stylish Pemingtons and their liveried driver, who was struggling to tie off the last cord binding the trunks in back.

"There you are!"

Sophia crunched across the gravel to me, holding out both hands to take mine like we were the most devoted of confidantes. Chloe and her mother, already seated inside the auto, eyed me suspiciously, probably expecting me to pick her pockets.

"Smile," she whispered. "They're watching, aren't they? Smile like you've just won all my money at whist."

I did, and Sophia smiled in return, laughing, and drew me into a hug.

"How do they look?" she breathed into my ear.

"Like you've shamed them for all eternity."

"Wonderful!" She made a show of touching her lips to my cheek.

"Time to go, pet." Lord Pemington ambled up from behind, placing a meaty hand on Sophia's shoulder.

"Yes, Papa. Oh, have you met Miss Jones? Eleanore, my father, Lord Maurice Pemington, Earl of Shot. Papa, Miss Eleanore Jones. She's the one who's going to be with Armand all summer."

"At the hospital," I added hastily.

"Of course." Lord Pemington granted me a cursory nod; clearly he had other things to do besides be introduced to a girl from the ghetto, even with Lord Armand's name invoked. "How do you do, Miss—er—miss. I'm afraid we really must be going, Sophia. You know how your mother dislikes to travel after sundown."

"I'll be right there." Much softer, as he walked to the auto: "And she's not my mother."

Sophia glanced back at me, unsmiling now, her blue eyes pale as glaciers.

"Have a grand summer," I said, because she'd called me *friend* before, even if it wasn't true.

"I hope to," she replied. "I suppose we'll just have to see."

She went to rejoin to her family without another look.

Chapter 9

Three lives shine below me. Of the nearly two billion mortal souls churning and sowing and reaping atop the curve of the planet below, most are muddy, lost to me. Only three shine up this far and high, tenuous as candle flames, bright as stars . . . which is funny, if you think about it.

I do. Think about it, that is.

I can't deny that I'm lonely without her. I can't deny, even a little bit, that I wish we were still together, me there below or her up high here, at my side. I never knew that mortal love could be so binding. That having her blocked from me would be so painful.

I try whispering to her, but she doesn't hear. I try shouting, but that doesn't work, either. Her dreams remain closed to me, and I don't know why.

The other two dragons in my care, males who haven't even mastered the Turn yet, who've come nowhere near her glory or power—*they* hear me. Even their sire does.

Lora doesn't.

It breaks my heart. It would, I mean, had I a heart still.

But I'm not going to stop singing to her. I can't. It would be like ceasing to be myself, or plain ceasing to be.

I tell myself that someday she'll hear.

Gods grant me this prayer, this one hope beyond our celestial realm: Lora-of-the-moon, stop looking down. Lift your eyes skyward. Turn your ears to me. With all the magic I can summon, I command you to hear this serenade. Feel my love, falling rose petals, white-hot tears, comet-tail sparks. All for you.

I miss you, too.

Chapter 10

Play a game with me. Imagine your most perfect home. Imagine everything you could ever dream for it, anything at all. It's going to be modern and expensive—because you're filthy rich—polished and fancy, all imported marble and mahogany and stained glass and hand-stamped copper trimming. It'll be wired for electricity in every chamber, even the servants' quarters. Its gardens will be tiered and grandiose, its motor stable as cavernous as a cathedral. It will be as huge as you could hope it to be, almost more rooms than you can count, with spires of limestone and wings that go on and on. It will dominate everything around it, and you yourself will have personally designed and presided over every square inch.

Oh, yes. One more thing: Imagine that you, the designer, are insane.

And that war comes before it's finished.

And all the men who used to be working on it are gone, dying in trenches in countries far away, so what there is of your dream sits half done and rotting through the seasons.

Tranquility at Idylling. My happy home for the next three months.

When I called it a monstrosity before, I wasn't exaggerating.

I climbed slowly out of the motorcar Armand had sent to Iverson for me, my suitcase clutched in both hands.

"No, I'll keep it," I said to the chauffeur when he tried to take it from me. He tugged at his cap and backed away to the front of the car again.

My feet seemed heavier than usual, dragging their way along the crushed-shell drive that left a pinkish residue on my boots. It was close to twilight, with a brisk evening wind that plastered my skirt to my legs and skittered through the grit. Tranquility was an elaborate sandcastle silhouette against the deepening blue.

Tranquility's butler, who always held his mouth in a flat, folded way that suggested he had something scandalous to say but never would, awaited me on the steps leading to the front doors.

"Miss," he greeted me, with a bow. "Lord Armand is in the west drawing room. Shall I take your case? . . . Are you certain? Very well, miss. This way, please."

The atrium was an elegant oval of space, with slick checkerboard tiles and smooth plastered walls and a curving, serpentine grand staircase that led to nowhere, because there was no top-story landing built for it yet. Leaping from that uppermost stair could possibly land you on the giant glass-and-wrought-iron chandelier suspended from a chain (it resembled a series of connected lanterns, or perhaps a bat), but then you'd still have a long drop back to the floor.

I'd seen it all before, but couldn't help gazing up and around until I felt a little dizzy. I wondered, briefly, if the maids had to dust and mop all the way to the top of the staircase, even though it could never be used. (They did.)

The butler led me to a door on the right, opened it, and indicated I should walk past him into the chamber.

"Miss Eleanore Jones, my lord."

"Thank you, Matthews."

Three people were seated before a low table, each holding a drink. One of them was Armand, but I didn't know the other two: a sandy-haired bloke about his age in a khaki officer's uniform, and an elderly woman in a beaded frock and long gloves and a colossal diamond-and-topaz brooch. Light from the sconces danced along the brooch, gold and white and yellow. I marveled that it didn't blind her.

Armand and the officer put down their glasses and stood. The woman didn't bother to move other than to aim at me a scowling look.

"Who is this person?" she demanded, querulous.

"*Miss Jones*, Aunt Lottie," replied the officer, speaking very loudly. "The girl we've been expecting."

"She is holding up dinner," the woman grumbled, sipping from her glass.

"I—"

I had been about to recite my standard apology to people of power, then cut myself short. I reckoned I'd done enough begging of pardons to last me some while, and anyway, I hadn't even known about the bloody dinner.

"I hope I am only fashionably late," I said instead, which still seemed a bit too groveling, considering, but the words were out and there was no calling them back.

Armand smiled. "Not even that. Please, join us."

I looked around, set my suitcase on the floor by a chaise longue covered in salmon chintz, and forced myself forward once again.

This room was one of the finished ones, apparently, because I didn't see any of the odd scaffolding or pallets of tools that littered the rest of the manor. In fact, it looked almost normal, with bronze-colored drapery and slender teakwood stands supporting ferns and busts of carved stone. Handsomely framed watercolors hung between the windows. The rugs were cream and rust and saffron, a flawless match to the striped wallpaper.

The undercurrent of madness was subtle here, seeping through in small, sneaky ways: how the rugs had been laid in a random patchwork, unaligned; how the woven patterns in the curtains didn't actually match from panel to panel; how all the watercolors were of gruesome hunting scenes, of wild animals being ripped apart by grinning men and dogs.

Armand was performing the introductions. I wrenched my attention away from the walls.

" . . . Lady Clayworth, Miss Jones. And you remember my friend from Eton, Laurence Clayworth? Lieutenant Clayworth now, of course."

The other fellow moved around the table to take my hand. I was gazing up at him, trying to place him—it wasn't as if I knew very many boys, after all—when he spoke.

"Good lord, is *this* that little beggar girl from the station? I would not have recognized you, I fear. How very grown-up you look, Miss Jones."

Then I remembered him. We'd met only once before, and that had been enough. It had been at the train station the night I'd first arrived in Bournemouth, and Laurence Clayworth, now Lieutenant, had been lounging about with Armand and Lady Chloe on the platform, waiting for their ride. He had regarded me then with the same interest as he might a bug on the bottom of his shoe. Less, really, because at least he would have bothered to scrape off the bug.

Although I recalled that it had been the charming Chloe who'd taken me for a beggar.

"Delightful to see you again," I said, smiling, and squeezed my fingers around his just hard enough to hurt.

His eyes widened; he dropped my hand.

"Laurence is here on leave for the next two days, helping to settle his aunt. Since the army nurses and staff have yet to arrive, Lady Clayworth has graciously offered to stay on at Tranquility until they do."

"Mind yourself, Miss Jones," said Laurence, with a smirking, sideways glance at me. "Aunt Lottie watched over each of my sisters during their debuts. She is a most vigilant chaperone."

"The light in here is far too bright," complained Aunt Lottie. "And I expect there will be trifle for dessert? You know it is my favorite. Foster, ensure that Cook knows about the trifle at once."

Laurence's smirk broadened; Armand wouldn't meet my eyes. As far as I knew, there was no one in the room named Foster.

"How reassuring," I said, "to know that all the rules of propriety are going be so rigorously followed."

"Drink?" Armand didn't wait for my answer, going to the sideboard to pour an amber liquid into one of the heavy tumblers. Our fingers brushed as I accepted it, and then he *did* glance at me—a brief, hard look—before releasing the glass and turning away.

It was whisky. I took a drop upon my tongue and let it sting a path to the back of my throat.

"How was your journey from the school, Miss Jones?" Lieutenant Clayworth inquired.

"Uneventful. Swift."

So swift that I hadn't managed more than a short goodbye to the only person who'd been in sight, a maid busy mopping the tiles around the front doors.

Mrs. Westcliffe had been pointedly absent for my scheduled departure.

Aunt Lottie held out her own tumbler to Armand, who quickly refilled it. "*Where* did she come from?"

"From *Iverson,* Lady Clayworth."

She brought up a pair of spectacles that had been dangling from a silver chain down her bosom and inspected me from head to toe.

"Gracious! Are we dining with the servants now?"

"She is a *student,* Lady Clayworth."

"She is *not* dressed for dinner!"

I smiled thinly. "And yet here I am."

"You look fine," Armand assured me. "But that reminds me. I was forwarded your allowance, Miss Jones. The one from the government, for your summer expenses."

The government would as soon send me an allowance as it would hand me the crown jewels.

I tried the whisky again. "Thank heavens. It's so difficult to afford to dress like a servant these days."

Armand's lips quirked, and Lieutenant Clayworth sniggered into his drink. Aunt Lottie downed her whisky and glowered at us all.

"Dinner is prepared, my lord," announced the butler, standing at the door.

"Finally!" With a creak of her corset, Lottie found her feet, reaching for Armand's arm. "I don't know what the world is coming to, when one is obliged to wait for the staff to arrive before being served dinner, and there is no trifle for dessert."

A bachelor living alone—even alone in a mansion—could not be allowed to host a single young lady of quality by himself.

It did not matter that there were approximately thirty servants of both sexes living within the mansion as well, or that I was considered hardly any sort of quality.

Even in wartime, the social niceties must remain observed. Therefore, Lady Charlotte Clayworth was also in residence.

Directly across the hall from me.

And she snored.

Piercingly.

Not that it mattered. I was awake anyway, staring up at the pressed tin ceiling of my chamber, little dots and florets repeated over and over until I lost the shape of them in the soft sable shadows.

I appreciated the shadows. I appreciated all that they hid.

The room I'd been given was grand and echoing, just as posh as I might have predicted. It was the kind of room that Sophia or Chloe likely would feel right at home in, but for me, it was just big, strange, and dark. I'd left the nearest set of curtains agape to allow in a sliver of sapphire glow; but for that hint of light, I might as well have been stranded in the middle of the blackest ocean.

A minnow in the ebony whale of my bed, curled up small in its center.

I did not belong here. Yet I had stepped right into the role Armand had created for me, and thus, I knew, into his and Jesse's plan. I would pretend to nurse sick men and I would pretend to be a normal girl who did not transform into anything else, certainly not a monster, and I would pretend I wasn't a coward who didn't want to do any of those things.

The very air of this place smothered me, pressed me down into the sheets with the weight of awful, awful expectations.

I had not Turned into a dragon since the night I'd been shot. I'd told myself that I needed time to recover, that I was still unwell. It was nearly true.

But the shadows lay everywhere, the thickest ones right over my heart, and beneath their suffocating darkness, the real cringing truth dwelled.

I didn't want to be a dragon again. I didn't want to fly anywhere or rescue anyone. I just wanted to be left alone.

I could still do it. I could still leave. I'd stuffed the cash from my pinecone behind the lining of my case. It would take me away from the war and the brothers Louis, all the way to America, if I wanted. South America, even. Antarctica. I could live by myself, cold and perfect as a snowflake, and no one would ever trouble me again.

"So do it," I whispered to myself, to the florets above me. "Go on, then, if you're so sure."

sleep, crooned the stars beyond the windows. *sleep now, beast, we have a dream for you.*

I am back at Moor Gate. I am splayed flat upon the table they use for killing people, my wrists and ankles bound by leather straps, another one hard across my neck. Yet although I'm on that table, I'm also standing beside it, looking down at me. I see myself there: the knotted mat of my hair; the sweat-stained smock, rucked up and torn; my clenched fists. The gag in my mouth. The wires attached to me, connecting me to The Machine.

My eyes, focused somewhere between terror and rage. I know what's to come.

I'm so skinny and dirty and fierce. No wonder everyone thinks I'm a beggar.

At the other side of the table, someone moves. Not one of the doctors; they're huddled to my right in their long white coats, a lumpy, indistinct mass, hissing to themselves like snakes.

No, this person is by himself. Golden and bright, serene. Just gazing upon him fills me with calm.

this was your worst moment, *Jesse says, lifting his eyes to mine.* here, in this room.

No, *I answer.* The worst moment was losing you.

but you've not lost me, lora. and you never will.

The Machine begins to warm into a hum, an evil sound. The skin on the back of my neck and arms contracts.

this moment, *Jesse says, returning his attention to the fettered me upon the table. He bends down lower, closer to my face.* and i promise you, beloved, i promise—it will never get worse than this.

His hand reaches out, strokes my cheek. I feel it even though I'm still the girl standing, not the one strapped down and about to die.

I turn my face toward his fingers. I want to smile because he's touching me again, finally. And I want to cry because even in this dream, I know it will not last.

i am above you, inside you, within and without, *he murmurs.* forever and always. that's the nature of true love.

But his words only sting. No. No, you left, and now I'm alone! I'll always be alone.

there is no shame in being alone. if this is the path you choose, lora, there is no shame. but there are more fates now than yours and mine to consider. there is one of your own beyond this place. he's trapped and in pain, much as you are here. will you leave him to his suffering?

The air tastes of copper. The Machine has reached a whine that means it is ready. I know that whine, that particular pitch. It has scored me in ways I will never be able to heal.

A doctor's hand reaches for the lever. I look desperately at Jesse, who straightens and sends me one last smile.

dragon-girl. feel free to hit him hard, *he says, and the lever is thrown and everything goes red.*

I jerked awake. Jesse's hand was still at my cheek, caressing.

"Jes—"

The hand slipped from my cheek to the collar of my nightshirt, to the first button at my breastbone, already undone.

"Eleanore," rumbled a voice, and the feather mattress sank with the weight of the person at its edge.

I sat up and struck out in one swift motion, my fist connecting with something fleshy that crunched.

Lieutenant Clayworth gave a cry and fell off the bed. Across the hallway, his aunt's snoring sputtered, stopped—then resumed.

Laurence had landed on his backside, both hands cupped to his nose. I flipped back the covers and leapt to the floor, ready to hit him again.

"What the hell . . . ?"

I believe that's what he said. It was pretty garbled from behind his fingers.

"Are you lost?" I whispered, unmoving. "Perhaps searching for a chambermaid up for a tumble?"

"I thought *you* were up for a tumble," he growled, coming to his feet.

"Yes. Because we got on *so* splendidly this evening, didn't we?"

Laurence lowered his hands, examining the blood that I could not see but could definitely smell.

I'd learned dancing and deportment at Iverson. At Blisshaven I'd learned how to punch: do it fast, do it hard, keep your thumb tucked and your wrist straight. Don't run away unless you have to. Make damned sure you win, because if you don't, you'll be watching your back for weeks.

"You're a ruddy bitch, you know that?"

"And you're a ruddy cad. I know you must know *that*. The only reason you're in my room is because you think I'm Armand's summer dalliance. That makes me fair game, eh?"

He leered at me, ugly. "Why should he have all the fun?"

"Because he's your *friend,* you jackass."

"What's the matter? Don't you want to give it a go with a real man? I'm not some blighter too afraid to enlist. I'm an officer, Eleanore. I'm out there fighting for us."

Some blighter too afraid to enlist. He meant Armand.

"Try it with me," Laurence cajoled, sidling closer. "Try it with someone sane. I'll make it ever so good for you, I swear."

My body went to ice. I couldn't believe what I was hearing.

"Or we can get as deranged as you want." He kept inching toward me. "If that's what you fancy. Howling mad, if that's what—"

"You think he's mad. You think Armand's mad?"

"Can't blame him if he's off his onion. Look at his parents. Anyway, better mad than a coward."

"You rotter," I breathed. "You stinking, prissed-up, preening bastard. You don't know anything about him!"

"I know what people say."

"People like *you*. People who've never even been to the front, I'd bet, who'd piss themselves with fear in a real battle. You're more someone's secretary than an actual fighting man, am I right? Rich boy like you, no need to get your hands dirty."

He surged toward me. "Shut up, bitch."

Dragon reflexes, dragon strength—I hit him again. It was easy. He didn't even have time to flinch as my arm came up.

He didn't land on the floor this time. But there was a lot more blood.

"You're going to leave this place," I told him, very quiet. "You're going to leave first thing in the morning, before breakfast. If you don't, I'll tell Armand everything. Let him realize what a great friend you are."

"Like he'd believe a slut like you—"

Something happened then, something I didn't understand at first. There was a flash of light, silvery purplish, very bright. It showed me Laurence's face and the blood smeared down his nose and lips, the walls behind him and the furniture and curtains. Everything intensely sharp and clear.

And in that split second of light, I saw myself reflected in his pupils, shining there, frozen. I saw a radiant-eyed monster caged inside a girl.

A Thing within me shifted. A Thing that was huge and twisting and hungry, rippling beneath my skin.

"Go away," I said. It came out strangled, hoarse. "Don't ever come back."

He backed up, one step, two, three—and then he was scrambling for the door. He ran down the hallway to the exact rhythm of Aunt Lottie's snores.

I stood there, my hands still fisted, ready to strike again at something. Anything. The rippling, twisting Thing shuddered through me, growing stronger, eating into my marrow. My skin felt too tight and my heart was hammering, *boom-boom-boomboomboomboom*, wild and fast as a hummingbird's.

I was panting. I was fever, I was ice. I was running to the closest window, shoving apart the heavy curtains. My fingers found the twin locks on the hinge and yanked, once, twice, until one released and the other broke apart in my hand.

I pushed at the glass. It opened just in time, air scented of night and mist bathing my face, and then I Turned to smoke and shot out into the dark like an arrow unloosed from the depths of hell.

Seconds later, the next Turn overtook me.

The one that uncaged the beast. The one that made me into a dragon.

Chapter 11

I've mentioned that I wasn't very good at the Turns, haven't I?

I materialized upside down. Falling. My wings unfolded and began a frantic flapping. I rolled and managed a drunken veer that had me only just avoiding a collision with a corner of Tranquility's roof. As it was, my right flank smacked into the leaden gutter, crumpling it like paper, and my tail whipped up and around and took out a row of slate tiles, sending them spinning like tops to the ground.

Better them than me. I flapped harder, gaining altitude. Soon I was flying straight, more or less, and Tranquility was a dollhouse beneath me, and the lawns and meadows and forests fell away, away, a map I no longer had to worry about or follow.

The rage that had driven me here, the feral anger and fear that had propelled me up into the sky, began to tear apart with the wind. Slivers, shards, blown into insignificance.

I thought, *This is me. This is the most honest part of me, if not the very best part.*

All those names flung at me recently, *beast*, *bitch*, *thing*, were true. If they were insults, then I would rip them inside out and make them my own. I was all of those words and a ferocious lot more, and right now—in this moment—I was glad for it.

I bared my teeth to the night. My talons clawed at the sky. The hummingbird hammer of my heart gradually calmed, becoming steady and strong, a constant guide.

I found a jet of air and let it snatch me south, opening my wings to it so widely they ached, but it was a good ache. I welcomed the pain.

I was a dragon of gold, by the way. Mostly gold, deep purple at my tips. My scales were glimmering, just as gorgeous as Jesse's pine-cone and flowers, and my tail was barbed and my wings—

My left wing had a hole it, I realized, craning my long neck to see. A bullet hole. Every beat of that wing brought a tiny whistle as the air rushed through. It didn't hurt, curiously enough, though it looked as if it should.

war wound, sang the stars, watching me as they always did, glinting their rainbow colors, as they always did. *war beast, dragon of war, fireheart. welcome back to us.*

I faced ahead again. I stretched out my chin and climbed higher, higher, until all I could hear was my heart in my ears, and all I could fathom was the endless sapphire line between heaven and earth, ocean and night, and the slim golden thread of me tearing a path between them.

Chapter 12

"This is most irregular."

Aunt Lottie frowned at the note the butler had handed her, the black pudding and poached eggs she'd been served slowly congealing into a single, oozy glob on her plate. She adjusted her spectacles and held the note closer, perhaps hoping for less irregularity via a shorter distance from the paper to her nose.

"*Most* irregular indeed," she huffed.

It was breakfast, a glorious full English breakfast, and for all of the massive sideboard jam-packed with platters of food, there were only three of us to dine. At the head of the table sat Armand, with Lottie to his right and me to his left. The rest of the chairs were empty, but like everything else about Tranquility, the table was huge. I'd wager forty more people could easily tuck in.

Forty orphans from the Home. I looked down the table and imagined them there, in the high-backed, buffed wooden chairs that all had carved lions for the arms, fidgeting and blowing their noses in the napkins, destroying the careful code of flatware arranged around the china, smudging the wax on the table with grubby fingers and sweaty palms. All wide eyes and growling stomachs and out-and-out disbelief, because, like me, not a single one of them would have been able to fantasize themselves from Bliss-haven into this room, before this feast of eggs and fresh fruit and pickled fish and toast and hash and meat, meat, meat.

For only three people.

I wondered if the servants would get to eat what we didn't fin-ish. Maybe they just tossed all the leftovers straight into the rub-bish.

And it wasn't merely the meal that was excessive. The dining room was filled with floor-to-ceiling windows, sky and glass every-where, with Armand's seat placed so that the biggest one loomed right behind his back. It made it seem as if he somehow sat sus-pended in midair.

But I guessed he was used to it. I hadn't noticed him glance even once out the windows. Instead he'd paused, fork in hand, and was regarding Lottie with polite interest. He was obviously waiting to hear what Lieutenant Clayworth's note said.

I, however, didn't stop gobbling down my latest helping of fried potatoes and sausage. I had no need to wait; I already knew what the note said, since I'd written it myself.

TERRIBLY SORRY, AUNT LOTTIE AND ALL. MUST DASH OFF UNEXPECTEDLY. WAR BUSI-NESS. HOPE YOU UNDERSTAND AND WILL SEE YOU SOON, NO DOUBT.

—L.C.

Another good lesson for you: When forging missives or signa-tures, it's always better to keep things short. The less there is to scrutinize, the less there will be to muck you up.

The lieutenant hadn't actually left a note. After I'd come back down to earth last night, I'd searched his empty room to be sure. I'd even done a quick perusal of both Armand's and Lottie's chambers to check that he hadn't slipped one under their doors before leaving, because I couldn't risk him writing something about me, truth or lie or anything at all. Not if I wanted this summer to keep going forward.

But he hadn't. He'd just fled.

Who, exactly, was the coward?

I had seen Armand Louis run into a hail of bullets for me. I'd seen him face mortal danger without recoiling, and I'd seen him weep for our dead. So to hell with sodding Lieutenant Laurence Clayworth.

During my hunt for the note, I'd come to the decision that I'd keep most of the facts of my encounter with Laurence to myself. I didn't know how close the two of them truly were, but hearing that a person you thought a friend considered you unbalanced at best, craven at worst, could only hurt. Whatever else I felt about Armand, I had no desire to cause him hurt.

Lottie sighed and held out the folded paper to Armand, who scanned it and then passed it to me. I looked down at it, allowed myself a fresh measure of satisfaction at the handwriting (which definitely didn't resemble mine), then looked back up.

"I trust everything is all right," I said, with what I hoped was exactly the right touch of genteel concern.

Apparently I'd miscalculated. Armand's focus went from his kippers to my face, instantly alert.

"'War business,'" Lottie muttered, slicing into her eggs. "And the boy couldn't be bothered to wait for a respectable goodbye."

"You know how things are these days, my lady," said Armand,

still watching me. "It's an unfortunate fact of the modern world. Matters change in the space of a breath."

Lottie squinted at him. "What's that you said?"

"Matters *change*."

"Did he receive a telegram in the night? We must ask Foster."

"I wouldn't," I warned Armand, low.

"Foster?" Lottie was looking around, annoyed that neither the footman by the sideboard nor the butler had come forward. "Foster? Where the devil is he?"

"Matthews," said Armand, "I believe Lady Clayworth would enjoy some trifle, if you wouldn't mind."

"Certainly, my lord."

Armand gazed at me, silent, while the butler offered a heap of cream and cake to her ladyship.

"Well?" he said as Matthews moved away and Lottie happily dug in.

I glanced at my own plate, now nearly empty, then back up at the sideboard.

Armand's tone went dangerously silky. "Lora."

"Yes, yes." I poked at a piece of potato with my knife. Now that the time had come, I found myself struggling with what to say. "We might have a problem."

"What manner of problem?"

"Your friend. I imagine his nose is broken."

"Oh? And why would that be?"

I gave up on the potato. I lifted my eyes and gazed back at Armand and let the silence balloon between us.

His face, already so pale, seemed to go even whiter.

"Are you joking?"

"No."

"Were you—hurt?"

I smiled, mirthless. "No."

He sat there without moving, staring at me. A cloud of small brown birds poured into view behind him, shrinking and swelling in unison, blurred wings and shrill chirrups. Pouring away again.

Armand had gone to stone. No, not stone, because I didn't think stones could emanate the black sense of menace I felt from him now. He was as stiff and frightful as he'd been that moment in the duke's asylum, when in the back of my mind I'd thought maybe, maybe I'd have to stop him from killing his own father.

I said, "I should have locked the door and I didn't. No harm done but to him. In fact, I likely did him a favor. He can tell all the girlies now that a Hun clocked him in a fight."

Armand stood; alarmed, so did I. He seemed fixed on a point beyond me, someplace where there were no birds or sky or anything civilized like breakfast. I looked into blue eyes and saw only sparks and darkness.

He'll come back to us stronger and stronger, Jesse had told me once. *He's going to crave you more and more, and not having you will eat him raw.*

How much worse, then, would it feel to know that someone else, his own mate, had not only craved me but had gone behind his back to act upon it?

It wasn't until then that I understood I'd accidentally revealed the worse betrayal, after all.

"Mandy. He's not worthy of you. Let it be."

"Lord Armand, have you taken ill?" demanded Lottie. "I cannot imagine why you're standing otherwise."

"Mandy," I said again, urgent, soft. Trying to pull him back to me. "There's more."

His lashes lowered. He looked down at his hand, at his opening fingers. The fork he'd been holding had been bent nearly in two. It clattered down to the table.

"Yes, indeed, I'm so eager to see the future therapy room," I said very audibly. "It's downstairs, you say? Do forgive us, your ladyship. I feel we must get started right away. For the soldiers, you know."

"What's that?" Lottie asked, but I ignored her, reaching instead for Armand.

I was counting on all those years of being raised as a gentleman, all that stiff-upper-lip training, Eton, London, any of it, and to my relief, it worked. Without a word he let me slip my hand through the crook of his elbow, and together we walked out of the dining room, leaving a confounded Lady Clayworth behind.

"What did that young woman say? Why are they leaving? Foster, did you understand her?"

I hadn't thought of where to go from there. No doubt there was a downstairs to Tranquility, but I had no notion of how to get there or even if there was going to be such a thing as a therapy room.

I was just walking, Armand rigid at my side, and my feet took us to the one other place I really recognized: the front parlor, where there was a piano.

Not an ordinary upright piano, either, but a shiny black grand piano, practically as big as a pond, with a bench long enough for two. I led him to it, waited until he sat, and then took my place beside him.

I didn't speak, and neither did he. Instead, my fingers touched the keys, and the music began to flow.

The duke had done up the parlor entirely in black and white. Floors, walls, furniture, drapes. It was probably the only reason the piano was there, fitting so neatly into his scheme, but as far as I was concerned, the piano was the only thing in the whole chamber that made any sense. Everything else was a black-and-white mess.

I closed my eyes to block it out and concentrated on the melody that drifted around us both, gentle and sweet, languid as a summer stream. I thought perhaps it belonged to the opal in Armand's stickpin.

Minutes passed. No one else came in.

"How do you do that?" he asked at last, his voice barely rising above the notes.

"I listen." And then, a while later: "Can't you do it?"

He shifted, not quite a shrug. "I don't think so."

"Have you ever tried?"

"No."

I stopped. "Here. Put your hands like this. That's it, right there. Now, listen to the melody. Let it surround you. It's lovely, isn't it? Do you hear it?"

He gave a short nod.

"So. Play."

He stared down at the keys, then tried a few tentative notes— the wrong ones.

"No, like this."

I traced out half a bar, but he didn't try to copy it. He didn't move at all, in fact, just kept staring down at the keyboard.

"Okay, then. Hands up again, like I showed you."

I rested my palms over the backs of his, our fingers aligned. I felt that slight, snapping shock that sometimes happened when we touched; he took a swifter breath, so I knew he felt it, too.

"Play," I whispered, and pressed my fingers down, showing him the way.

Slowly, haltingly, we caught the easiest snippets of the song.

"Lieutenant Clayworth saw my dragon eyes," I murmured, without looking away from our work. "I couldn't help it."

"Dragon eyes," he echoed, emotionless.

"When they flash. Everything lit up."

"I've seen it."

We kept playing. We weren't getting any better.

"And after that, he hared off. But I think it'll be fine. After all, if he says anything about it, who's going to believe him?"

"Only a lunatic," answered Armand gravely.

I shot him a glance. He was smiling a little.

"Precisely." I smiled back. "But—Armand. I think you should be prepared for him to . . . that is, he's really not the sort of fellow who . . ." I shook my head, back to stumbling over my words, searching for the ones least likely to wound. Eventually I had to settle for the same thing I'd told him before. "He is unworthy of you."

"Lora, if and when I see Laurence again, you may be confident that if his nose isn't broken now, it's going to be."

"Excellent," I said, and drew my hands away.

He tried it on his own for a few minutes longer, blundering along, before giving up.

"I'm no good at this."

I let out a laugh. "You're really not."

And then we were laughing together, hushed and real, like we were thieves who'd gotten away with stealing something special. When it ended we were leaning against each other, our faces inches apart. All those sparks, the danger and darkness, had lifted from his eyes; everything was blue and bright once more.

The last tickle of laughter died away in my throat.

Armand said my name. He lifted a hand to my hair, cupping the nape of my neck.

"Eleanore," he whispered again, tilting his head to mine, his lips skimming past my cheek, his breath in my ear. "I'd wait forever for you, you know. If it mattered. If you'd care."

"I do care," I whispered back, miserable.

His fingers tightened, warm and firm. "No, you don't. Not the way I mean. Not yet."

He pressed a kiss to my hair, then got up and left, taking all the heat of the room and the final floating notes of the opal song with him.

Chapter 13

The military descended upon Tranquility like a plague of extraordinarily organized locusts. Men in uniforms and shiny black boots trod in and out of the rooms, every location swiftly evaluated, every servant assessed, every unfinished chamber and hallway and stairwell marked with tape across the entrances, so that doctors and patients and nurses wouldn't topple through and break their crowns.

That part alone took up all of their first three days.

Then the wounded began to arrive.

Truck after truck pulled up the drive, spilling out broken soldiers. Men on stretchers, men with crutches or canes, men wrapped in so many bandages they might have been living mummies, blots of scarlet bleeding through.

The war had truly come to us at last.

"Miss Jones," barked a voice at my back, and I started, turning about.

Mrs. Quinn, chief nurse of the newly christened Tranquility at Idylling Recovery Hospital, stood behind me in her wimple and somehow always spotless white frock, scowling. We'd met only two days ago, and it seemed she was always scowling—at me, at least.

"Are you here to help, or are you rather more a tourist?"

I forced a neutral tone. "To help, ma'am."

"Then do so. You may take this wheelchair to Nurse O'Donnell over there, and assist her with that young man."

Unlike me, Nurse O'Donnell (*Call me Deirdre!*) was a real nurse, probably in her late thirties. She had hazel eyes and a round face and a quick polished smile, which she directed at me as I walked up to join her at the back of the latest truck.

"Emma!"

"Eleanore," I corrected her, but she wasn't listening, focused instead on the wounded man trying to ease out of the truck on only one working leg. The other was encased from hip to toes in a plaster cast.

"Lovely! Let's have you escort this gentleman to the induction room, eh?"

"Induction room" was the military's term for the front parlor, which was by far the largest chamber on the main floor besides the dining room. It had been transformed from a hideous black-and-white room with a piano into a hideous black-and-white room with rows of beds and chairs and portable privacy curtains . . . and the piano, which had been pushed back against a wall, since it was too large to fit through any of the doorways. It seemed the duke had had the parlor constructed around it.

"Here you go, then, sir, off with our Miss Ella. She'll take fine care of you, get you settled in."

I offered a smile to the injured man, who offered a wan smile back.

"Very kind of you, Emma-Eleanore-Ella," he said, proving that at least someone had been paying attention.

"My pleasure," I replied. I rolled the wheelchair into position behind him, then leaned in close to help him sit.

It was hard not to retch. Like a lot of the wounded, he stank, *really* stank, of something elusive yet familiar. Something that reminded me of the grimy butcher's alley a block from the orphanage, green bottle flies swarming over skinned animals, hot rotting meat.

I wheeled him into the manor.

The days went on like that. Since I had no true nursing experience, I was relegated to the least important tasks, most of which involved cleaning things or fetching things or relaying messages from one part of the mansion to another. By the end of each day I retreated into my bedroom with a sense of weary, guilty relief.

And no matter how I scrubbed, I could not rid myself of the dreadful meat smell. I tried scented soaps, borrowed perfume from Deirdre: no use. It was always there.

By the eleventh day, I was beginning to wonder if I shouldn't have gone to Callander after all.

Armand was busy with his new role as lord of the manor, but it seemed to me he was more of a specter haunting it than an actual person. We'd not spoken since the morning at the piano. Whenever I saw him now it was always from a distance, at the top of a flight of stairs or down long, gloomy hallways. He remained surrounded by others, the lone figure dressed in black or gray instead of khaki. They were all men with strict schedules and lives to save. I barely warranted a glance from any of them.

I'd smoked to his bedchamber once since everyone else had arrived. Only once. I'd Turned to girl beside his bed and looked down at him sleeping, hoping he'd wake, hoping for some stupid reason that I wouldn't have to put my hand on him for him to wake.

I'd read somewhere that people always appear peaceful in their sleep. All the cares and worries of the day slipped away, temporarily forgotten or buried beneath dreams.

Armand did not look peaceful. He looked shadowed, stark. He looked much like the dragon-boy I'd glimpsed weeks ago in the forest, when he'd lit that lantern and offered me caviar and trouble.

Out of curiosity, I leaned over him, inhaled; I smelled only soap and wine and him.

Hungry? he'd asked me that night in the forest, watching me with that dark dragon look.

Hungry?

I realized, unsettled, that I was. A flicker, a small stirring of my blood. Nothing like what I'd felt with Jesse, but . . . I was.

I stood there awhile longer with my insides roiling and that flicker growing, growing, my hand hovering above his shoulder.

In the end, I didn't touch him. I left him to whatever dreams may have lulled him.

As I said, we hadn't spoken in some time. Even so, I don't know why I was surprised at what happened next. Looking back, I can see that it was absolutely inevitable.

The man with the cast was named Gavin Raikes. He was nineteen years old and in the process of dying inch by excruciating inch. Everyone now, not just me, could smell it.

"No," he kept saying, staring up wildly from his bed at his doctor, at Deirdre. At me. "No, no, no, I won't let you! I won't let you, I say. Keep away from me!"

"This is just the cast now," Deirdre was trying to tell him. "The cast, that's all. It must come off. Be a good lad and let Dr. Newcastle take it off."

"I won't let—"

"Raikes," warned the doctor, very stern, "if you don't calm down, you won't like what comes next. We must have a look—"

"No!"

Gavin began thrashing about and within seconds a couple of soldiers were on him, grabbing him by the shoulders and ankles, pinning him down.

"Quickly," said the doctor to Deirdre, and like they'd done it a hundred times before—perhaps they had—they moved over the man, wielding saws, hammers, something that looked like a long metal claw.

I stood ready with clean linens across my arms because that's what I'd been told to do. Although as soon as the plaster cracked apart, all five of us, even the doctor, gagged and tipped back.

There wasn't much left of his leg. What there was was shredded, melted, sickly gross green. I looked away before I did something awful, like heave down Deirdre's skirts.

Before I knew it, everyone else had recovered, was busy moving again, and Deirdre swiveled about and deposited something in my arms: a section of the plaster with a saw still attached, all of it slimy with decomposed flesh.

And something else. Small somethings, wiggling through the slime. Squirming.

I had seen maggots before. At Moor Gate there had been a boy—I hadn't known his name—who'd been kept alone in his cell for so long that when they finally brought him out he'd been a papery skeleton, with big red sores on his lips and his hair mostly missing because he'd been tearing it out and eating it. Eating even his eyelashes and eyebrows.

I'd been pressed up against a hallway wall when they'd passed (that's what you were supposed to do: press yourself thin against a wall when the guards came, hope hope hope they weren't coming for you), a pair of men half dragging the boy down the corridor because his paper skeleton legs either couldn't or wouldn't work right any longer. They kept buckling, and it made the guards angry. They'd yelled at him and he'd giggled back at them. I'd reckoned then that he must have been actually barmy, because every patient at Moor Gate knew not to anger the guards. Not to make eye contact. Not to speak to them, not to plead.

Not to laugh at them.

The boy wasn't really laughing, but the guards didn't care. He was so young, probably only around eight. Maybe he hadn't been at the Institute long enough to learn the rules, but anyway, one of the guards made a sudden movement and there was the sound of snapping twigs and the boy screamed, because the man had broken three of his ribs.

Three. I remembered that, because three weeks later I saw that boy again, but on a stretcher in the hall. They'd pulled a sheet over him but it wasn't long enough to cover his face, and I'd crept close enough to confirm that he was slack and dead, and there were maggots crawling all along the sores around his mouth. Crawling out from the black-toothed, swollen-tongued *inside* of his mouth.

Little white wormy squirmy—

———

"Nooo," Gavin wailed as I staggered back a few paces. Then, to my horror, he spotted me between the doctor and one of the soldiers. He held my eyes and cried out, "Miss! Miss! For God's sake, help me, please, please, get them off!"

I shook my head, unable to look away, unable to say *Sorry, I'm so sorry* or to even part my lips at all, because if I did I was certain I was going to start screaming high and squeaky thin like that boy. The maggots writhed and the stench from the plaster shimmered up before me, bending the air into swirly shapes.

I was about to faint.

Someone new crossed in front of me. In the slow, syrupy suspension of the moment, she looked exactly like Chloe Pemington.

Whoever it was, she approached the bed and blocked my view. A crashing noise reached me from a distance; I had dropped the plaster, spattering maggots and putrefied skin and pus on us both.

A hand grasped my elbow. I was guided backward, one step, two, three, until I was across the room, near enough to the main doors that a blast of fresh air hit me, washing away the worst of the stench.

I sucked it in—*don't faint do not faint do* not *faint*—battling the big black spots in my vision until they gradually receded into pinpricks.

"I will admit I thought you had asked Lord Armand to accept you here as a way to avoid the orphanage," said the person holding my elbow. It was Mrs. Westcliffe, as fresh and smart as if she'd just stepped out from an audience with the king, maroon silk and matched pearls, not a hair out of place.

I licked my lips and swallowed hard, testing myself, but it seemed the danger of heaving had passed, too.

"Yes," I rasped. "I know."

"But now, Eleanore . . . now that I see this . . ."

All on their own, my lips glued shut again; I could not look at her. I glared up at the ceiling, down at my dress—my white nurse's dress, as clean and new as anything I'd ever owned—and took in the spray of Gavin Raikes' flesh across its front.

It seemed all the maggots had fallen off.

Mrs. Westcliffe's voice gentled. "Child, it's not too late. You need not stay."

"No, I do. I promised I would."

"A noble promise, indeed. But no one will think ill of you for deciding this is more than you bargained for."

I sucked in another lungful of air. "I'm staying."

"Very well. As you can see, at least you'll have company. It seems Lady Chloe and Lady Sophia were inspired by your example. Both have volunteered to become nurses at Tranquility for the summer, too."

I stared. Good heavens, it *was* Chloe, beautiful as ever, holding Gavin's hand and murmuring something mollifying as the doctor did his work. Sophia looked on with her arms hugged across her chest, hanging back from the crowd as I had done.

"Since I was on my way here anyway, I offered to escort them. Yet this is my final day in Wessex until the autumn comes. Miss Jones, I want you to know that I sincerely wish you well. And I hope you know what you're doing."

I definitely, definitely don't.

"Thank you," I said.

"Perhaps we'll meet again," Westcliffe said, and gave my elbow one last squeeze before moving off.

"This is very hard, I know," I heard Chloe saying. "But you're a good man, a strong man. You're going to be fine. Look at me, now. You're going to be fine."

"Oh God, oh God, I wish I were dead. I'm going to die, aren't I?"

"No, of course not," lied Lady Chloe, and smiled.

Chapter 14

Sophia was here now. *Chloe* was here now.

So, naturally, dinner became an exercise in exquisitely mannered persecution.

For evening meals the dining chamber was aglow with candlelight, twelve silver, twisty-armed candelabras stationed in a row down the center of the table, twelve more reflected back at us from the shiny black windows, countless dancing bright flames. There were vases of flowers dotting the table as well, along with salt cellars and frilled glass dishes holding rainbows of perfectly arranged hard, round candies that I was dying to taste but knew better than to try. They seemed like someone's idea of cheerful decoration.

At Iverson, Sophia had been at the far end of our table and her stepsister at another table entirely. But tonight Sophia sat directly across from me and Chloe was just two chairs to my left, a hapless young army fellow stuck between us. It was clear by the time the soup was served that she'd already fixed stars in his eyes.

To my right was yet another officer, but silver-haired and mustachioed, who'd granted me a nod and a grunt before getting down to the business of eating.

Mrs. Westcliffe would not have approved of dining sans conversation, but I did. If only I could as easily avoid Sophia's knowing gaze, and Chloe's light, venomous chatter, which kept floating my way.

" . . . so happy to be here, of course! To do my part. It's the least one might expect of a girl in my position. After all, you boys are doing all the *real* work. Only a fool would imagine that a mere summer of volunteer nursing would compare to *your* sacrifice."

"Er," said the man.

"But I told Mamá I simply *had* to do *something*. I simply *couldn't* spend the summer acting as if everything was normal. You know, attending dances and dinner parties and all those silly things. So I told her I was coming here to help, and no argument about it, if you please!"

"That's awfully kind of you, my lady."

"Oh, it's nothing! Nothing at all! And naturally my little sister had to come along, too. She's so *adorable,* simply has to follow wherever I go! Isn't that *adorable*?"

"Quite," replied the man, practically melting in his chair.

"But both of us followed Eleanore," pointed out Sophia, smiling with exaggerated benevolence over her sauced turbot. "And that's even more adorable, don't you think?"

"Who?" said the fellow.

I concentrated on my own turbot, taking apart the fish flake by flake with my fork.

Chloe murmured something, and the army man said, "Oh!" and shifted and darted me a look.

" . . . rather a wretched case, really." She slanted closer to the man, ensuring that neither of us would miss a word. "I heard she had nowhere else to go. Poor dear, she's just the most piteous creature. A charity girl, you know. It was either here or the streets for her."

"A shame," said the man.

Chloe shook her head sadly. "And she's just so *hopeless*, you know? Of course, I don't mean that in an unkind way!"

"Of course not!"

"It's just . . . well, did you see what happened today? When I first arrived?"

"No."

"She made a *huge* mess of things in the induction room. Couldn't listen to anyone, couldn't follow orders. Even at school, she was always the girl who couldn't manage to get anything right."

"There's always someone like that around," whispered the man conspiratorially.

"True," Chloe agreed, pouty and ravishing, batting her comely brown lashes. "There's always someone."

I leaned out of my chair, pried loose one of the decorative hard candies from its place, and popped it in my mouth.

It tasted a lot less like sugar and a lot more like salt, but I kept eating it. It was either that or chuck it at Chloe.

Across the table, Sophia only smiled.

He watched her at dinner.

He watched her all the time, he supposed, but dinner was easiest, because they were both stationary at the table, trapped for five full courses at least, and even though he could no longer seat her at his side—the chief nurse now had that honor; Lottie Clayworth, who seemed thoroughly happy to remain at Tranquility for the duration of the war, as long as she got to complain about it, had his other elbow—anyway, even though he could no longer have her next to him, Lora was still at the table, which was good enough.

So he could watch her. Providing he was stealthy about it, he could do it for minutes at a time.

Armand had perfected his stealth years ago. He knew all the tricks: how to keep his lashes down but his gaze up; how to smile without smiling; how to listen without reacting. How to walk without sound, to embrace the shadows. He even knew the trickiest trick of them all: how to shine in public so brightly that no one noticed what he was really about, because all they saw was dazzle.

He was especially good at that.

Every evening, Armand and the officers and doctors and nurses gathered at the table to enjoy Cook's best efforts. The conversation tended to be vague and genial and unequivocally impersonal. Charts, medicines, village life. Most of the men balked at discussing anything more serious with the women around. Had Mandy nothing else to consider, he'd be bored out of his skull.

But he had *her,* just seven chairs down to his left. Eleanore Jones, who ate with such a tension about her that he wondered she didn't crack apart into pieces, and even that was fascinating. Head down, unspeaking, quick small bites. Like someone was always about to snatch away her plate.

He'd noticed how she winced at the electrical lights, so he'd banished them from the meals, relying upon candles instead. He'd told the colonel in charge of the hospital that he thought it best if they reserved the generator oil for the soldiers' needs, which got him another *Dashed good thinking, old chap* from the military machine.

But Armand was a charlatan, a dazzler. The soldiers could have all the oil; he didn't care. He'd wanted the candles for *her*. Because she winced at the electrical lights. Because when they were on, she wouldn't look at them or walk beneath them.

And because, for some reason, that hurt him. The lights themselves never hurt him—he had no notion why they bothered her—but watching her having to be so careful, watching her eat like a starved dog on a chain, watching her coiled so tight in her chair and avoiding the eyes of everyone around her, finishing first, waiting without words, never asking for more—

It hurt him. It infuriated him. He wanted her to have everything she ever wanted, and he wanted to be the one to give it to her. And how delightfully ironic, how ridiculously sidesplitting it was that the only thing she really wanted was something—someone—Armand could not give.

it is to you now, Jesse had told him, that first night she'd come to stay at Tranquility. *i give to you her earthly cares, her beating heart and mortal life. she's rich with magic, rich with possibilities. be careful, louis. protect her. she's more fragile than she looks.*

Right, he'd thought. *Thanks for that, you bloody damned bastard. She looks about as sturdy as a dandelion tuft, so you're bloody reassuring.*

Then again, Armand heard talking stars now. So nothing was exactly reassuring.

From her place down the table, Chloe released a musical laugh. Sophia echoed it, sharper. They sat up straight and ate only what they should, smiling and chatting, practicing their English-rose charm. He knew from experience that Chloe would have half the men in love with her by dessert, and those she didn't manage to ensnare, Sophia would scoop up in the following days. They were well matched in their mutual hatred: both attractive in their different ways, both witty, both relentless.

Yet when he found his gaze drifting to them now, all they inspired in him was a vague sense of weariness. He couldn't help but think there wasn't anything genuinely interesting about either of them. He'd known girls like them forever and ever.

The secret dragon at his table took her final bite of salad and glanced up and around, candlelight tangled pink in her hair, gold along her lashes. He watched her tighten into her silent coil, still and taut until the next course was served, then bend her head and begin again.

I smoked back to him that night, and this time I didn't hesitate to shake him awake.

"We've got to work on a plan to get Aubrey," I said as soon as his eyes snapped open. "I can't stay here and be a nurse."

Armand's hand reached up and covered mine, pressing my palm to his shoulder.

"All right," he said.

We met just after dawn at the swimming bath. I thought it'd be belowground (even the term "swimming bath" made me think of dank, moldy places), but it wasn't. It was located at the back of the mansion, up against one of the unfinished wings. I'd glimpsed it from the air and thought it a hothouse, because it was long and rectangular and, like Prince Albert's famed Crystal Palace, composed almost entirely of glass. Tall glass walls, peaked glass roof. A glistening sparkler set upon the emerald lawn.

Perhaps someone else had considered it a hothouse as well. Inside there were palm trees in elaborately enameled Chinese pots, and some sort of fleshy, flowering vine crawling up stakes secured in all four corners. The air was moist with the scent of plants and disinfectant and loam—a considerable improvement over the meat smell any day.

The light around us bloomed lustrous soft, colored with the new day. Condensation from the bath formed a thousand crystal tears that trickled slowly down the walls.

"Ready?" Armand asked. He was in his bathing costume, standing upon the first tiled step that led down into the blue-green pool.

No, I wasn't. But I shrugged out of my robe anyway, approaching the steps.

I'd never swum in the ocean. I'd never had the luxury of a hot bath. Even at Iverson we washed ourselves with sponges, because that's what ladies did.

Yet thanks to Moor Gate, I had nearly drowned too many times to count.

I thought of Jesse in my dream, telling me about fate. I thought of Aubrey, who was suffering, and how endless the Channel looked from Iverson, slippery chopped water that went on and on and on, a skin over bottomless depths.

"You remember how to swim?" I asked Armand, which was dumb, because of course he did.

"Yes," he said, holding out a hand to me.

Armand's bathing costume consisted of a skintight black tunic that stopped at his shoulders and midthigh. It was the least amount of clothing I'd ever seen on him. On anyone.

My costume was similar, but red with white stripes and a belt above bloomers and a short ruffled skirt. I looked like a stick of peppermint candy. It was all Armand had been able to find in storage, a forgotten leftover from someone's long-ago summer visit.

Fashions changed, but even so. I could not imagine the woman who'd first spotted this rig in a shop and thought, *I'll look stunning in that!*

"Right," I said, steeling myself. "Let's get this over with."

I walked forward, took his hand. His fingers closed over mine.

I touched one foot to the water and jerked it back again.

"You said it was heated!"

"It is," he soothed. "It feels a bit brisk now, I admit, but you'll get used to it. Trust me."

I lowered my foot back into the water, fighting the goose bumps that raced up my skin. I held his hand hard and brought my other foot in. The water sloshed up to my shins, and I stifled a shriek.

Heated water should be warm, and this wasn't anything close. Only Armand's hand felt warm, and I fancied that was just because the rest of me had gone so cold.

"Come on," he coaxed, and took me down another step, and then another one.

Ice water to my thighs, my hips, chilling me in places I refused to consider. My feet halted in place.

"Who'd have thought," Mandy said, laughing, "that a girl bold enough to take on the Huns themselves would be so frightened of a little water?"

"I'm not frightened," I bit out. "I am freezing."

"Sorry, waif. Only describing what I see."

"I am *not* frightened."

To prove it I took another big step—too big. My foot skidded off the tiles and I lost my balance and plunged all the way into the pool. Water flooded up my nose, into my mouth, my eyes and ears.

Armand yanked me upright, still laughing as I sputtered.

"Oh, God," I said, my teeth chattering, my body trembling, my hair fat dripping ropes down my face. "Oh, crikey. Crikey!"

Smooth as satin, he glided in front of me and took me in his arms. He pressed me to his chest and kept me there, both of us bobbing in place.

Water to my shoulders, neck. Shoulders. Soft lapping water, the steadily brightening light. His arms around me. My cheek above his heart.

Mandy wasn't laughing any longer.

I became abruptly, acutely aware of my breathing. Of his. Of how my own arms had stolen around his waist.

Of how wherever we touched, I was no longer cold at all.

I felt his hand shift, his fingers weaving though the floating mass of my hair. His touch along my shoulder blade, satin again . . . but it brought back the shivers.

"Bad news," he whispered, not letting go.

"What?" Was that my voice? It sounded so reedy.

"I'm afraid this is the warmer end of the pool."

I tried to laugh, but it came out mostly choked. He pulled me closer.

"Lora—"

"My, my," said someone behind us. "You *do* realize the walls are made of glass, don't you?"

We broke apart at once. I ended up on the deeper side; Armand had to pull me back until I could stand without the water smacking me in the face.

"Good morning, Sophia," he said evenly. "What a surprise to see you up and about so damned early."

She stood at the edge of the tiles in a vanilla lace dress that already looked wilted, smiling a cool, cool smile. "Well, you know. The early bird and all that. I've found that one discovers the most *interesting* sights first thing in the morning."

"I'm teaching Eleanore how to swim."

"Oh? Is *that* what you're teaching her?"

"So far. Perhaps you'd care to shove off so we can get back to it."

"Back to what, exactly? The swimming or the lovemaking?"

I said, "We weren't—"

"Both," retorted Armand. "And if you don't mind, I'd rather we didn't have an audience."

"Then don't do it *under glass*."

"Stop it, both of you." I slapped my hand against the water for emphasis. "We're just swimming, Sophia. Honestly."

"*Honestly*, Eleanore, apparently neither of you has realized that half the mansion is already awake. So unless you're planning a wedding in here—"

I bobbled back and choked again, water filling my mouth.

"—I think it's best that I stay. I'm an excellent chaperone. Pious as a saint. Ask anyone."

"Bugger you," Armand muttered.

"Language, Lord Armand! I'm shocked."

"I doubt it, since you're the one who taught me that word."

Her smile returned. "Chloe was right about one thing. This summer would have been positively wasted on dances and social calls. Why, I might have missed all of this! Shall I go wake her to join in our fun?"

Armand shook his head in disgust. "Stay, if you must."

"Smashing!" She clapped her hands. "Swim away, children. Swim away. I'll just be *right here.* Chaperoning."

I looked at Armand standing inches from me, water breaking against his chest, all ivory skin and toned muscles, his jaw set, his eyes narrowed.

I couldn't tell if it was me or the pool, but suddenly I was much, much warmer than before.

And I knew I should be glad that Sophia was going to stay.

My almost-but-not-quite fainting spell from the day before had been noted by more than just Chloe. I wasn't three feet into the induction room before Deirdre cornered me.

"Ah, Eliza! There you are." She gave me that quick smile, which I'd come to realize didn't necessarily mean she was pleased. "How are you?"

"Fine." Knackered, actually. I'd been up practically all night and then had my first swimming lesson this morning, and nearly everything about me right now ached.

Armand had been patient with me. Sophia had not. I'd endured her heckling (*You call* that *a forward stroke? Eleanore, you're useless!*) for almost an hour before wading near enough to splash her pretty dress all down the front.

"Good, good. Listen, dearie, I think perhaps you might be better suited for a position slightly less . . . strenuous than assisting Dr. Newcastle and me."

"Oh," I said, partly offended. Mostly relieved.

"There, now, don't you fret! There are still many important tasks left undone! Why, Mrs. Quinn was just mentioning that we're always running short of properly rolled bandages. And many of these poor lads are sorely lacking for books and games. You might have a hand in distributing those!"

"Games," I said.

She clasped me on the shoulder and lowered her voice. "Not everyone is cut out for the realities of war, Eleanore. It is a grim business, a grim business indeed. You're still very young. You've not dealt with death before, and that's perfectly normal. A slip of a child like you shouldn't have to dwell on such things. You're more concerned with bonnets than bullets, I daresay! Have a go at the bandages, won't you? There's a good lass."

Another smile, and she was gone. I watched her until my eyes were caught by someone new: Chloe, seated in a chair by a bed, a man's hand clenched in hers, speaking something I could not hear. She felt my stare and returned it with a smirk, still talking. A duo of doctors worked frantically around her, both of them spattered with blood, and no one was giving *her* the boot.

I turned away, my chest tight. I walked a few aimless paces one direction, then another, until I found myself by the piano.

Someone had arranged a sheet over it, but it was already sliding off. A tray of dirty scalpels and clamps had been set haphazardly atop the sheet. A fly buzzed around it, hopping from blade to blade.

I was *not* useless. I was small and marked with a strange magic; I was different, but I would not be made useless. Not by Sophia, not by Deirdre or Chloe. Not by anyone. I had my own kind of power, and even if practically no one else knew of it or understood it— even I didn't fully understand it—it was real. It existed.

I scooted the bench into place. I took my seat and raised the cover from the keys.

It took a moment, but eventually a song did come. I followed it with my hands, soft as I could at first, just in case someone noticed and got angry. But no one stopped me, so I kept playing, my eyes closed, swaying in place because this was a meandering, sweeping sort of song, with parts that danced far and near and then doubled back on themselves, echoing, and I needed to concentrate to catch the smallest of the notes.

I wasn't sure where it came from. It seemed more permanent somehow than the bits of gold and silver worn by the people swarming around me. Perhaps it belonged to the limestone base of Tranquility itself. Perhaps Tranquility was trying to assert its own voice. After all, it wasn't the house's fault it'd been designed by a crazy person.

I finished and opened my eyes. Nothing in the chamber had changed. Same bustle, same noise, same smell.

Well, almost nothing had changed.

"I liked that," said a soldier dreamily from his bed. "Reminded me of home. Of the rye fields in autumn. All the frost on the stalks, and the sun coming though."

A new man spoke, sitting up as best he could with his torso and both arms swaddled in bandages. "Miss, can you play 'Tillie down the Lane'?"

"Um, no," I said. "Sorry. I don't know that one."

"How about 'Always Love a Sailor'?" called out a different man.

" 'Green Apples'!"

" 'Follow Me to the River'!"

" 'When She Said Yes'!"

"No." I felt my face begin to heat. "I'm terribly sorry. I don't know any popular songs."

During all this Chloe had come to stand nearby, her lips pursed, her hands on her hips. She practically radiated triumph, a goddess towering over my hunched-up humiliation.

"Oh, get up, Eleanore. I know them."

I ducked my head to hide my blush and swiveled off the bench. Goddess Chloe took my place, smoothed her dress, and smiled at the room. " 'Green Apples,' did you say?"

I left to roll bandages.

Chapter 15

I was asleep without dreams this time, cradled in a deep and dark silence, when I felt the hand at my cheek.

I sat up and swung out. Armand danced instantly out of range, nimble as a seal in water.

Or a dragon in air.

"Lora!" he whispered, both palms held out, staying well back. "It's me! Peace!"

I rubbed my eyes, wondering if this was the beginning of some unlikely new dream.

"What is it? What's wrong?"

"Nothing," he answered. "It's time, that's all. Come on."

"Time for what?"

"Time to plan, love."

Lottie emitted a particularly powerful snore; we both glanced at my door.

"Now?" I wasn't fully awake, nor did I want to be. I was tired. I wanted more sleep.

"It was your idea, remember? Or would you rather keep playing nurse?"

My shoulders sagged, and he nodded.

"Get dressed. Bring a coat. I'll wait in the hall."

"What are we—"

"Hurry. There are only so many hours left to hide us."

We were outside in a place I'd never been before, camped near the border of a tall crumbly cliff, ocean below, the woods rambling behind us thick and untouched. I assumed this was all still part of Armand's holdings, but I wasn't sure. All I could tell for certain is that we were miles from both the village and Tranquility, and that Iverson and its isle made a small, lonely blot against the water to the east.

He'd motored us here, guided by nothing more than the hazy starlight (the stars themselves oddly, stubbornly silent behind the haze) and the blurred cream half smile of the moon. Armand had refused to turn on the headlamps. I'd prayed the whole drive that his night vision was significantly better than mine.

He'd brought a blanket, a basket, and me.

The blanket was spread upon the grass, the basket was emptied of its bread and ham and cheese, and I was the one eating and listening and biting my tongue, because he'd made me promise not to interrupt until he was done explaining.

I'd agreed. The honey-smoky fragrance of the ham had been too much to resist.

But now the food was gone and he was done, and I had resorted to staring down at my clenched fingers in my lap.

"That," I said to my fingers, "is an abysmal plan."

"What?" He sounded indignant. "No, it isn't. Which part?"

"All of it, Mandy. You can't come along, and that's that. There's no safe way to keep you with me when I fly—"

"I explained to you about the saddle—"

I straightened. "I am not a horse! And anyway, every time I go to smoke, then what? I'll tell you: you and the saddle—" I made a plunging motion with my hand. "Straight down to earth. Splat."

"So you won't go to smoke while I'm on you. You can take off and land as a dragon, can't you?"

"No! I mean, I don't know. I've never tried."

"Aaaand . . . that's why we're here, far from prying eyes. Practice."

I groaned and flopped back upon the blanket, covering my face with both hands. "You don't understand!"

He didn't speak right away, but I felt his gaze. I felt the warmth of him through my new cotton dress and old battered peacoat, though he sat feet away. "Explain it to me, then."

"I'm not good at it. You know that I'm not."

"At what?"

I threw my hands back to my sides. The stars shivered in the misty black sky, distant as unspoken wishes.

She's just so hopeless . . .

Eleanore, you're useless . . .

A slip of a child . . .

"I'm not *good* at any of it yet. Half the time I think I'll be smoke, but I Turn to girl instead. I've only managed to be a dragon a handful of times, at best."

"A glorious handful," he said quietly. "A damned brilliant handful."

"But—"

His voice took on a harsher note. "Don't be dense, Lora. If I could do this for you, don't you think I would? I can't even manage smoke. There's no hope of *me* Turning into a dragon to fly halfway across Europe. It has to be you."

I glanced up at him, hard edges and burning blue eyes, that absolute focus it seemed he had whenever I caught him looking at me. Like I was something shimmering right at the brink of his understanding. A mirage, bright and unbelievable.

"Mandy, I'm saying . . . that you can't be with me. This idea of yours, to ride on my back, it can't happen. If I lose control—if I Turn to smoke or girl in midair—"

"You'll Turn back and catch me," he said, calm.

"That's easy for *you* to say."

"Not really. Frankly, I feel queasy just thinking about it. I've never liked heights."

"This isn't funny!"

"I should say not. I rather enjoy myself all in one piece. But . . ." He sighed and pushed his hands through his hair. "Look, waif. This is the way it's going to be. This is the way it's *meant* to be. The two of us together. Besides, do you even speak German?"

I averted my eyes, then gave in. "No," I confessed. "French. Very bad French. I've only had a couple of months of it."

"*Das habe ich mir gedacht, mein Liebling.* You need me. I need you." His lips curved, although it wasn't quite a smile. "I think fate and the stars would agree. We're a pair. It's time we acted like one."

A salt breeze skated up the cliff and pushed hard against us; the blanket flipped back, covering the empty plates and our feet. He went to his knees to resmooth it.

"That's not all," I said, following his hands, his back and arms, pale sleeves rolled up, an economy of grace even in these brisk movements.

"What else?"

It killed me to admit this. "I'm not entirely well yet. Dr. Hembry says I lost a good deal of blood. I still get weak."

"I know," he said, and sat back, cross-legged. "Did you think I hadn't noticed?" He sent me a sidelong look, then knocked his knee against mine. "It's one of the reasons I'm always feeding you."

I laughed unhappily. "Nice to know it's not merely that you think I'm insatiable."

"No," Armand said, and turned his gaze out to the mist-clotted sea. "You're not the insatiable one."

The surf crashed against the shore, a hard tinny sound. I hoped that it covered the noise of my heartbeat, how it had stuttered and started again, one tiny instant of betrayal.

"Practice," I said brightly, and leapt to my feet. "Watch my clothes, eh?"

His brows raised.

I Turned to smoke. I swirled up above the tips of the trees, thought about it, then flowed out past the cliff, over the open water.

I couldn't yet swim, true. But if I accidentally Turned back into a girl while floating in the sky, I thought the Channel might be a softer landing than oak trees and birches.

The mist drifted below me. I could see flashes of sea beneath it, dark waters sprinkled with faint silver coins.

Dragon, I thought, intent. *You are a dragon. Not a person, not smoke, dragon, dragon, you're a—*

I Turned, and it worked.

Right side up this time, wings out, diving down a steep, invisible slope. I flew so low that my tail scratched a line though the mist, dividing it into parts.

It felt cool and wet. It whipped up in a riot of curls behind me, marking my passage like an ovation of raised and dissolving hands.

I glanced down at my feet, golden scales a tarnished glimmer, my claws reassuringly wicked and sharp.

The stars had called me Fireheart. I liked that. A being with a name like that could surely handle something as basic as flight and landing.

Right?

Higher, lower, testing my wings. It was easier to soar as a friend to the wind, so I faced the other way and tried it like that for a while, until the crenellated outline of Iverson looked less like a chess piece and more like a real castle. There were lights shining from some of the windows, and I wondered who had to stay on for the summer, rattling around that cold hollow place.

Not the headmistress, apparently. Maybe Almeda, the housekeeper. The always-charming Gladys.

Mr. Hastings, the groundskeeper—and Jesse's great-uncle. He lived alone above the stables; from here I could nearly see it, nearly make out the smudge of light peeking out past the doors . . .

I turned about, telling myself I had to before someone caught sight of me.

I circled up and back and found the cliff with Armand motionless at its edge. There was the blanket behind him, the motorcar, and a small clearing behind that. Not much, but it would have to do.

I sailed closer, concentrating on the scrap of land I wanted, feeling my wings adapt to my target, shorter beats, a higher arch.

Closer. Closer . . .

I passed over Armand, ruffling his hair and shirt and trousers. I was by him in a breath, past the auto, sinking to the clearing—

Too fast. My body realized it before my brain did. My legs stiffened and my wings tried to reverse but they couldn't, and the ground rose up so quickly that all I could see were blades of grass and—

I struck the earth and went end over end, and my right wing got crushed and my tail hit something solid that squealed, and the next thing I knew I was on my back seeing stars—fake ones, woozy orange balls, up and down, up and down—and when I could focus again my brain was screaming, *Breathe!* So I did.

A human was running toward me. No, not a human.

Armand, his eyes gone an incredible, luminous blue.

I turned my head and looked at him, dazed and happy in some weird, detached way, despite the fact that I felt broken in about a dozen places.

Armand's eyes could *glow,* just like mine.

Armand was just like—

"Lora!"

He fell to his knees beside me, his hands roaming frantically along my face.

"Lora! Are you hurt?"

I smiled. Well, I would have. It was more like I showed him my teeth, which didn't have nearly the same effect. He scowled down at me, and his eyes reverted to normal.

"Eleanore, it's me. Don't you know me?"

I sighed, then Turned back to girl.

"Ouch," I said.

"Oh!" He lurched away from me. "Oh, ah, you're—you don't have any—"

"Just toss me my coat, will you?"

I kept my eyes closed until I heard him return and the rough wool weight of the peacoat was draped over my torso. The ground was lumpy and there was a rock digging into my thigh, but I didn't feel up to moving yet, so I ignored it.

"Mandy. Do you know what just happened?"

He settled down at my side, running a hand along my arm. "You managed to destroy my father's favorite car?"

I sat up, clutching the coat to me. The motorcar had a series of long, gaping gashes angled down its side, all the way from the bonnet to the back door. The tears were as neat and clean as if someone had taken shears to the steel.

My tail, I realized. My *barbed* tail.

"Uh . . . ," I said.

"Don't worry. There are a dozen more you can go through before we have to start buying new ones."

"No, not that. I mean, I'm sorry about that, of course—"

"As long as you're not injured—"

"No, listen! Armand, you . . . your eyes. They were dragon eyes! Just now, when you came to me."

He looked confused; I dug the rock out from beneath me and threw it toward the sea.

"Dragon eyes," I emphasized, smiling. A real smile this time, one I couldn't have stopped if I'd wanted. "And they were *beautiful*."

"Are you certain?"

"Yes."

And only then, with the wind whispering and the sea crashing and the mist rolling along the waves . . . only then did the stars come to life.

not alone, was their sudden chorus, a wily, sparkling tune. *not alone, beast, not alone.*

I rose to my knees and hugged him, the coat trapped between

us. His arms came up and encircled me; he turned his face to my neck.

"A dragon," Armand said against my skin, so soft and awed I barely caught it.

"Not alone," I said back, but without sound, because I wasn't ready for him to hear it yet.

After that, everything changed.

We still met at night, because it was obvious I needed all the practice I could get. The owls and herons were our witnesses as I shifted from one form to the next, over and over, mostly getting it right but sometimes not. Armand was always there for that.

During the day, however, he avoided me. I didn't notice at first; I was busy with my vastly crucial duty of ensuring that long strips of woven cloth were rolled precisely to measure. I spent hours in what once was the reading room but now housed (according to the sign on the door) "Necessary Supplies." The sage-green window treatments and white paneled walls had been hidden behind temporary metal cases holding everything from iodine to powdered gravy. My workstation was exactly in the middle of the room: one table, one chair, reams of cloth.

It wasn't unpleasant. I didn't have to see Chloe, and I didn't have to deal with maggots or scrubbing up blood.

Even Sophia lost me for a while, though once she realized where I was and what I was doing, she brought another chair and joined in—if you could call sitting beside me and doing none of the work *joining in*.

"It's so much cooler in here than out there," she commented, taking a sip of iced tea from the service she'd insisted we have on hand.

"No, it isn't," I said.

"No, it isn't."

"Quieter," I noted, adding one of my finished rolls to the pyramid I'd been building on the table.

She tipped her head to the side, musing. "Less . . ."

Death, I might have said. *Suffering. Dying men wasting away in their beds with nothing to be done.*

"Fuss," she finished, flat, and I nodded.

She placed her empty glass on the nearest shelf. "Where is Armand?"

"I don't know."

And I didn't. That was one of the things that had changed. It wasn't that I couldn't feel him around in a general way. I still did. But he'd become less than even a specter to me now. He'd become someone who shunned me. No more swimming lessons; he'd told me that since we weren't likely to drop into the Channel, I didn't need them. No more taking meals together; Sophia'd overheard the butler informing the chatelaine that Lord Armand was much too busy to formally dine.

When we met now at night, I noticed how he kept a firm distance between us. How he would stand at the edge of the cliff and watch me fly, but never touch me again, not even to offer me my clothes.

I was accustomed to his bridled admiration, I admit. I'd come to expect it.

Losing it irritated me.

"Lovers' quarrel?" Sophia inquired, rising to get more tea.

"We'd have to be lovers for that to happen."

"You're blushing."

"I am not. I am hot."

"Yes, indeed. Rolling bandages must be such awful exertion!"

"Perhaps you'd care to try it," I shot back. "Then you could find out."

She sent me a cat's smile. "No, thank you. I'm quite content over here with my nice, cold drink."

I slapped my latest roll on top of the pyramid, destroying its fragile unity. It broke apart into bouncing pieces, bandages unfurling down the table and all across the room.

"Lovers' quarrel," Sophia said wisely, and left it to me to pick everything up.

"This time I'm flying with you," Armand told me that night upon the cliff.

He said it without inflection, without even looking at me, standing with his arms crossed to confront the rising yellow moon.

No mist tonight; the moon threw a flickering path along the waves that led straight back to us.

"I don't know," I hedged.

"Don't argue. It's past time for it. You've done fine for the last two nights, haven't you? No unexpected changes?"

"That doesn't mean they won't come now."

"And it doesn't mean they will. What are you scared of, waif?" His eyes glanced back to mine, heavily shadowed; I couldn't read them at all.

"Killing you," I said bluntly.

He shrugged. "Everyone dies sometime."

"Oh, am I supposed to be impressed with that? You're so brave and noble, willing to leave me with your blood on my hands?"

He looked at me fully. "Is that what you envision will happen?"

Yes. No. I couldn't bear thinking about it long enough to decide.

"Tonight," he ordered, in that cool, distant tone he used with me now.

I turned on my heel, stalking back toward the motorcar. "Fine. Your funeral."

"We'll find out."

I Turned without waiting to reach the car, smoke to dragon, just like that. I stepped carefully around my scattered garments, my talons scraping against the hard-packed dirt.

I had no words in this shape; I'd discovered a while ago that I didn't have any manner of voice whatsoever. I couldn't even growl. So I lowered my head to glower at him and thought my dare.

Come on, then. If this is such a cakewalk for you, come on.

He walked over to me and placed a hand upon my shoulder. Damned if I was going to make it easier for him by bending down. I felt his feet slip for purchase on my scales, some tugging, and then he was up, straddling me.

I wiggled in place, adjusting to the weight of him. His feet hooked in the space behind my front legs and in front of my wings. His fingers entwined with my mane.

"Golden Eleanore," he said quietly, leaning forward along my neck. "Fairest of the fair. I'm so tired of waiting. Let's get on with it, shall we?"

My irritation drained away. I flicked my ears at him, took an uneasy step. He remained perfectly balanced.

I opened my wings. I tried a few tentative beats, letting him get the feel of it, of how my muscles would shift beneath him. I didn't like his grip along my mane but couldn't imagine how else he was going to hang on; my scales were slick as glass.

Suddenly the saddle didn't seem like such a bad idea.

"Fly with me, love," Armand whispered, a warm and urgent pressure upon my spine.

I crouched, bounded, and took us up into the heavens.

Chapter 16

It was a very different thing to fly with another. I learned that right off.

He slipped back some but held on tight, which was good, because if he'd fallen off as I ascended I didn't think there was much I could do about it. I climbed and climbed so there'd be time for me to twist about and catch him if I needed to, then had the grisly thought that if I went too high, I might suffocate him.

I chanced a look back. Armand was windblown, beaming. He met my eyes and blew me a kiss.

Cheeky, but the relief danced through me light as bubbles.

I leveled out, unwilling to try anything too daring. I felt him adjusting in place; every movement threw me off by degrees, and I had to compensate by tilting this way or that.

I caught a stream of wind and the roar in my ears subsided into something close to silence. There was only the hiss of my wingtips scraping edges off the air. His breathing. Mine.

The sea was a reflective floor, occasional ships adding dollops of light. We skimmed below clouds plated in gold, because the moon was huge and lovely, pulling me toward it with a yearning that tugged soul deep.

Fireheart. Lora-of-the-moon.

I was meant to be here. I was meant to be this way. And even with Armand clinging to my back, I was glad. Up here I was as free to be myself as anywhere in creation. No rules meant to bind me, no gossip meant to make me feel small. No adults chiding me for never being quite what they hoped; no toffee-nosed girls mocking me for what I'd never have or never become.

Beyond the clouds, the stars had been arranged in a high, brilliant lattice of glitter. They were singing without words, a symphony as glad and ferocious as I was.

I gazed up at them and imagined plucking them one by one, wearing them as debutants did diamonds: a necklace of stars, a coronet, a glinting fan of them trailing behind me like the train of the most breathtaking gown. The queen herself would weep with envy.

There was one star in particular that caught my attention, brighter than all the rest. It blazed with light, a rare green and gold. I'd wear that one over my heart . . .

Wait . . .

"Jesse?" I gasped, and then screamed.

Because I'd Turned to girl, of course.

We tumbled down together, two bodies pinwheeling, the air sucked from our lungs. For a few long, terrifying seconds—much too long—I was trapped in the black breathless vortex of my impending death. I was senseless, powerless. The words *Turn! Turn!* screeched through my mind with no results.

Then I went to smoke, instantly suspended.

Armand continued his tumble, smaller and smaller against the waiting sea.

I Turned to dragon and plummeted after him.

I'd done something like this once before. I knew to fold my wings as close to my body as I could, to keep myself stiff and straight, a knife blade, a sword. He had his arms and legs spread out, which gave me the only small advantage I had; I was gaining on him, but not swiftly enough.

He toppled upward, his face toward me. His eyes had that same blue glow that had thrilled me days ago, but now only served to fill me with an infuriated fright.

He was *not* going to die. I was *not* going to lose the lone person who understood what I was and liked me anyway—

The sea was so near. I was too far. Armand reached up an arm toward me and in desperation I reached back, my claws flashing.

I felt the pull of him, an abrupt yank of weight. I opened my wings and tried to rise but couldn't get high enough in time. Armand hit the water and then so did I, but the difference was that I broke apart into smoke as it happened, shattering far and wide.

I didn't know what had happened to him.

The pieces of me bobbed about, gradually mustering back into one. Seawater splashed through me, atoms of mist adding to my vapor.

Where was he? I funneled up, searching, seeing only pewtered water and slippery waves.

Where is he? I called silently to the stars. *Jesse, help—where is he?*

As if in answer, I felt myself beginning to solidify. And even though I tried to stop it, I Turned into girl again.

I splashed down almost gently. It was a bit preposterous how leisurely it happened, and how utterly unable I was to keep my head above the water.

My one brief lesson in swimming deserted me. I thrashed about, sinking fast, the entire world sheathing me in smothering dark.

Sophia had been correct. I was useless.

My lungs burned. My limbs had gone to stone.

Smoke, I commanded myself, but it seemed like such an impossible feat. All my magic was cold and lifeless, already drowned.

My lungs were on fire. My heart was a dying ember. I had to breathe. I had no choice, I was *going* to breathe—

The air rushed out of my lungs just as he found me. I was hauled upward and we broke the surface together and I was able to cough and wheeze and cry, and I did all of them at once.

Armand had slung an arm under both of mine, our sides pressed together.

"Use your feet, Lora," he was panting in my ear. "Kick your feet, like I showed you!"

I couldn't feel my feet, but I must have been doing it because I was sort of floating, and he swam about to face me, still holding on.

"I believe"—he kept panting—"I ended our lessons—a tad too soon."

I was shivering, aching, mad as spit beneath it all. "*Now* do you understand? I need to do this alone!"

"No." He shook the water from his eyes. "You rescue Aubrey. I rescue you. See how it goes?"

"You stubborn, brainless—"

He pulled me to him and mashed his lips to mine. It might have been a magnificently romantic gesture, but I knew he only did it to shut me up. Anyway, my face was so numb I didn't even feel it.

"Turn to s-smoke. Dragon." His teeth were starting to chatter. "Hang low. I'll—c-climb up. Fly back t-to shore."

It was as good a plan as any. And it worked, more or less.

I was able to hover just long enough for him to cling to my front leg. I flew as slowly and steadily as I could and eventually we made it back to land like that, both of us exhausted and chilled to the bone.

I warmed myself by thinking that if he caught pneumonia, at least I wouldn't have to worry about him coming along to Prussia and ruining everything.

And even though I searched the skies, I didn't glimpse the gold and green star again.

Chapter 17

Wire transmission from His Grace the Duke of Idylling, Bath, to Miss Eleanore Jones, Tranquility at Idylling

01 *JULY* 1915 13:04

MY DEAR MISS JONES STOP KINDLY CEASE DAWDLING STOP ALL BEASTS MUST HAVE COURAGE STOP I AM TOLD IT IS IMPERATIVE ARMAND GO ALONG STOP FOR HIS SAKE HURRY STOP

Chapter 18

The cable arrived the following afternoon. I would have burned the damned thing before Armand had a chance to read it, but since he was the one who handed it to me, it was too late for that.

"Whatever does *that* mean?" asked Sophia, peering over my shoulder to make out the typed words. She rattled her glass of iced tea in my ear.

"I don't know," I lied, and crumpled the paper in my fist. I directed a look up at Armand, still standing over my other shoulder and my table of miscellaneous bandage rolls.

Why hadn't he waited to give it to me? Now Sophia would never stop pestering me about it.

His smile was slim and as hard as nails. His cobalt gaze seemed more piercing than ever, almost unnaturally vivid.

"The doctor informs me that Reginald's delusions are as real to him as this"—he gestured to the cramped supply room—"is to us. No doubt you play some mysterious role in them, Eleanore. I'm sorry for it. I'm surprised he was allowed to send this at all."

"Oh," said Sophia. She bit her lip. "We don't have to discuss it, Mandy."

"No, we don't," I agreed. I stuck the wad of paper in my pocket. "Was there anything else? I have to say, you're looking a bit peaked, Lord Armand. It'd be such a pity if you took ill. Perhaps you should go have a rest."

"I feel fantastic," he said, and turned around and left.

Sophia waited until he was no longer in view. "You might be kinder to him."

"Pardon?"

"His father's illness isn't Armand's fault."

Empathy from Lady Sophia. Was it snowing in hell right now?

"I know that," I said.

"It's a shame you've been drawn into it, but sometimes parents do things well beyond our control. Queer things. Reckless things. It's not his fault," she said again.

I touched her on the arm. "Sophia. I know."

She shrugged me off. "Good."

I returned my attention to the table, to the tiresome, interminable strips of cloth waiting to be transformed into useful rolls. Sophia walked to the tea service and stood there without reaching for any of it.

"They hadn't any money when he met her," she said suddenly, not looking at me. "I mean, *none*. Just bloodlines and a bankrupt estate and I must suppose some sort of womanly charm to lure him in. And it worked. He was lured, hook, line, and sinker. And they married and she and Chloe moved in and every day after that became some version of *Of course you must call her Mamá, since she's your mother now. Just forget about your old one*, and *If Chloe prefers your room to hers, then you must let her have it. Or your riding pony. Or your hair ribbons. Or your favorite necklace. Because we want her to feel like part of the family, don't we, pet?*"

"I'd kill her before I'd let her have my pony," I said after a moment.

"Yes!" A hand raised; she wiped at her eyes. "I considered it. But I thought they'd know it was me."

"Truly? It seems to me there must be any number of people out there happy to strangle your stepsister."

She let out a watery laugh. "There are two of us, at least."

"Cheers to that. Pour me some tea, will you?"

"All right."

The final stages of our plan required a late-night consultation over maps and nautical charts. Armand had managed to procure ones far better than anything I'd discovered at Iverson. We needed maps for England, France, the Netherlands, Belgium, and the German Empire, which included Prussia. Towns, geography, trenches. He'd even found an etching of the Schloss des Mondes ruin itself in an old travel journal in Tranquility's library. Apparently tourists a century ago found decaying castles incredibly romantic.

Altogether, the floor in front of his bedroom fireplace and a good deal more beyond was covered in paper. I studied them from my hands and knees, the gray blanket wrapped and knotted at my chest.

I traced my fingers along one of the trench maps, which showed the battle lines of the front, along with inked-in dates. Dotted red lines for us. Solid blue ones for the Huns. The most recent date was five days ago.

"Where did you get this one? Are people just allowed to have these?"

"Don't ask, and no. But I'm not people. I'm sure the colonel won't miss it for a few hours. He should have locked his desk."

My lips wanted to smile; I fought for a straight face. "Larceny. I'd say I fear for the state of your character, but I'm rather too impressed."

Armand didn't look up, anyhow. "Thank you very much. But look here, Lora. See?" He poked at some town in Belgium with a name I couldn't pronounce. "I think that even if we take our time, we can make it to here by the first morning. It's far enough from the front to probably be safe, and rural enough that we can find a barn to hole up in during the day."

"A barn," I said, unenthusiastic. "Sounds comfortable."

Now he glanced at me. "We could try for an empty house. But if it's empty, there's probably a good reason for it. Like Germans nearby."

"No, I love barns. Horse sweat and all that prickly hay. Let's do that."

"I'm only being practical."

"Can't we fly it all in one night?"

"No." His finger drew a new line across the papers, traveling across the Netherlands and most of the German Empire before getting to East Prussia. "We have to get all the way over here, and once we're there, we'll need to be ready for whatever comes. Even if you fly at top speed—and I have no idea what that might actually be— you'll end up worn out and hungry just as we've landed in the heart of enemy territory. We'll need stay alert at all times, but especially then. If you're too fatigued, it won't do anyone any good."

"Speaking of that." I sat down upon a portion of Berlin, crackling the paper. "I wasn't jesting before. You look . . . I don't know. Not quite yourself."

"I told you. I feel fine."

"You don't look it," I stressed. "I'd say you look like you have a fever, except you aren't flushed. But your eyes are strange. They're too bright. And your complexion is paler than ever."

"Eleanore—"

"No. If you're ill, or even just coming down with a cold, it might be the thing that destroys us both. You're the one preaching about safety. I couldn't agree more. We need every advantage, and you out of sorts is *not* that."

He sat back, somehow managing to avoid all of the scattered papers. He sent me a long, level stare; firelight draped him in orange and black, fiendish dancing shadows. "I swear to you. I feel fine."

I waited but he didn't back down, so I surrendered, lifting a hand.

"We'll need—"

Someone knocked on the door.

We both jolted in place, startled, and then the knob turned and the door opened and Chloe was saying, "Mandy?" in a soft, sweet voice.

I Turned to smoke. My blanket fell in a puff across the maps.

"Are you awake?" she asked, coming all the way in, so of course she could see that he was.

She wore a dressing gown of brick-red damask trimmed with jet beads. It was tightly wrapped and belted and covered her from throat to toes, but she still managed to make it look alluring. Her hair had been pulled back into a loose braid, suggesting *bed* and *desire* and *forbidden* all at once.

Armand had climbed to his feet. He, at least, was fully dressed, all the way down to his polished shoes. If she thought that peculiar, she didn't say so.

I lingered near the top of the hearth, making myself as thin as possible.

"Forgive me," Chloe said. She smiled, tremulous. "I know it's frightfully scandalous of me to come up to your room like this. But I—I had to see you."

Armand threw a nervous glance in my direction. "It's late."

"After two, actually. I couldn't sleep." She walked closer, noticed the maps on the floor. "What's this?"

He bent down, scooped up all the ones he could reach, and snapped them into a pile. "Nothing. Just some research."

"I didn't mean to interrupt."

"Chloe." Exasperation crept into his tone. "Why are you here?"

She went stock still, her hands clasped before her as if in supplication. Her eyes got bigger and bigger; it almost appeared as if she would cry.

"Don't you know?" she asked, hushed. "After all these years, don't you know?"

Apparently he did. He took a step toward her but then stopped, shaking his head.

"I'm sorry," he said.

"Don't say that. Don't say it."

"Listen, I—"

"No!" A single tear leaked down her cheek, perfect as a dewdrop. "Everything can still be fine between us. I know you have this—infatuation—with Eleanore. I don't pretend to understand it, but I can accept it. Temporarily. Gentlemen have all sorts of wants, I realize that. Sometimes they make sense and sometimes they don't, but even Mamá tells me it is our duty as wives to—to accommodate." Her fingers began a slow, painful twisting upon themselves. "So I will, Armand. I swear to you I will. You can have me *and* her. And I won't ask you about it, and I won't bother you about it. Just—*please*, Mandy. I've loved you since we were twelve years old. Since the day we met. The hour. The very minute." Another tear. Another. "How can that mean nothing to you?"

She was weeping openly now, doing it just as beautifully as she did everything else. Her nose was barely pink and her eyes glistened like jewels, and she never moved otherwise. Just her hands, twisting and twisting.

So he went to her, and stilled her by cupping his fingers over hers.

"Don't you think you deserve better than that?"

She tilted her face to his. "I don't want better! I only want you."

"How could you want to marry a man who thought so little of you that he'd keep you at home while chasing someone else?"

"It's not *little*. It's how it *is*!"

"Not for us. Not for me, and, I hope, not for you. You deserve someone who loves you without conditions. Who would never look at another woman for the rest of his life with anything but indifference, because you are the sum of his dreams. The one girl whose eyes shine with all the days and nights he prays will come. His stars and his sun and his moon. His happiness, his true heart." His voice roughened. "His everything."

She gazed up at him, her lips trembling. "Is that it? Is that how you feel about *her*?"

"Yes," he said, and dropped his hands.

She swallowed, looked around. Gave a pained nod. She licked the tears from her lips and turned about, walking back to the door.

Opening it, passing through. Closing it.

He only watched her go.

I hesitated, then poured back into my human shape. I picked up my blanket and held it to my chest.

"Armand . . ."

"Not now, Eleanore." He spoke to the wall; I was granted only his profile, chiseled against the shadows. "Let's continue this tomorrow."

"I—"

"Tomorrow. Please."

I nodded, realized he couldn't see it, and murmured, "As you wish."

Then, just as Chloe had done, I slunk out of the room.

Chapter 19

I didn't run into him the next morning or afternoon. I didn't seek him out, though, figuring it a good idea to allow him his peace. Just remembering what he'd said about me to Chloe made me feel hot and awkward and disturbingly exhilarated. I knew I likely needed some time away from him as well.

. . . his stars and his sun and his moon . . .

Had he really meant for me to hear all that? How was I going to look him in the eyes now?

In any case, I didn't need him for the next part of our plan.

All I needed was Lottie Clayworth.

It was well known that Lady Clayworth enjoyed midday sherry and sandwiches in the gardens if the weather was satisfactory. A pair of footmen set up a table for her in the same spot at the same time every day, and sure enough, that's where I found her: in a gazebo beneath a massive, droopy plum tree gravid with purple-frosted fruit, eating and drinking in regal isolation as various men and their nurses crisscrossed the grounds to take in the air.

I approached the gazebo with confident steps. It was important that anyone watching believe I was welcome.

"Good afternoon, Lady Clayworth."

She peered up at me from beneath the brim of a hat adorned with stuffed canaries, a cucumber sandwich paused halfway to her mouth.

"Who are you?"

I put on my best *you-can-trust-me* smile. "Miss Jones, of course. We met the other night, when your nephew was still here."

"Who?"

"Miss *Jones*."

"Ah, yes." Up came the spectacles; she gave me the up-and-down. "Your looks are somewhat improved."

I sank into a half curtsy. "I am dressed for tea, my lady."

"Hmph." She took in my frock and was apparently none too pleased that she couldn't find fault with it. I'd chosen my best day dress—the best I'd been able to find ready-made in the village, that is—which was collared and beribboned and utterly inoffensive. Even the color was inoffensive, a bland shade caught somewhere between gray and dun.

"What is it you want, young lady? As you can see, I'm busy."

"Why, only to sit awhile with you."

She heard *that* well enough, and smiled in triumph. "Alas. There is but one chair, and I am in it."

"True," I said breezily. "So I'll just rest here against the railing, if you don't mind."

Her lip curled; she ate chippies like me for breakfast. "But I *do*."

"No." I scooted until I was very close, close enough to lean down and capture her eyes and speak darkly, deliberately. "No, you don't mind."

"No," she confirmed, with faint, offended disbelief. "I . . . I don't."

A butterfly landed on the beveled rim of the sherry glass, a teal-and-brown striped tigress. Her wings opened and closed and opened, absorbing the sun.

"Lady Clayworth, listen carefully. You have a cousin. A dear, dear cousin who's taken ill. You must go to her at once."

"Oh, my," she said, her brows wrinkling.

"You will find her back at your own home. And that is where you will go. Tell me, where is your home?"

"Tewkesbury. Just north of the Severn. Oh, my. Oh, my."

"You'll find her there. What is her name?"

"It's . . . is it Gracie? Is it my own Gracie?"

"Yes. Gracie needs you, but you do not feel quite right about going there alone. You need me to come along as your companion. Do you understand? You've invited me to come with you. To stay with you. Until Gracie is better."

"Oh, I'm so grateful you can come," she said, and took my hand.

I patted hers lightly. "One does hate to travel alone these days."

Lottie nodded, and the canaries on her hat nodded with her. "One does hate to travel alone."

"We'll leave on tomorrow's train. Is that time enough for you to be packed?"

"Yes. I shall have the maids attend to it at once! My Gracie!"

"Very good." I reached around her and grabbed two sandwiches, sending the butterfly aloft. "I'll see you soon. Enjoy your meal."

I'd bought a new travel case when I'd gotten my new clothes, an arbitrary purchase, like all the rest. The sleepy fishing village that served Tranquility wasn't precisely known for its haute couture, and I'd had to make do with whatever was available. But at least all my garments now fit, and the case was sturdy, if ugly, with leather sides and thick-stitched seams and brass brads holding everything together along the edges. It looked as if it might survive a sinking ship.

Perhaps it'd have to.

"Eleanore Jones. I think we ought to have a chat."

I looked up from folding a blouse over my bed, discovering Sophia sauntering past the door.

"I thought ladies knew to knock before entering someone else's boudoir."

"That eliminates the element of surprise." She was dressed for dinner in the sort of gown that wouldn't be for sale around here in a million years, a long black satin sheath, tight metallic lacework over the bodice and sleeves.

Dinner. The clock on the desk informed me I was about to miss it; my stomach growled.

In perfect counterpoint, a rumble of thunder came from beyond the windows. It was still miles off, but the sky above Tranquility had gone a bubbly deep soot, leaving only a feeble, jaundiced wedge of light stuck between the sea and clouds.

Sometimes I heard that rumble and it wasn't thunder at all. It was the sound of the Germans bombing cities and towns far, far down the coast, a sound that only I could perceive. But tonight it was just thunder.

Rain was coming. Bad timing, but it was too late to switch things up now.

"What is it?" I asked absently, realizing I was going to need to change my dress yet again. Morning dresses, tea dresses, dinner dresses, dance dresses, different wraps and hats and gloves for each . . . I was beginning to understand what upper-class women did all day.

My armoire was empty. I'd already packed nearly everything, so I went back to the case and began to rummage through it.

"I understand you're leaving us soon."

"Uh . . . yes. I'm afraid so."

Sophia reclined sideways along the settee against the windows, ankles crossed, one arm slung over the top. She looked like she was posing for a painting.

"Accompanying Lottie Clayworth to Tewkesbury?"

"That's right."

"To help with her sick cousin Gracie."

There. A jade brocade number. That would do. I grabbed it, shook it out with both hands.

"Not sure how much help I'll actually be," I said, working at its buttons. "But when she asked, I thought it was the least I could do."

"How generous of you." Something in her tone warned me at last; I glanced up, and she gave her sly cat's smile. "But, say, here's a quandary, Eleanore. Charlotte Clayworth doesn't have any living cousins. Not a single one."

Damn.

I returned to the buttons, nonchalant. "I don't think that's right. She was very specific about it. Perhaps she meant a second cousin, something like that."

"I've known the Clayworths my whole life. There *was* a Gracie, as it happens, but it turns out she died about forty years ago."

Damn, damn.

I took a breath. "Perhaps this is—"

"I looked it up in *Standish's Peerage of the Empire* to be sure. Lottie is the last of her line. And since she's going on and on about her dear cousin and dear Miss Jones who's going to help her, and what a relief it will be not to have to travel alone, I find myself pondering what, exactly, is going on. Are you thinking of robbing her?"

My jaw dropped. "What did you just say?"

"Because as much as I find her a stuffy bore, she's ancient and obviously potty and I can't allow it."

"I wouldn't do that." *So openly.* "Grant me some bloody credit."

"I'd be glad to." She abandoned her pose to sit up, regarding me with flinty eyes; the metallic lace sparkled and bit into her skin. "*If* you tell me what's really going on."

"She told me she needed help with her cousin!"

"And *I* told *you* she doesn't have one."

I was desperate; I darkened my voice. "Yes, she does."

"No—"

I let loose my gown and grasped both of her hands in mine, holding hard. "*Yes*, she does. She does, Sophia." I made a decision. Trying to fool her with my voice hadn't worked—I might have known it wouldn't—but I needed her cooperation. I chose my next words carefully. "And Armand will be gone, too. And we are absolutely *not* going somewhere together for the next few weeks. Do you understand?"

She pulled her hands free.

"Is that it?"

"Yes. That's it."

"An elopement?"

I felt the blush climbing up my neck. "No."

Her head tipped; she looked at me coldly. "That's too bad. Eloping with him would likely send Chloe around the bend."

"You can't tell her. You can't tell anyone."

She stood in a swish of satin, walking past me to examine the mess of my things upon the bed. "Aren't you the most cunning little fraud? *We're just friends, Sophia! Really, truly, honest-to-golly-goody-good-goodness!* What a lot of tosh." She picked up one of my garters, pinching it between two fingers, then let it fall. "You very nearly convinced me. Butter wouldn't melt in your mouth, would it?"

"Well . . ." I struggled to think of an explanation that wouldn't sound too blatantly false. "You can imagine how it went. Secret trysts, forbidden love. You yourself called it the definition of rebellion, remember? The last thing I needed was for Westcliffe to catch me upsetting her lovely applecart of rules. We weren't sure whom to trust."

"I believe my feelings are hurt."

Like hell they were. "Sorry."

"How on earth did you manage to induce Lottie to have anything to do with this?"

"It—it turns out she's more romantic than she lets on."

Sophia released a throaty laugh. "No, she isn't."

"You're right." The lies were flowing more smoothly now. "Armand is paying her. I guess her funds are short or something. She agreed to cash quick enough."

"Now, *that* sounds like the truth. How very sordid!"

"Sophia, you can't, *can't* tell. Think of the shame poor Lottie'd feel."

She raked her nails across the covers, then sighed. "Fine. I'll keep your secret. But you owe me. You and Mandy both."

"Fine!"

She pushed off the bed and walked to the door. "Tell him to buy you some baubles to go with those frocks. You look naked without them."

"He didn't buy—"

She sent me a steely, testing look.

"Right," I said. "Good idea."

"Have a nice *holiday,* Miss Jones. I *will* be collecting on your debt to me when you get back. Don't forget."

I stood there with the jade gown a wrinkled spill at my feet, hearing the dinner gong sound from stories below.

Don't forget.

Bugger me. As if I could.

Even though the rain descended upon us in a powerful, steady pour, the train station bustled with people. Tranquility's chauffeur had unloaded our trunks to join the stack beneath the platform awning, but I'd dismissed him before he could hail a porter. I had no desire to lose what few belongings I had to the train to Tewkesbury.

I reached from beneath my umbrella to hand him a pound note and got a cheerful "Gor'bless, miss!" and a tip of his sodden cap before he left us.

"These three, not that one," I instructed the porter who approached, likely drawn to Lady Clayworth's evident wealth, if not her damp glower.

"I do so hate to travel." She grimaced at all the people splashing past. "Such a bother, all the mud and cinders and the hoi polloi. How does any civilized person abide it?"

"Lottie," I said loudly, and she faced me. I summoned my dragon voice. "You're going home now, my lady. You are happy about that. You're relieved. You can't wait to get there, and once you're there, you will feel nothing but contentment."

"Ah," she said, her grimace fading.

"You will forget about Gracie and her illness. You will forget my name and my face. Everything now is wholly agreeable, even the rain. In fact, you feel a deep, unshakable joy."

"How marvelous," she said, and looked around at the hectic people, the shiny-wet train gushing its smoke, her eyes bright.

"Should anyone at home inquire why you've returned, you will tell them you missed Tewkesbury too much to stay away. You've missed your friends and servants and the familiar sights of home."

"Even the ghosts?" she inquired matter-of-factly.

"Er . . . yes. Even them."

She gave a nod. "We have so many of them, you know. Oh, that reminds me! She said to tell you good luck. And to thank you for saving her sons."

My mouth opened, but no sound came out. A corpulent man in an oilskin coat bumped into me without apology, sending me staggering. My umbrella dumped streamers of rain down the side of my skirt. "Who—who said that?"

"Reginald's wife. Wispy thing. Looks rather like you, doesn't she? Anyway, I've told you, so my duty's done."

"Yes." I gave a small cough. The train let out a whistle, and the porters were calling for stragglers. "Yes, just so. You're done."

"Last call!" hollered the steward by the first-class doors.

"Time to go." I aimed her toward the steps. "Be well, my lady."

But she was no longer listening. She was boarding the train, looking forward to her future, and I was forgotten, reduced to something even less than a rain-fogged memory. I was a ghost, too.

Armand found me about two hours later.

I was seated on one of the filigreed iron benches lining the platform, snacking on cold fish and chips that I'd bought from a vendor disembarking from the last train.

My feet were propped straight out upon my case, soles to the world. My lips and fingers were smeared with grease and my hat was a soggy ruin, since I'd run out into the storm to stop the vendor without my umbrella. Men of all stations clipped by me without a second glance; respectable matrons, however, had been giving me the evil eye for the past half hour. I was dressed too nicely now to pass for a beggar, so I must have been instead a single young woman of questionable upbringing.

But the battered, vinegary fish was delicious, and the chips even better. I'd eat them every day if I could.

People had been coming and going. I scarcely noticed when a new someone sat on the bench beside me, until he reached for my chips.

"I haven't had these in ages," Armand said, taking a bite. "Not since Eton."

"Leave off. These are mine."

"Ages," he said again, and reached for another. I held the cone of oily rolled newspaper out of his reach.

He laughed. "I'll buy you more."

"The vendor's gone."

"Lora, I'm going to buy us both supper. A huge one. Here in town."

I lowered my arm, and he ate all the rest. Then he stood, whisking the crumbs from his coat. His hat and shoulders were sprinkled with raindrops; his smile was altogether rakish.

"Come on. The auto's in the lot, the pubs are open, and I'm starving."

Chapter 20

He'd meant it when he said it'd be a huge meal. It was.

I'd never dined in a pub before. As far as I recalled, I'd never dined in any manner of public place, but if they were all like this one, I'd gladly return.

Everything was dim and smoky and loud and smelling pleasingly of cider and ale. The tables were worn smooth, their deep coffee-colored varnish marked with paler rings upon rings, proof of generations of sweating drinks. I didn't even mind the electrical lights, since they were mostly over the bar. Our table was lit by a single drippy candle stuck to a saucer that had a series of nicks along its rim.

I definitely fit in here.

I'd allowed Armand to order for us. Roasted chicken, duckling, corned beef. Jacket potatoes and rice and smelts and bread, mutton chops and meringue, potted shrimps.

We devoured it all. Then he ordered more.

"Cor, right away, luv," said our server, completely smitten because she was plump and plain and he'd smiled at her, and even from across the table, I'd seen that it'd been blinding.

"You're awfully cheerful," I said, mashing up the last few grains of rice with the tines of my fork so they'd stick.

"Am I? I suppose I'm relieved, mostly. To be doing something. To be going at last."

I understood that. There was a certain wretched tension to waiting. I'd felt it, too.

A different woman came by with fresh ales for us both, cold and topped with froth, and when Armand finished his first draw there was a line of foam tracing his upper lip. He wiped it away and looked at me and gave a much tamer version of the blinding smile, but it was still handsome and bright.

Thank you for saving her sons was Lottie's message from her ghost.

Sons. Plural.

"Mandy," I said slowly. "Are you still all that hungry?"

"I am, actually."

"Did you not eat today?"

"No, I did." He sat back and surveyed the table, picking up the last slice of bread and running it through the mutton juice. "Breakfast, at least. Some luncheon. But I had to clear out by noon if they were going to believe I was headed to London."

That had been the story we'd agreed upon: I was to go away with Lady Clayworth to Tewkesbury, and Armand was to go alone to London, to rattle the cages of any Important Persons there who might have news of his brother. Both reasons might legitimately keep us away from Tranquility (and each other) for weeks. We didn't know how long rescuing Aubrey might actually take, but we'd figured the bigger the cushion of time we gave ourselves, the better.

I watched him fold the bread in half and shove it into his mouth. "And do you feel . . . restless?"

He stopped chewing, looking back at me. Then he swallowed, and his next sentence came flat.

"What do you mean?"

"Like your skin doesn't fit. Like it's shrunken too small and you're going to burst through."

He said nothing. But oh, his eyes were so, so wild and blue.

"And your heart," I went on, accusing. "It's beating so fast now. Did you think I wouldn't hear it?"

"It's the same as ever, Eleanore. The same as it's been since I met you."

I shook my head. "This isn't good. Not now. Not tonight."

"Everything is fine."

Anger was coming awake inside me, a small growing flame. "Are you going to lie to my face now, Armand Louis? Are you?"

His brows lowered. He leaned forward to reply, but right then the plain server returned, platters of food stacked up both arms all the way to her shoulders. She winked at Armand and began to sling the dishes to the wood. Someone at the table next to ours produced a noisy belch and a guffaw, and the server winked again before moving off.

"Everything will fall to pieces," I said, biting off each word. "If the Turn comes to you now, while we're on this journey, it will all fall to pieces."

"You needn't worry about me, Eleanore. I can handle myself."

My voice began to rise. "I think we should wait until it happens. I think you're very near to that edge, and it's a bloody dangerous thing and we should wait."

He pushed back his chair and held out his hand. "Come with me."

"No. The food just—"

"To the window, Lora. That's all."

So I let him lead me across the pub, both of us angling through the crowded tables until we were next to the panes. He bent his head to mine.

"Look," he said in my ear, and I didn't even have to ask where.

The storm had broken apart. The clouds were swept into tufts, into somersaults, and the twilight sky beyond them glowed a pure, unmistakable amethyst.

And there, right there in the middle of the clearest patch of heaven, was a golden green star. The brightest star I'd ever seen.

Brighter than life, brighter than death. Brighter than comets or forgotten hopes or any of my futile dreams.

"He says we must go tonight," Armand murmured, so near our shoulders touched and the heat of his face warmed mine. "I hear him as clear as I hear you, Lora. Clear as ever. He says it must be tonight."

"Have you—" I had to fight against the knot in my throat. "Have you always heard him?"

"Yes."

"You blighter." I lowered my gaze and stared at the girl in the glass: white as a sheet, rain-bedraggled hair, a face etched with betrayal, hurt, betrayal.

The boy in the glass beside her answered the question I hadn't asked. "I don't know why it's me who hears and not you. It should be you. Obviously, you. But this is how it is. And Jesse says tonight."

He hesitated, then turned his head so his lips grazed my cheek, a kiss and not, because it was warm and soft and over before it began, and he was walking back to our table without me.

I threw a last look up at the star (green! gold! green! gold!), then went back as well.

I sat down, my hands on my thighs. Armand regarded me through half-lidded eyes and didn't speak another word.

"Keep eating," I said, reaching for the nearest platter.

This is what I knew about the first Turn of a *drákon*:

It was meant to hurt.

Not a little pain, either. A great, great deal.

Nearly everything Armand and I had discovered about our species had come from a series of letters authored by one of his ancestresses, letters that his mother had hidden before her death and that he had recently found.

In them, a woman named Rue had warned her great-great-granddaughter about the alarming facts of her impending first Turn. How it would feel as if the flesh was being flayed from her bones, her body ripped asunder, pure torture. How the agony would consume her, unbearable, and of how she wouldn't be able to even scream because by then she'd be smoke or she'd be nothing at all.

If you didn't manage to control the pain and rule the Turn, you'd simply float away as vapor. Dispersed. Forever.

The pain of my first Turn had come to me more slyly than Rue had implied, but that didn't mean it would be the same for Armand.

Reckless, audacious Armand.

But he was young and male and strong. I told myself that over and over the next few days.

He was strong.

I hoped it would be enough. Because despite whatever the ghost of Reginald's wife might have said, I didn't believe for a moment I was going to be able to rescue both of her sons.

We registered at Bournemouth's Sea Vista Inn as Mr. and Mrs. Pendragon, an alias so ludicrous that I rolled my eyes when Armand announced us to the innkeeper. But it was too late, he'd said it, so I'd smiled and turned my eye roll into a flitting of my lashes because the innkeeper was beaming at me and congratulating us on our recent nuptials, and promising us a suite that surely would inspire our honeymoon to grand matrimonial heights.

Or something like that. I wasn't really listening. I'd perked up when he'd mentioned sending along some champagne, until I realized I wasn't going to be able to drink any since I'd be flying most of the night.

The "suite" was boxy and charmless but did boast a balcony with a fine view of the beach and breaking surf. We waited until the champagne arrived—fat strawberries, too—and then Armand was pressing a wad of notes into the innkeeper's hand and spinning a short, slippery tale about how not to expect to see much of us (wink!) and we'd not require maid service or anyone's attention for days to come, thank you very much.

I swear to God, money makes everything so much easier. When you can toss it around as easily as false compliments or blown kisses, the world becomes a wide-open place.

I sighed as the door quickly closed.

"*That* was embarrassing."

"It's fine. We're married." Armand began to pull at his tie. "Anyway, if you think it's bad now, just wait until the next time he sees us."

I flopped into a chair. "Lovely."

"Let's have a drink."

"I can't. I need my head clear."

"One drink. One toast. That's all." He worked at the cork. "If someone does pop in while we're gone, the glasses should be used and the bottle tapped. And the bed, needless to say—"

I cut him off. "Right."

He poured the champagne, brought me a flute, and pulled me back to my feet.

"To Mrs. Pendragon, light of my life."

"That's enough. If we're going to do this, give a real toast."

"To Eleanore," he said, instantly serious. "Light of my life."

Would there ever come a time when I'd be able to hold his eyes when he looked at me like that? When his gaze burned with that deep blue fire, with that intensity that seemed to strip me to the core?

I didn't know. It wasn't tonight.

I stared at the bubbles marching in lines up the sides of my glass. "To success," I said, and tipped the rim of my flute to his.

He didn't echo me. I suppose he'd already given the salute he'd meant most.

The Sea Vista Inn apparently had any number of romantic couples staying on. They lingered upon the beach until long after midnight, promenading and holding hands, ladies giggling, men stealing kisses. There was a boardwalk leading to a pier lined with glassed candles, a gently glowing path of them stretching out over the sea.

But eventually the couples were fewer and fewer, until there were none, and the candles all guttered out. Then it was just Armand and me and the deep purple night.

And that star. Star-of-Jesse, burning above us.

We waited until we were well and truly alone. Anyone stumbling across us now would hardly mistake us for newlyweds out for an amorous stroll. I was in a thin calico dress, no coat despite the brisk breeze, while Armand wore a leather driving duster, gloves, goggles, and sturdy boots. There was a compass in his pocket, a knife in one of the boots, and a pistol in a holster around his waist. He had a knapsack, too, because we'd thought it would be the easiest way to transport anything else.

It was heavy. *Anything else* included my spare clothing, his, tinned food, water, a blanket, aspirin, iodine, bandages (expertly rolled), cotton wool, bullets, and the maps.

We took a final look around to ensure we were alone, then faced each other.

I wanted to say something but couldn't think what. We'd already gone over our plans so thoroughly they were seared into my brain.

Off we go seemed woefully inadequate. So did *Don't forget to hold on.*

Perhaps it was the same for him. He only lifted a hand to my face, an unhurried stroke of his fingers along my cheek, and smiled.

I went to smoke. He knelt down, retrieved my dress and chemise and stockings and shoes, and pushed them into the knapsack.

rise up, urged the stars (and I still could not pick out Jesse from among them). *rise up, beloved beast!*

And then there I was, a dragon in the sand, gleaming and actual for anyone to see. Armand climbed up quickly; he knew as well as I that we were most vulnerable like this, fixed to the earth. I felt him nestle into position. The weight of the knapsack was a new adjustment for us both, but there wasn't time to fret about it.

His legs clenched my sides and his hands grabbed my mane. I gave a nod and took us up.

We'd decided to hug the coast as far as we could until Dover, when the span of the Channel shrank as much as it ever would and the risk of me drowning would be significantly lessened. It was the same route the zeppelins took, but there was no helping that. The moon was bright tonight, so the airships probably weren't out. If they were, we'd just have to avoid them.

I'd been cold as a girl on the ground. In the air, though, I felt fine. The wind was my ally, its chill diluted now that I had scales. But I was glad that Armand had thought to wear gloves and a coat. It's what the pilots wore, and after all, we were flying nearly as high as they did.

I glanced back at him. He was slanted over my neck, an extraordinary aviator indeed with the glass goggles over his eyes and his hair whipped into spikes. He released my mane long enough to give me a thumbs-up. Moonlight feathered his edges in silver; all the rest of him was purple, like the sky.

We were probably visible from the coast. I could see the rough line of the shore, the occasional inviting lights of villages or towns, but I hoped we were far enough out that anyone getting a glimpse of us would think we were a very large bird. Or an illusion.

We weren't really liable to be anything else.

Moon above, England to the left, a deceptively velvety-looking sea below. Jesse, like Armand, somewhere behind my shoulders. My wings found their rhythm and kept it.

And time passed.

The stars changed places. The moon set.

Armand and I soared alone through the center of the universe, no aeroplanes, no zeppelins, no birds or seals or boats or fish. Just us.

It seemed a very quiet sort of war.

I felt the sun wanting to rise, right as we neared the end of our passage over the sea. It was a peculiar sensation, a building, bulging pressure against the eastern horizon, like a giant on the other side of the world pressing his fist against the thin glazing of night. I'd never felt anything like it in my human shape—but then, I'd never kept my dragon shape as long as this before, so who knew what other strange *drákon* skills I was about to discover. In any case, the sun wasn't up yet; heaven and earth were still thick with dark. The only way I knew we were near land again was that the scent of salt water became mixed with that of seagulls once more, a great many seagulls, and also sheep. And the stink of coal. Which must have meant people.

We had about another hour before the sky would begin to catch fire. Armand knew it too (to be fair, he had a watch). With his compass in hand he pointed the way we should go, and I veered north, following the invisible path he'd set for us.

The sea gave way to bumpy, broccoli-topped forests, quilted patchworks of fields, and somewhere over the tip of France I had my moment of grace: Only a few weeks ago I'd been the outcast charity student seated on a stage before some of the most wealthy and powerful people of the kingdom, but now I, Eleanore Jones—a girl without a true home or a past or even a middle name—was on my way across enemy lines to save the life of a man I'd never met. Because I could.

And *that* was power.

I was proud of it. Pride was a sin; I'd been told that over and over again at Blisshaven, at Moor Gate, even during services at Iverson.

Pride is a sin, Eleanore, especially in a woman. Women must be modest and meek. Only the meek shall thrive.

I doubted *meek* would get me to Prussia. It was pride curled up warm inside me, ticklish and pleasing, and if that made me bad, so be it. I planned to thrive just fine without bloody meekness.

We located a rickety, leaning barn in a pasture, exactly as Armand had predicted, and settled down tight with our blanket amid mounds of sweet-smelling hay. I fell asleep right as the giant had his way and the night cracked apart, letting in the morning sun.

Everything had gone so smoothly.

I should have known it wouldn't last.

Chapter 21

I was asleep. It was quiet and dark. Then I was awake, and it was quiet and bright.

But it was raining wood all around me. A plank struck me hard and silent on the arm; hay swirled everywhere in a straw storm, sticking to my hair, my eyelashes. Where there had been a roof overhead before—surely there had been one?—there was now only a gray cloudy sky.

Armand was standing above me, impassioned, his lips moving, but he wasn't making any sound. It was the most curious thing.

He reached down, hauled me upright. He grabbed the knapsack and pulled me with him toward the open doors of the barn, which hitched back and forth and back and forth as though a brutal wind had them in its grip.

I began to cough on the hay. Again, no sound.

Breaking free from the walls of the barn, I realized that everything was bright because it was daylight still, and I was deaf because a bomb had just carved a crater only feet from our shelter. It was a sizeable crater, too, deep enough to prevent a man from climbing back up should he fall in. Singed rocks and dirt formed spokes around it, a black smoldering starburst.

Armand still had my hand. We were running for the woods at the edge of the pasture when the next shell went off, farther away but still near enough to send us both to the ground.

We scrambled back to our feet. The woods beckoned, hardly sufficient protection from falling bombs but surely better than the fallow, open land we sprinted through.

We reached the first trees as the third bomb hit, and this time I was able to grab a trunk instead of falling down.

The forest around us trembled. Birds screamed from far away, and suddenly I could hear again, and Armand was yelling, "Come on! Come on!" and dragging me deeper into the shadows.

I don't know how long we ran. Until I had a stitch in my side and I refused to keep going. I pulled free of him and bent over, puffing. The ground smelled of mulch, and my boots were covered in grass and dust, and I was *so* ruddy glad I'd had the sense to go to sleep fully clothed in Jesse's old shirt and trousers.

Ashes began to drift down around us, soft and serene as snowflakes.

"This—" Armand was out of breath as well. "This should do."

Another bomb, not near. The birds screamed and screamed.

I slithered down to the ground, legs out, and pressed my palms over my eyes to hide from the ash-laced light.

"Where are we?" I asked from around my hands.

I felt him sit beside me, the solid *thud* of the knapsack plopping down.

"Belgium. Far past the front. I thought the fighting would have moved on by now. This area was secured months ago."

"Apparently not," I said, as a new sound reached us: *pop! pop! pop!*

Gunfire.

I lowered my hands. Armand wasn't actually sitting; he was coiled back on his heels in his black leather duster, ready to spring up in a second. He looked lean and sharp and feral, even with the hay in his hair.

So pale. His gaze glittering.

And his heart, his heart—

"Steady on," I warned him. "Stay calm, all right?"

"I am entirely calm," he said, and beneath the trees' groaning and the gunshots and the screaming, he sounded it. "You?"

"Of course."

"Your eyes are glowing."

"Merde."

I covered them again, rubbing hard. Everything smelled of ashes now. My mouth tasted of it, mixed in with dust and grit. I realized that the screaming I'd thought was birds had been going on for too long and was too high-pitched. It was people. Children, mostly. Women, too.

"We've got to fly out of here," I said shakily. "Right now."

"Too late, waif."

"No, it's not! We'll fly fast. We'll be up and gone before they—"

"Eleanore. We have company."

I dropped my hands a second time, and the pair of women standing before us screeched and skipped back.

One turned and fled, vanished at once into the depths of the woods.

The other went to her knees, gaping at me. She crossed herself and began to babble in French.

"Your eyes," explained Armand, in that same calm voice.

"I can't control it!"

The woman began to creep toward me, her hands up in prayer. She was speaking so rapidly I had no hope of catching any of it. Her clothing was ragged and her eyes were bloodshot and her skin the exact color of the ashes floating between us. As soon as she was near enough she grabbed at my sleeves, my hands, and brought them up and buried her face in them.

I felt it then, what she wanted. I felt it as sure as I felt her tears and her hot breath on my fingers and the deep, dire desperation that had given her the strength to approach a demon girl in the woods and beg for help.

I felt her desperation, and it was the heaviest thing I'd ever known.

"One of the men from the village killed a German soldier last night," translated Armand, toneless. "He did it to stop the soldier from raping his daughter-in-law. But now the Germans are retaliating."

"They'll shell everything," I whispered. Her breath was so hot, fluttery hot and frantic. It felt like I'd trapped a sparrow in my hands.

"Yes," he said.

She lifted her face. She was younger than I'd first thought. Probably a mother to one of those screaming children.

"You'll have to leave." I tried to find the words in French. "*Se cacher. Se masquer.* After this. All of you. For as long as the war lasts, you'll have to hide like animals, because if they do this for one man, they'll never rest if it's all of them." I swiveled about to find Armand. "Will you tell her?"

He looked at me, at her, and then at the trees. Slowly he shook his head.

"Armand," I pleaded.

"She thinks you're an angel."

I laughed, and felt my own tears well up.

"She thinks you have some holy power to end this," he said. "And you don't. You don't, Eleanore."

"It's not holy," I agreed. "But it's something."

"It's your *life*," he said through his teeth. "And I won't let you imperil it for *this*."

I disengaged my hands from the woman's, climbing to my feet. She sagged in place and watched me without blinking.

"Not for *this*," I said to him. "But for *your* cause, it's fine."

"That's not what I meant."

"I know what you meant. This is our path, Mandy. This is where we're supposed to be. You know I'm right, because you're the one who charted it for us. Didn't Jesse insist we leave last night? He knew we'd end up here. We've been tapped on the shoulder by the stars themselves. Gifted with powers we don't yet fully even realize and have done nothing to deserve. Do you truly doubt what has to come next?"

He still wouldn't look at me. I went to him and wrapped my arms around him, resting my forehead to his chest.

Boom-boom-boom-boom-boom—

The sparrow now was his heart. I covered it with one palm.

" 'All beasts must have courage.' I'm not an angel of any sort. But what am I if I refuse this woman? What am I then?"

"Only all that I love," he answered finally, low.

"Thank you." I stepped back. "I'll see what I can do to earn that."

He spoke a few words to the woman, who answered in her raspy babble.

"It's not a large company," Armand interpreted. "The village is small and starving, so most of the soldiers moved on last month. Only a core group left. Rifles. Bayonets. Cannons. They plan to execute the remaining menfolk within the hour."

"Find the rest of her people," I told him. "Tell them they're going to need to hide."

He arched a brow at me, a right proper lordling once more. "I rather imagine they already know."

"Good. I'll be right back."

And this time, for the first time, it was I who kissed him on the cheek.

Then I Turned to smoke, and the woman cried out (*Un miracle!*), and I swept over the top of the forest to find the source of all those shells.

.

She vanished in a spiral of pearly gray, gone from his view so quickly it was as if she'd never been there. It felt, oddly, as if a part of him had ripped away with her. As if he'd lost an arm or a leg or an eye.

An old saying from his childhood popped into his head: *In the twinkling of an eye.*

That's how it was. Lora was gone from him in the twinkling of an eye. He might never see her again.

"God will protect her," said the woman, crossing herself again.

"No, I was supposed to," Armand replied, but in English, so she wouldn't understand. He looked back at her now, trying not to hate her, her bony emaciation and her tear-streaked horsey face and the damned sprigs of daisies printed on her dress that might have once been pretty but were now just dirty and brown.

"Where are the villagers?" he asked.

"The men are being kept in the millhouse—"

"No. Everyone else."

She nodded. "I'll show you. This way."

He followed her through the brush, ignoring his racing heart, ignoring how his body felt alien and sluggish. Ignoring, most of all, the constant, itchy whisper in his head that kept repeating, over and over, *Shed this skin. Shed this skin. Finish this life in the twinkling of an eye.*

They'd set up their artillery at the end of the main road that sliced through the village, not bothering to conceal themselves or move to a safer position because, after all, they didn't have to worry about retaliation. Half the buildings were already in flames—the source of all the ash—and what was left was a cratered disaster. A scruffy yellow dog picked its way around the pits, tail between its legs.

The soldiers weren't firing very quickly, taking the time to laugh and chat in between loading and shooting the cannons. There were about twenty men, but only half seemed to be working. The others were standing about and sharing what looked like jugs of wine.

The screams of the children had begun to die out. I hoped it meant Armand had found them, was moving them to a safer place.

One of the drinking soldiers spotted the dog. He pulled out his pistol and took a shot; the bullet struck a wall and sent chips of plaster flying. The dog yelped and tried to run.

I'd had no firm plan. I still didn't. But when the soldier grinned and raised his rifle this time to aim again, I materialized as a naked girl right beside him.

"Bonjour," I said, and punched him in the face.

I was smoke before the other men had finished whipping about, guns up. They weren't laughing now, by God. They were shouting over each other, and the man I'd hit was shouting loudest of all.

I Turned behind them, standing against a stack of wooden crates filled with shells.

"Over here now," I called in English, and ducked behind the crates when all twenty of them aimed their weapons at me.

"*Cochon!*" I yelled, which I was almost certain meant *swine* in French.

"*Menj a fenébe!*" I shouted next, and I didn't know what that meant, but it sounded insulting.

And just as they were pounding toward the crates—because, even drunk, they weren't stupid enough to fire at them—I Turned again, stole above them, and became a dragon next to the cannons.

A dragon in daylight. I'd never done it before, but I didn't have time to celebrate it now. If I'd glimmered by moonlight, by day I was afire, nearly too bright to behold. I lifted my tail (my lovely sharp tail!) and swiped it at the nearest cannon, flipping it over, the wheels of its base broken off, a nice big hole in its side.

I found the eyes of the dog-shooting rotter and sent him my own evil grin.

All the men screamed. About a quarter of them peeled off and pelted away. The rest began to fire.

Smoke, dragon, smoke. Two cannons gone. Three. I was Turning more quickly than I'd ever done, but still the bullets zinged by me, some bouncing off my scales. When they came thick as flies I knew I had to stay as smoke; a lucky shot between my scales could kill me.

I made myself sheer and silent and drifted over the remaining men, a natural part of the smoke-choked sky.

There was still one cannon and fifteen soldiers to go.

The problem was, now they knew what I wanted. Two men were hunched over a tall black box that emitted an unmistakable electric hum; one cranked a handle as the other shrieked into a mouthpiece.

The others had rallied around the cannon, round-eyed, fingers on triggers, scanning the sky.

"Listen to me! Listen to me, all of you!"

The horsey-faced woman was standing in the doorway of what looked to be a decrepit granary that had been long forsaken to the woods, medieval thick-cut stones eaten over with moss and wild ivy. She was holding up both arms, her raspy voice gone strident.

Armand couldn't discern much beyond her. He had the impression of bodies crammed in the space past the doorway. Of children sniffling, old men with creaking bones, women in kerchiefs, babies squirming. The stench of fear and feces rippled out, engulfing him. He cupped a hand over his nose, then forced himself to lower it.

"We have been saved," the woman announced, solemn now, and backed up so that Armand could take her place.

He took a step forward, straining to see through the darkness. Why was it so opaque?

Whoever was in there, they were quiet as a tomb. All he heard was breathing, theirs and his own. The rise of nervous heartbeats. An infant suckling. Blood pulsing through veins—

"Who are you?" called a woman, and as if her question had lifted the shadows from his eyes, he could see her now, see all of them, in a clear blue, almost otherworldly illumination. The darkness melted back and he was faced with close to fifty people of all ages and shapes and sizes. All of them filthy. All of them greasy with sweat.

But for one. There was one face that didn't match any of the others. A girl in the far back, half hidden behind her grandmother, perhaps. She had long reddish gold hair and a face as white and clean as—

"Sweet mercy! His eyes!" cried someone.

"What is it? What is that light?" whimpered someone else.

"Is it witchcraft?"

"The devil!"

"Not the devil, but angels!" claimed the horsey woman at his shoulder. "Do not fear! I told you God would deliver us!"

"No." Armand was tired and jittery and his skin felt like it'd been crisped with hot coals and he couldn't think of a single good reason to lie. It was too late to pretend now, and anyway, what these people wouldn't witness firsthand, they'd hear about over and over. "Not angels, not devils. We're English. We are dragons."

"Drákon," gasped the redheaded girl, and slammed back hard against the wall behind her before she disappeared into thin air.

Disappeared. No smoke. Only gone.

In the twinkling of an eye, he thought absurdly, exactly as the crowd flared into panic.

Here's the thing about cannons.

They're worthless without their shells, aren't they? Without the bombs to fire, they're just big, bulky, useless contraptions of metal.

I Turned into a girl behind the crates, lifted a pistol one of the deserters had dropped, and began to unload rounds into the wood.

Chapter 22

I found the village men trapped in a large stone building with a waterwheel attached, a river running brown and stagnant beside it. It was a mill, about a mile from where I'd just taken care of the rest of their company, and the dozen Huns guarding it had obviously heard the commotion. All those shells exploding at once—it might have been heard all the way to Prussia. Even as smoke, it felt like my ears were still ringing.

They were armed to the teeth, these blokes, rifles pointing in every direction, bayonets flashing. I became a dragon in front of them, plain as you please, and whacked my tail against the ground.

It was almost as earthshaking as the shells going off.

Only one of them thought to charge me. The others, happily, simply scattered. A couple actually jumped into the river.

As soon as the lone soldier noticed he had been abandoned, he skidded to a halt, halfway between me and the potential shelter of the mill.

I stalked toward him, twitching my tail. He was stocky and short, a patch of blond whiskers on his chin. I opened my wings and reared up, and he was too dumbfounded to even fire; he only stood there with his mouth hanging open, gawking up at me.

So I flicked him with a claw. It knocked him back to the dirt in a stir of dust, his rifle jarred free. His helmet rolled away down the lane, hollow as a tin can.

He was out. I Turned to girl, ran to the millhouse door, and strained to hoist free the heavy slab of wood that sealed it shut.

"Bonjour," I called breathlessly through the door. At that point it was the only French my scrambled brain could remember. *"Bonjour, bonjour!"*

As the first of the village men began to edge past the doorway, some small, shamed remnant of Iverson flushed through me; I was young, I was nude, they were all males, and I was supposed to be a lady.

I Turned to smoke.

Their fields were burned, their village was rubble, and even behind those stone walls I had no doubt they'd heard all the ruckus. Surely they'd figure out for themselves that it was time to flee.

Besides, I had a strong and uneasy feeling it was time for *me* to return to Armand.

I followed the fragrance of his blood.

In my smoke form, I didn't have what I'd term an actual sense of smell, yet I could recognize certain aromas. Like everyone, Armand had his own unique scent (sea salt, pine woods, lemon and clouds and spice) . . . yet what I chased now wasn't that. It was him but not him, more an essence than a scent.

It had a heat to it, a coppery tang, which felt to me like urgency.

I flew first to the last place I'd seen him, that anonymous spot in the woods where we'd run into the women, but of course he wasn't there. So I floated around until I felt him again: a dull tugging to the west. That ominous sensation that I needed to hurry.

Ash settled upon the crowns of the trees twitched upward as I passed, an acrid dry flurry. I dropped down lower, into the heart of the forest, weaving swiftly around trunks and boughs, because he was down there somewhere and I was getting closer, closer—

I found him. He was slumped against a log, head down, along with a pair of girls with messy braids and patterned skirts. One was holding his face. The other rifled through the knapsack, half its contents strewn along the ground.

Blood stained his forehead, his cheek. Blood made a scarlet river down his neck.

The sight of it did something to me—and that scent, that dreadful scent, so copper-hot. Rational Eleanore vanished; animal Eleanore swelled with rage.

He was hurt. He was bleeding. They were *hurting* him—

I became a person at his side and backhanded the girl nearest me, the one holding him. She sprawled flat, red palms to the sky.

"Stay away from him," I hissed, and lunged for the second girl.

She squealed and dropped the knapsack, clambering backward on her hands and heels like a stranded crab, but before I could reach her my ankle was caught.

"Lora! No! They're helping!"

I was snared, hopping in place. When his hand fell away I stumbled forward to my knees, catching myself with both hands. I glanced back at him with my hair in my eyes; he'd collapsed against the log again. He was breathing hard, watching me. The blood was flowing from a gash above his left eyebrow.

"They're helping," he repeated, making certain I understood.

I got up, pushed the hair from my face. I brushed the leaves from my body, then walked over to the girl I'd hit and pulled her to her feet. She was younger than Armand and I. Both of them were. I'd guess they were around twelve or thirteen, bony thin and fragile like the pleading woman had been.

Her cheek was pink. I hadn't struck her as hard as I could have, but I'd still meant it. She stared up at me with her lips compressed and something that might have been hatred in her eyes. Or terror. Or awe.

"Sorry," I tried. "Er . . . *je m'excuse.*"

"Pardon," she answered, short, and pushed by me to return to Armand.

"What happened?" I asked Armand, following her. The second girl slunk cautiously closer, picking up the knapsack again. "Who did this?"

"Do you remember, once upon a time, telling me never to let anyone see me as a dragon?"

I stopped probing at the gash, shocked. "You Turned?"

Without me? Without me being there or knowing it or feeling it—

"No. But I told them what we are." His lips smiled; it looked ghastly. "They didn't appreciate it much. Bit of a riot ensued. Somebody has rather good aim with a rock."

"You told them we're dragons. Come to help. And they *stoned* you."

"Dragon," sighed the red-palmed girl, as deeply and irrevocably besotted as only a twelve-year-old could be. She stroked her hand down his cheek and smudged the blood to his chin. *"Un prince de dragons."*

"Well, my prince, it looks like you made at least one friend. Good thing you haven't lost your touch with the ladies." My voice sounded harsh even to me. The skin around his wound was shiny hard and swollen. Beneath all that gore, it was turning a nasty shade of beet.

If he lost too much blood, if the blow had injured his brain—

I kept talking so my fear wouldn't show.

"Why'd they even believe you?"

"My eyes."

"Oh. And then you . . . what? You fought them off?"

"Then," he said dryly, "I ran."

"You still have the pistol. Why didn't you shoot them?"

He gave me an incredulous look. "Because I'm not like those soldiers. I am a nobleman. I don't shoot unarmed people."

I rolled my eyes. "Right gallant of you, your grand magnificence! Do be sure next time to remind them of how principled you are as they beat you to death—"

"Ici," interrupted the girl with the knapsack. She lifted up the cotton wool, along with a roll of bandage, and trotted over. I took them from her with blood-sticky fingers and realized a few things at once: that I was the eldest and presumably most responsible person here unharmed; that despite my exasperation with Armand, my body was sapped and my reason gone to mush; that I had no clue what to do next.

Bind the wound, my mind instructed. That's what I'd seen Deirdre do over and over, wasn't it? Bind the wound, stop the bleeding.

I pressed the pad of cotton in place, seized the besotted girl's hand, and made her hold it there while I wrapped the linen bandage tight around his head.

As I worked I felt something soft settle over my own shoulders and back. Jesse's shirt, the one I'd slept in. The knapsack girl had crept up and draped it over me. I'd completely forgotten I was nude.

"Merci," I grunted, not looking away from what I was doing.

"Vous êtes une princesse dragon?" she whispered.

A princess. Hardly.

"No." I met Armand's gaze, finishing up. *"Paysanne."*

I would have shot those stoning bastards for certain.

"You're not a peasant," he protested, but it was weak. If I'd thought him pale before, it was ten times worse now. The red on his face stood out like war paint.

"Nothing wrong with being from the gutter. At least we're raised to know the odds." *And when to keep our bloomin' mouths shut about monsters in our midst.* I stood. "The odds are now well stacked against us, I'd say. So I'm the peasant who's going to get us out of here."

We'd have to fly. Somehow he was going to have to hang on to me and we'd fly, because if the people here had been willing to stone him once, they'd do it again. Now that I listened carefully, I actually heard them. Footsteps not that far off, the forest floor crunching. Voices calling names—*Bibiane! Yseult!*—edged with frenzy.

I gathered everything back into the knapsack as quickly as I could, then shrugged out of the shirt and stuffed that in, too.

"Think you can still carry this?"

"Yes."

He climbed to his feet, supported instantly by either Bibiane or Yseult. Whichever was the moony one.

"Get ready," I said to him, assessing the girls. They reminded me far too much of the paper skeleton boy from Moor Gate, but I hoped they were more resilient than they looked. "It's one thing to imagine a dragon, and quite another to see one. They might come undone."

"Lora." His fingers were tracing the bandage across his brow. "Give them something."

"Like what? Money? They can't spend pounds out here."

"Food. Give them some tins."

I wanted to protest, then bit back the words. No matter what trouble swept these woods next, we were going to leave. These girls would be trapped here for a while to come. Maybe months. Maybe years.

I stuck my hand into the knapsack and dug around until I found the tins. I grabbed a few without looking to see what they were and passed them to the whispery girl.

"Bonne chance," I said. Good luck.

She clutched the tins to her chest, brown eyes alight. *"Et vous."*

I stepped back and Turned into a dragon, and to my absolute wonder, neither of them screamed or bolted or did anything but make O's of their mouths and squint at me like they'd just accidentally looked straight into the sun.

Then, together, they smiled.

We were fortunate the day was so overcast. Otherwise, we would have been forced to escape in plain view of anyone on the ground.

And, as I now knew, plenty of those anyones were armed.

I ascended as fast as I could, my wings beating hard, so that by the time we reached the bottom of the clouds I was drawing the air past my teeth because it was so cold and I wanted it so badly.

When you're earthbound, clouds look fluffy and soft, like dreamspun pillows, but the truth is that they're wet. And not soft so much as dense. Choking. I blinked away the drops that pearled my lashes and climbed higher, knowing it'd be harder for Armand to breathe the soupy mix of air and water than it was for me.

Breaking free was like exploding into a new day. We went from a world of cool, murky gray to brilliant sunlight and blinding azure sky. I had to narrow my eyes against it.

I had no inkling of which way to go. The sun was not quite directly above us—I thought it might be shortly before noon—but north, south, east, west . . . who knew? All I could really tell was up and down. Everything before me was either boundless firmament or white-crested clouds. There weren't even any birds this high.

Armand inched forward along my spine. From the corner of my eye I saw his hand lift, a finger pointing to our right. I didn't know if he still had the compass or not, since he'd lost his coat somewhere in the forest. But it seemed as good a way to go as any.

I tilted us to the right. Our shadow zoomed sharp below us, boy on dragon on clouds.

I couldn't keep him up here for long. In just his shirt and trousers Armand was going to get very chilled very quickly, and besides, I was worried he might pass out. We needed shelter and we needed it soon.

Yet the cloud cover remained uniformly opaque. I wasn't going to be able to see a good place to land. I'd have to use my other *drákon* senses as best I could to perceive it.

We couldn't come down near a town, obviously. Or a village, either. I hoped for more woods, a nice heavy stretch of them. Someplace with another barn, perhaps, or an abandoned farmhouse. Even a shepherd's hut would do.

I supposed I should try to sniff out some livestock. Sheep or cows.

Stupid, stupid, you're not that good, my mind scolded.

But I had to be.

I closed my eyes. *Stupid!* my brain reprimanded, unyielding, but I could tell I was flying straight, and again, there were no birds or anything. Nor were there any aeroplanes or zeppelins. They were loud—you could hear them from the ground, even—so I was positive I'd notice one up here before it was upon us. Closing my eyes helped me to concentrate on everything beyond sight: the touch of the wind against me, how it jostled me this way or that. The silence of this bright heaven, where the only two living creatures within miles made the only noise.

The taste of sunshine and vapor.

The scent of . . . nothing but clouds.

Try harder.

There was land below me. I knew that without doubt, so I concentrated on it. I knew how trees smelled, and how soil smelled. I recalled with acute precision the powdery black pungency of gunpowder, how it parched my tongue and burned my nostrils and clogged the back of my throat.

We passed through a whiff of that, then more than a whiff. I sneezed and shook my head and angled beyond it.

Trees, yes. Fields, very dry wheat or something like it. Woodsmoke suddenly, apples. Were we over an orchard? Orchards tended to be dense and mostly empty of people. That might be good—

Horses. Unquestionably horses, or rather, the product of them. I was from the city; I tried to remember if horses went with orchards . . .

And then, quite abruptly, Armand made the decision for both of us.

His hands loosened. He fell backward. He slid down my side but by some miracle didn't fall off. I realized my wing was holding him in place, but only barely, because he was sliding again—

I twisted my head around and managed to grab him by the cuff of his trousers just in time. His eyes flashed open and he struggled to get upright, but the wind was so strong. Slowing down would mean we'd descend, but I didn't have a choice.

The cuff began to rip. The bandage blew off his head, a graceful, looping ribbon that danced down and down and became swallowed by the clouds.

His hands slapped against my neck until he found my mane. His fingers dug in. I opened my jaws and he clambered up into place just as we plunged into the gray.

It no longer mattered what lay below. I had to get us to land.

Blind again, beads of water spangling my lashes again. My brain was now commanding, *Hurry! Hurry!* but I was so afraid of suddenly materializing in the open air. What if I was wrong and we were above a town? What if we were above the front? What if we were above just some farmer with a rifle and frayed nerves and a keen eye?

Armand wilted once more, this time forward. Then the mist streaked away and all I could see were trees, rows and rows of them, bright rosy dots of apples. Birds erupting from the branches and leaves, flinging themselves every which way.

I slowed as rapidly as I dared, trying to judge if I could fit between one of those rows, but Armand started to fall, so I just dropped.

Like a stone.

I snatched him up by the leg with my head lifted high so he dangled there from my mouth. Talons scraping the earth, feet, body, tail. We slammed down and apples pelted the grass around us, a hard thumping rainfall.

Somehow I managed not to roll. We skidded to a halt sideways but upright, my lungs scorched and my wings trembling. When I could, I lowered my head, placed him down as gently as possible. Then I Turned and collapsed beside him, done in.

I'll tell you this: The aroma of apples mixed with horse dung had never, ever smelled so sweet.

Chapter 23

"What an appalling trip," complained a voice near my head. "Bone-rattling ride, rotten service. Next time I believe I'll take the train."

I wanted to smile, but it seemed too much effort, so instead I only opened my eyes and gazed up at the ocean of clouds.

They churned far away from us now, their own separate realm once more.

"Eleanore, are you alive?"

I cleared my throat. "Just. You?"

"Aside from the fact that there's a welt the size of a cricket ball on my forehead, and some rather impressive puncture wounds along my leg—"

"What?" I sat up, reenergized. "Where? Show me!"

I'd tried to bite down carefully, but I'd had to catch him, after all, and we'd been plummeting and I'd been mostly focused upon how much I didn't want to die.

"It's fine," Armand said. He was propped up on his elbows and smiling, that small ghastly smile, his face still painted red and white. "Hardly hurts at all. I say, do you think you might, er, put on some clothes before stripping me of mine?"

"No," I snapped, vexed. "Just be a ruddy gentleman and look away."

"I am the ruddiest damned gentleman you'll ever meet," he retorted, all wounded dignity. "You have no idea. You're naked nearly all the time and I *never*—"

I laughed. "Righto. *Never*. Will you be still? I need to examine your leg."

He gave up, falling back to the grass. "You're the nurse."

I pushed up the tattered remnant of his cuff. The punctures weren't insignificant; my dragon teeth were very sharp. But neither were they as deep as I'd feared they'd be. Some were more like scratches. If I had a chance to clean them and wrap them, they likely wouldn't require stitches.

I thought. I hoped. I'd gladly take on another round of soldiers before I'd shove a needle and thread through Armand's flesh.

I was categorically not, *not*, anyone's nurse.

"We need cover," I announced, looking around. Trees everywhere, as far as the eye could see. No people. No horses. Only trunk after trunk ringed with manure and scraggly, uncropped grass. A misty, silvery haze wafting through, making a phantom wall of the distance.

Furrows from my claws scored long lines through the dirt that led straight to us, ending at our feet.

"Thought I saw a lake when we were coming down." Armand was staring directly up at the sky. "Perhaps a house beside it."

"Really?"

"It was quick. I might be wrong. The orchard ended and the

area seemed more like a forest. I think it was in that direction." He pointed to the left.

"I'll investigate. Hold on."

I Turned to smoke.

Except I didn't. Nothing happened.

I released a breath, frowned. Tried again.

Nothing.

Armand's gaze cut to mine, then swiftly away.

"Are you going?"

"I'm trying! It's not . . . it's not working for some reason. I'm so . . ."

Exhausted. Hungry. Scared.

I scowled up at the sky, my fists on my hips. I had to do this. We were in danger out here in the open, in daylight. So I had to.

Come on. Smoke. Smoke . . .

"Eleanore."

Smoke!

"Lora."

"What?" I snarled.

"We need to eat," he said. "Both of us. Hand me the knapsack, will you?"

I pressed a hand to my forehead, then flung it away. The knapsack had torn off him before we'd landed, but it hadn't gone far, stuck in some lower branches of a tree nearby. I stomped off and jumped for it until I could grab it, then jerked at the straps.

It broke free. Twigs and leaves bombarded me. A few more apples plunked to the ground.

"No need to kill the tree," Armand called.

"Shut it," I replied, but under my breath.

He was right. I needed food and clothing and rest, but as I

walked back to him I realized he probably needed all those things even more. Well, not clothing. But he looked as if he might go down under a good stiff breeze.

I set the sack before him. My shirt was still on top, so I tugged it free. The buttons felt fat and unyielding; my fingers groped at them clumsily. By the time I'd managed the trousers and boots, Armand was sitting up, an array of tins before him. The knife in his hand stole the weak daylight, condensing it into a stab of silver along its blade.

He speared a tin and sawed it open, then lifted it to his nose.

"Minced peaches. There should be some hardtack, too."

I searched for the hardtack while he lifted each tin and examined the labels.

"What are you looking for?"

"The caviar," he said. "But it's not here. It must have gone to the girls."

"Thank heavens," I said feelingly, then paused. "You brought caviar on our rescue mission?"

"It was in a tin." He sounded defensive. "A perfectly logical choice."

"Too bad. It's peaches for you instead."

I handed him one of the flat hardtack crackers. He dipped it in the open tin, then took a huge bite.

"Delicious. *Much* better than caviar."

It was. So was the next tin of beef stew, and the next of poached salmon, and the next of lobster. We washed it all down with one of the flasks of water, sharing sips. I wanted to open another tin but was growing more and more uncomfortable sitting there so exposed, plus I knew we'd need to save something for later.

I took up the empty tins and chucked them as far from us as I could. Then I gathered up handfuls of apples and stuffed them into the knapsack.

The day was darkening. Wind began a long, slow whistle through the trees, a strange and melancholy sound.

"I'm going to try to Turn again," I told Armand. "Stay here."

"Not a problem."

I wiped my hands down my thighs. I lifted my face to the clouds and the wind took my hair in a wild dancing swirl and I thought, *Smoke!*

I remained stubbornly, unmistakably, a girl.

"I can smell the lake," Armand said. "On the wind. It can't be that far. We can walk it."

I sighed. "Can you? On that leg?"

He rose to his feet. "Let's find out."

It wasn't a house, after all. It was a hunting lodge by the lake, a rustic and gloomy and conveniently unoccupied one. It took us nearly three hours to get there, Armand's arm slung about my shoulders, both of us lurching along through the mist. I'd rewrapped his head with a bandage and done what I could for the bite marks, but truly what we needed was a place to bed down.

The lodge was certainly that. It was two stories of stacked logs and glass, a fringe of moss clinging to the northern slope of its roof. We watched it for a while before venturing too close, but there were no lights glowing inside, no movement. No scent of people or meals cooking or anything but wood and water. I supposed it wasn't hunting season yet.

We stole forward, ducking from pine to pine, just in case. I dashed up to the nearest window and pressed my palms against its frame, but it didn't budge.

I'd scarcely discovered a good-size rock to break the glass when Armand murmured my name.

I looked over. He was standing at the front door, which had swung wide open.

"Sometimes the simplest solution is the actual solution," he said.

I dropped my rock to the dirt and followed him in.

It was far more elegant inside than I would have expected. The walls were still obviously rough-hewn logs, but the ceiling had been plastered, and the furniture was ornately carved and padded and polished. Green foggy light from the windows revealed a collection of crystal goblets glinting in a hutch. A medieval-looking shield hung above the hearth had been painted with heraldry, two peacocks and a knight's grim, gray visor. A rusted sword hung above that, fixed with hooks into the stone.

Glass eyes gleamed from every wall. There were mounted animal heads wherever I looked. Deer, boars, rams. Bears and birds.

A single cobweb, delicate as elfin lace, stretched between the antlers of a buck.

"Enchanting décor," I whispered, because beneath my sarcasm, I couldn't shake the chill of those dead, watching eyes.

"Makes you think, doesn't it?" Armand had limped over to a bookcase, studying the titles.

"That the person who owns this place is rather too fond of murdering innocent animals and chopping off their heads?"

"That without these human masks we wear, it might easily be *our* heads on those plaques."

I shivered, enveloped in a sliver of that cool, greenish light.

"Let's find a bedroom," I urged. "Someplace soft."

"Lora." He ran a finger down the side of the case. "All of these books are in German. I think we've crossed the border."

German books in a German lodge, in a hushed German wood. It felt awfully real to me then, even more real than bullets or cannons. Odd, I know. But standing there in that room, in the home of someone who no doubt would happily see me dead or, at the very least, subjugated, it made me realize how very far from my own home I was now. How far we both were.

And now, without my Turn, how vulnerable.

A mouse poked its head out from a gap in the timbers, saw us, squeaked, and jerked back.

Armand swayed. I caught him by the shoulders once more; he leaned heavily against me. I spoke into his shirt.

"I bet the bedroom is up that stairway over there. Can you do it? Come on, lordling, one step at a time."

I'd been correct. Upstairs was a series of bedrooms, and I led us to the biggest, because it was the only one with a vantage overlooking the hazy lakefront. Should anyone approach, hopefully we'd see them or hear them before they made it to the door.

If we didn't . . . there was still the pistol.

The bed was enormous, easily large enough for four (which made me wonder about both the size and the inclinations of its owner). The mattress had been stripped bare, but all the clean linens and blankets were in a trunk at its foot, so it didn't take long to make it up.

"You're quite good at that," Armand observed, seated in an ugly leather chair by the door. He'd wanted to help, but I'd made him sit. I was glad I had when I saw how he tried to hide his wince as he stretched out his leg. He reclined and with those unnaturally bright eyes watched me work.

As soon as this was done, I was going find some water to scrub away all the dried blood on his face.

"Experience," I said. "We suffered a scandalous lack of maidservants at the orphanage."

"I'm beginning to suspect this orphanage of yours wasn't nearly the utopia you've always boasted it was."

"Oh, right. You know me, forever boasting about what a ripping good time it is to be an orphan."

"It always is in fairy tales," he said innocently.

I snorted. "Have you actually *read* any fairy tales? Orphans fare the worst of anyone. We were lucky they didn't decide to roast us and eat us for dinner, come to think of it."

"Ah, dinner," Mandy said, closing his eyes.

Of course. One more task before I could rest. I hoped Mr. Hunter kept his larder well stocked. One couldn't live off chopped-up woodlands creatures alone, surely.

"There's something I forgot to tell you," Mandy said, eyes still closed.

"What?"

"Well, I didn't forget, precisely. But I . . . I wonder if it really happened."

"What?" I said again, impatient, tucking in a corner of sheet.

"Back there this morning, back in the woods with the villagers, before everything went so wrong . . . there was this moment. This girl, I mean."

I glanced up.

"And she . . . I could swear that as soon as I told everyone that we were dragons—hardly, I don't know, an *instant* before it all blew to hell . . ."

"What?" I demanded, crossing to stand before him.

"I said that we were dragons, and she said, '*Drákon.*'"

I stared at him, speechless. His eyes opened. He looked up at me soberly.

"She was fourteen. Fifteen. Reddish hair. Different from the other villagers, you know? Different. Like us. And I . . . I couldn't see all of her, but I don't think she was wearing any clothing."

"Are you saying—"

"Then she vanished. Right in front of my eyes, she vanished. Without smoke, without anyone else even noticing."

I sank into a squat before him, my hands light atop his knees.

"Sounds like a hallucination," I said carefully.

"I know."

"But you don't think it was?"

"I was struck on the head *after* that, Eleanore."

"Then perhaps you heard her wrong."

He eased back again, evading my gaze. "Perhaps."

"And perhaps she *seemed* to vanish but was merely caught up in the crowd. They were rushing you then, weren't they?"

"No."

"Armand!" I dropped all the way down to the floor. "I'm sorry, but you're asking me to believe that this girl, this villager in the middle of bloody Belgium nowhere, knew what you were, what *we* are, that she *herself* may have been one of us, and then, poof, she's gone? No smoke or anything?"

"I told you I wasn't certain that it really happened," he grumbled.

I regarded him without speaking. It had to be close to dusk, because the room around us was dimming from greeny gray to greeny charcoal, and Armand was dimming with it, a wraith in the big dark chair.

Outside, a water bird began a low, piping warble that bounced off the lake before fading into nothing.

"Suppose it was real," I said finally, quiet. "I don't see what we're supposed to do about it now."

"No," he agreed, and closed his eyes again.

I moved through the night shadows. I didn't want to risk any sort of light, even though I'd found candles and matches stashed inside a cupboard. The lodge had plenty of windows, and the woods were plenty dark. A single flame would be all it'd take to reveal us to anyone, anything, out there.

I'd located the pump for the well and gotten us buckets of fresh water, which was handy, but I'd figured the lake would be a good enough source even if I hadn't discovered the well.

The larder was the problem.

Most of its shelves were bare, but for four sealed canisters and a great many mouse droppings. The canisters contained four different things: sugar, noodles, something fetid that might once have been powdered eggs, and strips of dried meat.

That was it.

The meat was a welcome find (I thought maybe it was venison), but I couldn't imagine what to do with the rest of it. I might soak the noodles in cold water and wait until they softened, then sprinkle them with sugar . . .

That sounded disgusting, even to me.

We still had some tins left in the knapsack, plus the apples, but we'd decided to save them if we could; neither of us knew what lay ahead.

I devoured a couple of pieces of venison as I rooted around to make certain there wasn't anything else hidden anywhere else (there wasn't, only more droppings), then carried the canister upstairs with me to check on Armand.

I walked slowly, my feet feeling the way step by step, the wooden banister smooth and warm beneath my hand. The bedroom was slightly less dark than downstairs had been, probably because of the series of windows meant to take advantage of the view. I was able to pick out the contours of the bed, the silhouette of Armand within it.

"Hullo," he said, and even though he'd spoken softly, it rang abnormally loud in my ears.

"Hullo."

"I don't suppose you've brought back some strudel?"

"Even better." I held up the canister. "Desiccated meat."

His voice held a smile. "My favorite."

"It will be."

I sat upon the edge of the bed and opened the lid. I had to admit, the strips tasted better than they looked. I reached in, took a few, and passed them to him.

Our fingers touched. His felt like fire.

"Mandy!"

"Beloved."

"Stop it." I reached for him blindly. "Come here. I need to feel your forehead."

Obediently he leaned forward. My hands found his neck, his jaw. The firm shape of his nose and then that welt on his forehead, which I'd cleaned and rebandaged, so what I really felt there was padding. I'd given him some aspirin then, too, but it didn't seem to be working.

I brought my face to his and touched my lips to a bare spot above the bandage.

I felt him go very, very still.

"Eleanore," he said, and if his voice had been soft before, now it was barely a sound at all.

I pulled back, unnerved.

"It's how you check for a fever," I explained, glad he couldn't tell that I was blushing. "My mo—"

My what? My mother? My mother did that? I shook my head, and the tickle of memory was gone.

"I think my mother taught me that," I finished. "Or someone. I don't know."

He bowed his head, seemed to be examining the venison in his hands that I knew he couldn't really see.

"Do I? Have a fever, that is?"

"I don't know," I said again. "Honest to God, Armand, I don't know how anything works anymore."

Likely it was the darkness freeing me, freeing my tongue. Likely it was that I didn't have to look into his eyes and acknowledge what I'd find in them, the constant hunger, the unwavering focus that made me feel both huge and tiny at once: selfishly pleased to be the recipient of his desire, inwardly terrified because I didn't know if I'd ever be worthy of it, or even able to return it.

I'd loved Jesse. I had. And it had been easy.

But now, with Armand . . . everything was topsy-turvy. Jesse was the star I couldn't hear. Mandy was the dragon at my fingertips, right here, right now, and he wanted me.

I'd never have to wonder what he thought. Where he'd gone.
I'd never have to wonder how he truly felt.

Only how *I* felt.

Which was . . . confused.

not alone, sang the stars, a refrain that shimmered through the
cool, dark air, chasing shadows.

"I think I need to sleep now," I said.

"I know," he answered, and moved over in the bed to make
room. "Come on, Lora. It's soft, just like you'd hoped."

"I should get you some more aspirin first."

"Later."

"But—"

"It can wait. Everything can wait until tomorrow, waif. When
there'll be sun."

I was too knackered to argue. I placed the canister upon the
floor and crawled toward him, not even bothering to remove my
boots. I let myself slump into the bedding, a downy pillow beneath
my cheek. Armand didn't try to get closer, only lay there beside me,
but eventually, after counting out more than two minutes silently
in my head, I felt his hand clasp mine.

Fire, still.

Weary as I was, it was a long while before I fell asleep.

Chapter 24

Shed this skin.

He didn't sleep. He couldn't. He felt wrapped in flames, tortured by the simplest sensations: the weave of the sheets. The revolting smell of the dried meat. The dampness of the night.

His heart, too large in his chest now, too large and too desperate to get out, because it hammered and hammered against his bones with such violence it would splinter him into a million pieces. Every bit of him smashed, right down to his cells.

Only her touch was still right. Only Lora's hand, lax around his, felt like the anchor he so greatly needed.

Armand remembered what Rue had written about the first Turn of the *drákon* as if he'd composed the words himself: *It's going to hurt. It's going to hurt so very much that you will wish you could die.*

But he couldn't die yet. He hadn't saved his brother yet. He hadn't confronted his father. He'd never even kissed the girl he loved, not really, and if he died here, tonight, she'd be the only one who'd ever truly know what happened.

It would ruin her, the burden of that secret. Somehow he knew that it would.

Finish this life.

The Turn was building inside him, a tidal wave of smoke and disintegration so colossal it blotted out everything but his fear.

He dug his fingers into the sheets and stared up at the black timbered ceiling.

Shed this skin. Finish this life. In the twinkling of an . . .

The dam of his willpower crumbled, spent.

The air went to syrup, too thick to breathe.

His heart slowed. Slowed.

Stopped.

He couldn't die—

Chapter 25

I jolted upright. I didn't even realize I was awake until I heard the mournful piping of the water bird again, and I looked at the windows because it sounded so near.

I was awake, and I was alone in the bed. I felt ill and sweaty for no reason I could think of, as though I'd just broken a fever.

A fever.

I looked down and yes, there they were: his shirt laid out flat, the bandage that had been around his head fallen to his pillow. Beneath the sheets I'd find his trousers and underwear, too.

I sprang from the bed.

"Armand! Where are you? Mandy!"

I didn't bother to keep my voice down. There was no one else here, no one at all.

All the windows were closed tight. If he'd left as smoke, it hadn't been that way. There was no fireplace up here, but there was the one downstairs, and the door—

I hit the stairway so hard my feet slipped; only my grip on the railing kept me from spilling all the way down. As it was, I had to skip and hop and finish the last few steps at an awkward run, my boots cracking against the floorboards of the landing.

The front door gaped open. The night sky hung beyond it, coal black dappled with treetops and stars.

I tried to Turn. It didn't work. I raced out into the open and scanned the heavens, searching for him.

There were some clouds, that persistent haze hanging over the lake. No smoke that I could see. But he had to be here. He had to. He wasn't going to be one of those unfortunate young *drákon* who Turned and dissolved into death, because I was going to save him—

"Where is he?" I shouted to the stars. "Where?"

rise up, came their response; even they sounded mournful. *rise up, fireheart.*

And then, as if they'd unlocked the hidden shackles that had bound me, I could.

I went to smoke, freed from the earth. I left my garments behind, the lodge, its mossy roof. I launched upward, and suddenly I could see all of the lake, the bristly stretch of forest encircling it, the mist that shifted and curled above the surface of the water . . .

Hold up. There was no wind, no reason for that patch of curl there near the center of the lake. I moved closer to better see. It spun and whirled like a miniature cyclone, no natural thing.

Armand.

I flowed over to him, became thin and hollow, and surrounded him as best I could. I couldn't tell if he realized I was there; now that I knew where and what he was, I felt him as strongly as ever. It was obviously Mandy, gone to smoke but in such a furious way. The force of his whirling was sending me spinning, too, tearing me into tendrils.

I was beginning to feel ill again, so I had to draw free and let him alone.

What was he doing? Below us both, the water grew stormy, thick wide ripples that slapped all the way back to shore.

I wished he'd stop. I wished he'd move away from the lake, because if I accidentally Turned to girl here, I probably wasn't going to be able to swim to safety. I was rotten sick of nearly drowning.

He went faster, faster. He was pulling a spiral of water up into his middle, sending drops in every direction. I hung back farther, baffled, as the spiral became a funnel, and the drag from his rotation became something stronger and more ominous.

What's happening to him? I asked the stars.

They didn't answer. I wandered higher and hunted the heavens, but Jesse wasn't anywhere in sight.

Tell me why he's doing this, I demanded.

shape and form, they sang to me. *form and shape.*

So . . . Armand was attempting to hold on to his shape? To not Turn back to a human or into a dragon, but remain as smoke?

Why would he do that? Unless . . . unless he thought that if he didn't, he'd have no form left at all.

this beast was never meant to be fully as you are. the thread of his life has always been destined to be severed here.

If I had had breath in a body, it would have left me then. I rushed upward, trying to see as many of them as I could.

No! You can't take him!

we do not take, fireheart. Their song was so sad now. So chilling. *he is a child of magic. by law of magic, he ascends to us.*

I sped higher and higher. *Where is Jesse? Let me speak to Jesse!*

Again, no answer. They glittered against a black, black sky, ice cold and remote.

You told me I wasn't alone!

you were not. your span of hours with this dragon was freely given. that time is done.

Far below, the cyclone that was Armand began to break apart. The waterspout grew shorter, splashing into diamonds upon the surface of the lake. The mist settled. Armand spread thin . . . then began to rise.

I arrowed back down to him, surrounded him. I tried my own cyclone to keep him in place. He only twirled with me and then beyond me; I wasn't able to stop him from flowing higher.

Please, he can't die now, I pleaded.

I had no hands to capture him. I had no words to encourage him. Within moments he was so diaphanous it was as if he had no substance at all, not even color. Zigzag rips began to cleave him; unvarnished night peeped through. A distant, horrified part of me wondered if it hurt.

I'm supposed to save him! I have to save him!

The stars burned in silence. I wanted to scream and I wanted to cry. I wanted to destroy the magic that was taking him. If I'd had a bullet or a bayonet, if I'd had a machine gun, if I could have killed this thing that was killing him . . .

I watched, helpless, as the smoke of the only living soul who loved me wisped away, molecules falling skyward, gone forever.

And I realized that I had no true power, after all. Not over death. I'd failed. I'd failed at everything.

A sudden new song swelled around me.

what do you give for this life? what sacrifice do you give?

My answer was instant, unthinking.

My own life. Mine for his.

agreed.

Have you ever done something so rash, so immense, that it takes an eternity of seconds for the magnitude of it to sink in?

I'd just committed suicide.

For Armand.

I had survived my youth immersed in storybook fairy tales. Spent the last few months of my life living one. The one thing I knew with absolute certainty about magical pacts was that they were binding, evermore.

I floated, suspended, waiting for it to happen. That same distant part of me that had been horrified for Armand was now cringing at my own impending pain, but I wasn't going to try to fly away or Turn to escape it. I was petrified and defiant, and if I'd been in my girl-shape, I'd likely have been huddled in a ball on the ground, covering my head with my hands. But what was done was done.

So I floated.

Slowly, beautifully, the shredded bits of Armand Louis sifted down around me, growing longer and denser until I was threaded through with him. Strands of his smoke coiling around mine, reshaping the mass of me until I was new and unknown, even to me.

We twisted into helixes together. We joined and separated and joined once more, dancers on air. Dancers *made* of air.

I thought, *I never knew it could be like this, this coupling. I never guessed. I wish I'd known, I wish—*

No. I wasn't going to waste the final few beats of my life wishing for impossible things.

Armand slipped free of me, sinking down to the water. I remained where I was, still waiting for the stars to claim me as he drifted toward the shore.

Eventually, since nothing else was happening, I drifted after him.

He Turned to boy in the mud. He was flat on his back, his knees raised, eyes shut. But his chest was rising and falling. He lived.

I returned my attention to the heavens. No songs now, only those brilliant flecks of light shining down.

If they were giving me another hour with him—blimey, another few seconds—I'd take it. I hurried to his side and Turned to girl, kneeling by his head.

"Armand?"

He moaned, deep in his chest. I touched my hand to his hair.

"Armand, how do you feel?"

In response, he rolled over and vomited into the water.

"Oh," I whispered. I kept stroking his hair. It felt so soft against my skin. Had it always been like this?

"That," he announced, guttural, "was truly, profoundly vile."

"But you're here. You're alive. You're going to be fine."

I said the words as if casting a spell. I said them and thought, *This is so. This is what must be true. My life for yours.*

Armand rolled flat again. His eyes were red and watery.

"Mind if we . . . walk back?"

"No." I shot a frightened look up at the stars. "No, don't Turn again."

"If you insist," he said weakly, and I helped him to his feet.

———

Daylight came. I must have slept through a good portion of it, because by the time I opened my eyes, the world was mellow and golden, as if the sun was already dipping to kiss the horizon.

I felt warm and comfortable. I was a lazy girl wrapped in woolly blankets and Jesse's arms and—

No, I wasn't.

I craned my head up. It was Armand holding me, not Jesse. He was awake, too, watching me. Our bodies were nestled close; he was the source of all that heat. Our legs had entangled.

"You looked cold," he said, as if that explained everything.

It might have been true. All I had on was my shirt. The bedcovers had rumpled down by my waist.

He was also wearing a shirt. I'd helped him into it last night after we'd made it back to the lodge. I remembered that. I remembered . . .

Oh, crikey.

I remembered it all. My warm lazy happiness swiftly evaporated.

I had changed something. Maybe everything. Armand was going to live now, and I was not.

It's fine, it's fine, I reminded myself, trying not to panic. *A fair bargain. Worth it.*

So why was I still alive? Why was I burrowed here in this bed with him and those generous rays of golden sun? How much extra time were the stars going to allow me, anyway?

Armand's palm shifted against my shoulder, a sweet, familiar pressure. His lashes were long and ebony. A shadow of blue whiskers roughened the planes of his face. He held my eyes and gave the smallest smile. It was crooked, almost shy.

Right then I made a choice. Until the stars summoned me, until my thread was severed, I was going to finish what I had come here to do. Because if I was going to leave this boy behind, the least I could do was leave him with his brother.

"Was it only a dream?" he asked, losing the smile.

"No." I sat up and pushed away the covers. Mud had dried into flakes all around us, grayish brown smears ground into the sheets. "It was real."

"I Turned," he said wonderingly. He picked up one of the flakes, which went to dust almost at once between his fingers. His eyes took on a fierce, faraway look. "I can't . . . quite seem to recall most of it."

I was surprisingly disappointed. "Oh?"

"Some. Perhaps you might fill in the gaps."

"Well . . ." I had to weigh my words; I didn't want to accidentally let him know too much. I could barely stand to think about what I'd done. I definitely wasn't ready to talk about it yet.

Mandy was waiting. My fingers found the bottom button of my shirt and began to pluck at it nervously.

"I awoke, and you were gone. I found you over the lake, er, spinning."

"Spinning? Like a top?"

I shook my head. "Like a gale. Like a windstorm that would consume the world."

"There was the mist," he said abruptly. "And the funnel of water."

I glanced back at him. The fierce look hadn't faded, but now it was directed at me.

"That's right. And then we—we danced a little."

"We did?"

I shrugged, embarrassed. I'd never danced with a boy before. All my lessons at Iverson had partnered me with Stella, because we were closest in height, and we'd had to take turns at playing the man. To be granted permission to dance in public was one of the most coveted ambitions of any young woman of any class. But to have your first-ever dance be with a genuine lord, no matter what form we'd had at the time—

I was sorry then that I wouldn't be able to tell anyone about it. I jolly well would've enjoyed the expression on Stella's face. It might even have made up for all the times she'd trod on my toes.

"Rather a dance," I amended. "That's what I'd call it, anyway. You don't remember flying?"

He sat up, his brows knit. Blots of mud stained the back of his shirt, too. "I remember the pain. I remember tearing about, unable to . . ."

I tugged and tugged at the button.

"I remember the colors of the stars. How they were every color I'd ever seen, and more. Colors I can't even name." That hint of slow wonder crept back into his tone. "How exquisite they were. How they sang, and how I hoped they'd never stop."

"What did they sing to you?"

"Just *come*."

"Oh."

He looked at me askance from beneath those black lashes. "I remember you as well. Now I do. I remember sensing you below me. Wanting to be with you so badly that I ached. Even more than the pain—more than the songs—I *ached*. And then it happened. I came down and we . . ." The crooked smile returned. "As you said, Lora. We danced."

The button popped free. I cupped it in the heart of my palm.

Armand said, "I suppose I wanted it badly enough, eh? To be with you. To live. That's what saved me."

"Yes," I said. "That must have been it."

At Blisshaven, at Moor Gate, I used to make bargains with myself all the time. Lonely little *if this, then that* deals to help me endure.

If I keep my shirtwaist clean all day, I can read an extra chapter of my book tonight.

If I can dodge Billy Patrick's pinches, I can think about my parents before going to sleep.

If I can snatch a piece of bread at tea, I can pretend it's cake. White cake, with pink and silver frosting.

If I make it past Lizzie and her lot down the hall, I can imagine I'm the queen. They'll be my slaves.

If I live through this session with The Machine, I'll find a way out of here. Tonight I'll find a way out.

If I don't mention my pact with the stars to Armand or anyone else, never ever, I can stay awhile longer. Exist awhile longer.

Perchance we never really outgrow our childhoods. Not the worst of them.

Chapter 26

Mr. Hunter kept a trunk full of spare clothing in the second bedroom. He was a bigger bloke than either of us, but we both got fresh shirts and trousers, and Armand a new leather coat. They were winter clothes, woolens and heavy twills, but I thought that a good thing. The sky was a much colder place than the ground, even in high summer.

Armand had gone through every book in the case searching for clues about where we were and had come up empty-handed.

"Philosophy, agriculture, crime novels. Quite a few monographs on waterfowl and guns."

"Imagine that," I said, gnawing at the last strip of venison.

"But this chap hasn't kept so much as a scrap of newspaper, local or otherwise. We could be anywhere."

"Anywhere in Germany," I corrected him.

He was seated by the crystal goblets, a book in each hand. Splintered light from the goblets threw prisms across him, across the pages of the books. He frowned down at them, then up at me.

"Right. Anywhere in Germany. But until we figure out exactly where, we don't know which way to go to reach Schloss des Mondes."

"I'll Turn to smoke and locate the nearest village. Sneak down there, find a daily or a placard, something with a name on it, then come back to you. Will that help?"

"It might," he said, "except that it won't be necessary, since I'm coming with you."

"You can't. I can't travel as a dragon in daylight, Armand, and I don't think either of us is up for another hours-long hike through the woods."

His brows arched. He looked at me without speaking.

"And you can't Turn!" I burst out, more strongly than I'd meant to. "I mean, it's too soon for you," I added, calmer. "There's likely to be more pain, isn't there? And what if you can't hold it? What if you Turn back in midair? What am I supposed to do then?"

"What if *you* can't hold it?" he countered, closing both books.

"I'm better at this than you are!"

"Only more practiced."

"Precisely." I folded my arms across my chest. "So I'm the obvious choice to go."

"No. We're a pair, remember? We stick together. That's the way it's meant to be."

I laughed, but it was mostly angry. "You can't stop me from doing what I want."

"And," he said quietly, rising to his feet, "you cannot stop me, either, Eleanore. Not any longer."

Stalemate. This was my thanks for sacrificing my life for his. He'd survived one Turn and was now convinced he was the master of it. Born into wealth, coddled by society, Lord Armand had always been granted power over whatever—or whomever—he desired. How could I have forgotten it?

We glared at each other as the light grew softer and the prisms laid their rainbows long across the empty chair.

"What if you Turn into a dragon?" I asked. "Right there, in the middle of town. What if *that* happens, your mighty lordship?"

It had taken days after my first Turn into smoke to make myself a dragon. It might be the same for Armand. It might not. I'd thought the world topsy-turvy last night. Today it was positively upside down, inside out, and sideways.

"Then let's hope I'm as lovely a dragon as you are," he replied. "I'll stun them into submission with my overwhelming splendor."

"You're cracked."

"No." He came forward, took up my hand. I half expected him to kiss it, shake it, something—but he only held on. "Merely stubborn. Heart-kin to you."

Heart-kin. Kin of the heart.

Was that why I was so afraid for him?

The nearest village seemed very near indeed, especially from the air. It lay approximately ten miles beyond the opposite shore of the lake, an attractive collection of brick buildings and cobblestone lanes. In its middle was a wide, fine square with a statue of a man holding aloft something that might have been a club.

We floated over it, two patches of haze against the blue sky, absolutely unnoticed.

I'd made Armand Turn twice at the lodge before we'd left. He'd been right, of course: Now that he could transform into smoke, I couldn't truly stop him from following me anywhere, but at least he'd decided to humor me and practice the Turns.

I didn't think the stars were going to steal him now, not really. Better that he be able to remain smoke with me than to suddenly manifest as a clothesless young man in the middle of a crowd.

The first time he'd Turned back into a human, he'd thrown up again, making a mess of the kitchen floor.

The second time, he'd held it in, but only barely—I could tell.

He'd refused a third practice, looking daggers at me from behind one of the reading chairs. It was clear I wasn't going to budge him.

"We're wasting time. It's already past six. We need to get going."

"All right. Stay thin," I said, and then thought better of it. "Not *too* thin, though. Thin enough to escape scrutiny. Not so thin that you—you blow away."

"Blow away?"

"Disperse. Pull apart."

Once more, that arched-eyebrow look.

"Just do as I do," I growled.

"As you wish, love."

"I *wish* you'd stay here and let me take care of this."

"*Nearly* as you wish, then."

Closer inspection of the statue in the square revealed that the man was holding up a spyglass. Since there wasn't an ocean anywhere nearby, I assumed it was meant for the stars. Perhaps this was a learned place. Perhaps the people here had their own special kinship with the inhabitants of the heavens.

If I could have shivered, I would have. Instead, I glided toward a whitewashed stall along one of the streets displaying broadsheets and periodicals. A collection of men and women loitered in front of it, some of them smoking.

Armand and I mingled with the blue-gray miasma rising up from the cigarettes and cigars.

Most of the people were clutching the same edition of a broadsheet, talking to each other excitedly. I couldn't understand what they were saying; then I glimpsed the broadsheet, and realized I didn't need to understand.

Ein Drache! blared the headline.

Beneath it was an illustration of a monster. It was exceedingly scary, with bulging eyes and savage, needle-pointed teeth. Flames were shooting from its mouth. Its tail was some sort of a cannon, its wings resembled those of an aeroplane, and the entire thing appeared to be cut up into segments joined by fancy clockwork gears and machinery.

It was a mechanical dragon.

It was me.

I sank closer, caught between outrage and flattery.

I hoped my eyes didn't bulge like that. I knew they got the rest of it wrong. But still, there I was. Soldiers had been drawn at my feet, firing up at me bravely.

That company from the village. Those soldiers who'd run. That's who they were supposed to be.

I was so enthralled with it that when the man I'd been hovering over folded up the paper and tucked it under his arm, I was annoyed. I moved over to the next man, who was still reading, and only then noticed that Armand was missing.

I made myself go still. I wanted to shoot upward, around. I wanted to fly, and fly hard. But if he'd been overcome and had to Turn back into his human shape somewhere, I needed to find him without drawing anyone's attention.

I inched away, away from the stall. I went as thin as I dared and cast out my senses, searching for him.

People everywhere. Horses and carriáges. A smattering of automobiles. Dogs, cats. Stoves stoked hot for dinners. Lives lived behind closed doors, the war so far away. The forest so near.

For some reason, I kept envisioning pastries. Delicious berry-chocolate-vanilla-pear-plum-cream pastries . . .

No, I need Armand.

Yeasty dough. Crumbly crusts.

Armand!

Apples and icing.

Strudel.

There was a bakery at the opposite end of the square. It had a garish orange awning and spotless windows that gleamed. Figures moved around inside, lost to shadows.

One of them had to be Mandy.

I flowed to the doorway, seeped through a crack between the door and the jamb. A man in an apron stood behind the counter, a young mother with a child attached to each hand before him, perusing trays of bread. The smaller child was bouncing on her toes and squeaking something in a treble, eager voice. Her free hand was pointing at the iced strudels, and bloody Armand was nowhere in sight, not as smoke or a boy or anything.

But he was *here*. I could *feel* him.

The baker reached over the counter to hand the little girl a bite of sweet. She accepted it with another happy squeak.

Below them, I realized. Below me. That's where he was.

I examined the floorboards, which seemed too tightly set to slip through. Would there be a basement down there? A door leading to it?

The answer was yes to both. Off to the right behind the counter was the door, slightly agape. I hovered against the ceiling a moment, judging, then—as the baker was handing a sweet to the other child, and the mother was settling her chosen loaf into her basket—I zipped past them, squeezing through the gap of the door.

Tight wooden stairs, no lamps or any light but for what came from a single small window up near the ceiling. I flowed down into the chamber, which I realized must be where the baking was done. There were vats of flour and molasses and salt, bowls of dough rising with dampened cloths covering swollen tops, an icebox, and an oven in the wall composed of blackened bricks and a blackened iron door.

Metal contraptions that looked like the scaffolding back at Tranquility hugged the walls, only these were filled with the baker's wares, everything from bread to cake to . . . strudel.

Armand was leaning against one of the racks, watching me with glowing blue eyes. The bruise on his head was more vivid than ever. A small puddle of bile near his feet had been concealed with a cloth.

I told you so seemed both mean-spirited and insufficient. Perhaps I'd try *Next time you might listen to me.* Or *Not as easy as you thought, is it?*

I Turned to girl. Before I could speak, the door above us opened—but a bell rang at nearly the same instant, accompanied by footsteps. Another customer must have arrived.

The door swung closed.

Armand really did look wretched. Although he was attempting to hide it, I could tell that the rack was holding him up. Chiding him now would be unsporting, I supposed.

So, instead, I reached out and took a pastry. It was one of the cream-filled ones, puffy and round. I tore off a piece of it and placed it in my mouth, never taking my gaze from his. I ate it like that, bite by bite, until it was gone.

Then I took another.

He straightened, swallowing. He removed a puff from the shelf beside him and copied me, eating it, looking at me, neither of us saying a word, until we'd each had five of them and the glow had faded from his eyes.

Then I wanted some water. There was a sink and faucet beneath the window. I found a measuring cup, blew away the layer of flour inside it, then carefully, carefully, turned the spigot.

Water trickled out. I filled the cup, drank, filled it again, closed the spigot, and carried the cup to Armand.

He accepted it. A dab of filling dotted the corner of his lips. I wiped it away with my thumb before he drank; he held still for that, unsmiling. His skin felt prickly with whiskers.

Something happened then. Something that started in my hand, the one that had touched him, and spread in a tingle up my arm. It was hot and heady, almost dizzying. It shook me awake to the fact that I wasn't the only one without a stitch of clothing on. And that we stood only inches apart, and his lips were so warm and we were wreathed in the aroma of molasses and freshly baked bread and if I took one step, even a small one, our bodies would brush.

And I didn't know what would happen after that.

Armand lifted his hand, drained the cup.

"Better?" I whispered.

He nodded.

"Think you can Turn?"

He nodded again.

"Last one to the lodge is a rotten egg," I said, and made certain he flew just ahead of me the entire way back.

Armand informed me that the German broadsheet had been giving an account of a dastardly new British weapon, a monstrous dragon apparatus recently employed to raze defenseless villages, incinerate vital food supplies, and slay sobbing children.

"How insulting," I said. I was resting flat upon the bed, trying to relax as best I could before we had to journey on later that night.

"War propaganda is hardly ever true," he noted. Instead of the bed, he'd chosen the chair by the door again. His voice sounded sleepy. Still . . . maybe I hadn't been the only one shaken back at the bakery. There was lots of room left in the bed.

"Even so," I persisted. "It doesn't make any sense. How could such a contraption possibly work? And why design a machine meant to do those things as a dragon? Why not a—a lion or a hawk?"

"Because dragons are the most formidable creatures of all. Because we exist at the fringes of their imaginations, nefarious and bloodcurdling and never quite fully defined. We can be shaped however they wish, assigned any horrific trait they dare to invoke. We're the accumulation of all that they fear, most of all themselves. Why not a dragon? It makes perfect sense to me."

"Idiots," I muttered.

"In any case, what's the alternative? It had to be a mechanical weapon attacking those soldiers. Everyone knows that dragons aren't real."

I sat up to see him. "My eyes don't look like that. Bulging like that. Do they?"

Mandy was slouched sideways against the leather, his head tipped back and his eyes closed. But he smiled. "Not in the least. Your eyes are gorgeous. You'd be the belle of the *drákon* ball."

"Are you mocking me?"

"Never."

I remained as I was, unconvinced. He shifted to the other side of the chair.

"Your dragon eyes are nothing like what the paper showed. They're almond-shaped, iridescent. The rest of your face is gold, but they're ringed in purple."

"Like a raccoon?" I'd seen a drawing of one once. It had looked like a rat with a sharp, pointed nose.

He laughed. "Not really. Just like . . . markings, I suppose. You've never seen your own face?"

"No. How could I have?" I'd barely noticed even my human face. Mirrors weren't exactly a vital part of my existence. I used them to ensure that I was free of smudges and that my hair was pinned tightly enough to avoid Mrs. Westcliffe's censure. That was about it.

"Belle of the ball," he assured me. "No wonder the other girls at Iverson snipe at you."

"Right. That's why."

I eased back down. Gradually the room melted into that greeny gray darkness, and Armand's breathing slowed. I watched the air condense into night. I listened to the insects in the forest clicking their tiny dusk songs. Frogs. The water bird by the lake, piping alone.

"Are you going to marry me, Eleanore Jones?" Armand asked, his words barely breaching the dark.

Yes. No.

How could I, and how could I not?

"Ask me again later," I answered at last. "Ask me when this is all done, and we're back in England, and the sun is shining."

Ask me then, if I'm still walking in this life beside you.

Chapter 27

Always she astounds me. Lora-of-the-moon, changing her fate yet again.

I can't believe I never realized she'd do it. I'd thought I'd tested her depths, known her true heart. There can be no sound reason I never anticipated this future, except, perhaps, that I didn't want to.

Her life for his.

And now all will be different. The path she was meant to forge ahead alone has been bent.

I am a furnace with the force of my desire, a fire so hot I melt my own limitations.

I need to reach them. I need to change the coming day.

But they're so entwined now. Because of her sacrifice, they're bonded in a way I never was with her, absorbed in each other's songs. Mine becomes harder and harder to distinguish.

I watch from my impossible distance, knowing the sun will exhaust me before I see these next few hours through; that I'll vanish from the sky before I know how it concludes. I spin a spell and sing the only song I need this dragon whelp to remember, the only command Armand must obey: *Don't leave her.*

Chapter 28

Armand had discovered the name of the village by the lake, consulted his maps, and figured out where we needed to go next. I munched one of the apples (very tart) as he suited up: the leather coat and gloves, the compass, the knapsack and goggles. The pistol in its holster, which I was starting to think would be better off in my hands than his. But since I wouldn't have actual hands for our flight, I let him keep it.

I took my dragon shape by the shore of the lake, the moon looming over us, a sharpened scythe imprisoned in rings of misty platinum and mauve.

Mandy climbed up and ran his hands down my neck before finding my mane. He felt too light to me. I knew it to be an illusion—he weighed the same as ever—but I wanted him to be heavier. Solid and substantial like a boulder. Like a mountain, so I'd never have to worry about anything harming him ever again.

I gazed at the stars and thought, *Don't take me now. Not while he's riding the clouds with me. Let him stay safe, please.*

safe, beast. tonight he is safe.

It would have to do.

We left the lake and lodge behind. I went up, up—the lambent lights from the village quite festive from here—making a wide, easy circle before heading in the right direction.

Northeast, toward Prussia.

Mandy had calculated that we could reach the prison camp by dawn. We weren't going to attempt to infiltrate it yet; we'd wait a day, hide and rest up, assess our situation. See if we could figure out exactly where Aubrey was being held before charging in.

I flew as high as I dared. With the moon out and no ocean or heavy cloud cover to protect us, we slipped along the wind, silent but painfully visible. Our route wouldn't take us over any major cities, but still I did my best to avoid any pockets of civilization below. I didn't know enough about guns to know how high bullets could be shot. Only that it hurt like the devil when they struck you.

A few hours in, I realized the land below me had changed from forest and roads to roads and clearings. But these clearings weren't farmers' pastures or plowed fields. They were too narrow for that, parallel strips that went on and on, bare of any vegetation. I puzzled over them, slowing some, and by the time I glanced ahead and noticed the aeroplanes stationed at their ends, Armand was already pressing his knees into me and wrenching at my mane.

It was an airfield. I'd never seen one before, of course, but it—

We'd been spotted. An alarm sounded; I heard it clear as the bell Mrs. Westcliffe liked to peal at Iverson to herd students from one room to another, only this was shrill and awful and went on and on and on. Figures of men spilled out from structures I hadn't even noticed, swarming the aeroplanes. A searchlight flashed on and pinned us in white light.

Bad luck for me—I'd been looking at its tower when it lit. I was blinded. Armand was pulling me left, *left*, and I veered that way without being able to see what I was doing, if I was getting free of that light or just moving into another one.

I heard the unmistakable sound of gunfire. The *tat-tat-tat-tat!* that I knew meant machine guns unloading their drums.

I supposed I'd find out the range of their bullets after all.

I climbed. The peaceful silence of before had been devoured, eaten up by the clanging of the alarm and the gunfire and the wind that now scoured me, fighting me. I felt Armand tucked close to my neck and heard him shouting, "Go! Go!" and God help me, I was.

Then came the worst sounds of all: engines sputtering to life. Propellers spinning, hacking the air.

I grimaced, trying not to imagine them hacking me instead.

My vision began to filter back, shapes and colors returning. We'd left the airfield behind and were over roads and pasture once more. I didn't think the searchlights had caught us again—hopefully we were too far beyond them—although I could still hear that blasted alarm.

And then the aeroplanes taking off.

I looked back. Two, three . . . five of them right behind us. Armand met my eyes, then twisted to look back, too.

Six. Seven.

And they were getting closer. The wind had turned against us and it made all the difference, but I'd wager it meant nearly nothing to the engines of those planes.

Tat-tat-tat-tat-tat!

Bullets strafed by. One zinged off a barb on my tail, sending me into a spin.

I spiraled out of it, ducking and dodging, dipping and soaring. At one point Armand lost his seat entirely and was floating over my back, holding on with just his hands, but I couldn't stop, because the aeroplanes were roaring closer and closer, and they were relentless.

I should Turn. I should go to smoke. But I didn't know if Armand would, too—if he *could*, even, but I didn't *know*, and since I didn't know, I couldn't do it. I wouldn't leave him and just let him fall and bloody well hope he figured out what I meant for him to do before he ended up a smear on the ground—

There! There was a town up ahead! Surely the pilots wouldn't continue to fire over their own people?

I slitted my eyes and straightened for speed, the wind screaming now, gunfire puncturing the night in wide-open arcs to the left and right and above.

So I dropped lower, and the dull yellow burn of the streetlights was just there, and the first of the buildings swept into view. I flew over rooftops so close my talons scratched sparks from their shingles. I couldn't tell if the pilots were still firing, but it didn't matter; I had to slow, so I opened my wings and fought the rush of the world whipping past us.

Not all the streets were lit. I aimed toward a section of shadows, finding a lane of cobblestones, plowing into them.

More sparks; the lane ripped apart. A brick wall hurtling toward my face, too late to avoid.

I angled my head and took the blow, and everything flashed white like the searchlight, then black.

I opened my eyes, or thought I did. Everything was still black.

Maybe I'd gone blind.

Maybe I was dead.

But someone was holding me. Someone who smelled of pine

trees and sea salt and desperation. His lips were pressed to my temple. His breath blew ragged against my hair.

"Wish I'd had a cannon for a tail," I mumbled, and passed out again.

The next time I regained my senses was much more unpleasant. The world was no longer so opaquely black, but murky and dingy and sickeningly blurry. Somewhere nearby dogs were barking, an entire army of them, with a weirdly jabbering chorus of human voices lacing through. My head felt as if it would split apart.

All of me, *all* of me, hurt.

Armand was gone. I lay alone on something itchy and hard.

Had we been captured?

I rolled to my side, made my way up to my elbows. Beneath me was a shabby felt blanket spread over a stone floor. A stale breeze swirled by, and I sneezed, cramping my stomach and sending everything even blurrier and more nauseating.

Where was Armand? What were they doing to him?

I tried to stand. The world tipped sideways, and I found myself on my hands and knees with my head hung down, gasping.

Very well. I'd sit first. That seemed . . . not entirely unreasonable. I leaned back carefully, making it to one hip, and that was when I realized I was wearing the calico dress I'd bought a lifetime ago back in England. Back when I'd been so secretly thrilled to have something as simple as a new dress all my own, and never once really thought for a second about the consequences of what I was about to do next, promises made, lords to save . . .

I exhaled past my teeth and covered my eyes with one hand. It helped to tamp down the nausea.

Armand was beside me suddenly, supporting me by the shoulders, urging me back to the ground.

"Stay there. Don't try to stand." He was speaking in a voice so low it was nearly a hiss. "I don't think anything's broken, but I couldn't be certain, and you took a nasty blow to the head."

"Where . . . ," I began, but couldn't seem to finish the thought.

"A warehouse. A vacant one, at least so far." His hands pressed me against the blanket. "We're a couple of blocks from where we came down. They haven't searched here yet."

"We need to . . ." Why couldn't I think straight?

"We will. Just—just rest a moment, all right?"

All right.

I lay back and covered my eyes again, listening to him pad away. He was moving swiftly, doing something with the knapsack, I could tell, because I heard the tins clinking around inside it.

A match was struck. I heard it, smelled it. I lowered my hand and turned my head and saw him crouched in a corner far from me, a pile of papers before him writhing with flames.

He was burning the maps.

As soon as the last one crisped to ash he stood, scattering the soot with the sole of his boot. Then he returned to me.

"I've stashed the rest of it. We'll come back for it later. Right now we need to disappear. Do you think you can Turn to smoke?"

I groaned. The sound of the dogs barking grew louder and louder.

"Then, can you stand?"

"I . . . "

"Come on, Lora. Come on, love. We have to get out of here."

"Out there?"

"Yes." He was pulling me to my feet. "They might not know where that dragon machine went, but they heard the crash and they'll be looking for its pilot. We can't be discovered hiding."

"I need . . . stockings. Shoes."

He'd dressed me in the frock but had forgotten that part. I wasn't wearing my chemise, either. If we were going to step out of this place with any hope of blending in, at the very least I shouldn't be in my bare feet.

He ran back to the knapsack, which he'd stored on a shelf beneath more of the felt blankets, and returned with my shoes.

That was fine. The thought of bending over to slide on stockings made my throat close with sick.

I shoved my feet into my pumps. I leaned against him and we made our way to the door, which was big and rusted and looked like it would squeal to the heavens if jarred. I heard people beyond it, rapid footfalls.

Armand was whispering in my ear as we walked. "You're my wife. You're shy, you're pregnant, and you're ill, got it?"

"Yes."

"Ja," he corrected me.

"Ja."

"Hell. Your accent is atrocious. Just nod, okay?"

I pushed a lock of hair from my cheek, glancing up at him. He paused, taking me in, then moved behind me. He gathered all my hair past my shoulders and began quickly to braid it.

"If anyone talks to you, asks you questions or anything, you look at me. That's it. Don't try to answer. Act like I'll beat you if you answer."

I nodded, managing to keep my head in one piece by holding

both hands against my temples. I didn't know where he'd learned to braid a woman's hair, and right now I didn't care. All that yanking and pulling; it was as if an elephant was attempting to groom me.

He finished and stepped around to face me again. He clasped his hands around my upper arms and bent at the knees until our eyes were level. He looked disheveled and determined, bruised and mussed. In the half-light of the warehouse, he looked like he felt worse than I did.

"We need to blend in for a while. There's a crowd gathered out there, and we need to be in it. But if things go bad and you can escape, I want you to. Turn if you can. Whatever it takes."

"Not without you," I said.

"*Yes*, without me! Don't worry about me! I can Turn, too, remember?"

I rubbed at my scalp. That's right. I'd forgotten. He could Turn now. Couldn't he? It had something to do with the stars. . . .

A dog snuffled up to the door. It caught the scent of us and let out a deep, frightened bark before skittering off.

"Time's up," Armand said, and pushed open the door.

He kept her as close to him as he could, their arms linked. She was a featherweight against him, her head to his shoulder, her steps matching his. He tried to walk slowly because he knew that would be better for her, but the people hustling past them weren't going slowly. They were running. Some sprinting. An enemy aircraft had been downed, right here in their very own town, and everyone wanted to be able to say, *Did you see?*

A mob of young men—too young to be soldiers yet, still just a shade too young—jostled roughly by, shouting and laughing, deliberately knocking elbows and shoulders. Light as could be, Armand snatched the hat off a straggler and slipped it behind his back, but the fellow didn't notice. He was calling to the others, hurrying to catch up with his mates.

Mandy settled the hat over his head and pulled the brim low, and the wound above his eyebrow was gone as if it'd never been.

Dawn had arrived in a sweep of green clouds above them, the sky brightening into blue turquoise. If there were any stars left out, he didn't see them, and he damned well didn't hear them.

Could use a spot of help right about now, he thought anyway. *Bloody Jesse. Wherever you are.*

But all he heard were people and dogs. A far-off whine of aeroplanes, likely out searching for their hides, too.

He was hoping for a pub, an inn, someplace where he could take Lora and tuck her away until that mirror-glazed look was gone from her eyes. It was so early in the morning, though. Surely there'd be a coffeehouse. Something.

He'd meant to steer them away from the crowd, but it was proving impossible. It appeared the entire population of the town had emerged from their beds to throng the streets, everyone flowing in the same direction. Before he knew it, they were at the beginning of the lane Lora had ravaged, the very place he had carried her from not an hour past. People were picking up chunks of cobblestone, exclaiming, as men dressed as soldiers and police attempted to keep them back. Dogs shimmied through legs, sniffing and winding toward the wall in the distance, which even from here looked as if it'd been struck by a train.

The dogs were bloodhounds.

Shit.

Lora's fingers tightened over his arm as the nearest of the

hounds fixed on them and began to howl. He pulled her closer and tried to angle them away.

Another dog approached on stiffened legs, hackles raised. It pinned them with wild eyes and joined in the howling. On the left came a third.

Armand swiveled all the way about. With Lora clamped to his side he began to ram his way through the people, as rude and fleet as the gang of boys had been.

"Sir," called a voice behind them. "Sir! A moment, sir!"

He didn't stop. He scanned the street for any way out, an alley, a store—but there were no alleys and all the stores were shuttered. The next intersection was a good thirty yards away.

Eleanore was breathing heavily. She staggered against him, losing her balance, and he hauled her upright and kept shoving through.

"Sir! You there, in the leather coat! Young woman! You are commanded to stop!"

All the damned dogs were baying at them now, baying but, thank God, not pursuing.

Animals distrust you, Lora had told him once, when she'd been trying to convince him of what he was. And it was true, they did, they always had; he'd never had an easy time of it learning to ride, he'd never had a pet of any sort, because animals wouldn't go near him if they had a choice about it, not since he was a lad. These hounds were no different, but by the gods, he wished they'd shut up—

He pushed past the elderly couple in front of them and came up short against a man in the navy blue uniform of a police officer.

Everyone else around them melted back into a circle.

"Good morning," said the officer pleasantly. He was tall and broad and black-haired, with a fresh nick on his chin from the morning's shave. He studied them both, from Armand's white-knuckled grip on Lora to her small, breathy gasps. "Perhaps you're unaware that my colleague behind you has been attempting to speak with you?"

"Has he?" Armand sent a glance over his shoulder, feigning doubt. "I fear we never heard him. It's chaos back there. All those dogs."

"Yes. All the dogs." Another look, longer, harder, at Eleanore. "If you would both be so good as to come with me?"

Despite the phrasing, Mandy knew it wasn't a request, and that there wasn't going to be a quick way out of it, either. There were policemen on all sides of them now, a handful of soldiers sprinkled in. One of the soldiers broke rank and came forward.

"These people need to be interviewed by the major."

"Certainly, if he wishes," responded the policeman, amiable. "Right after I'm done with them."

"Sir, I must insist—"

"Do you imagine this man and woman are the enemies you seek, Captain? Do they look like daredevil pilots to you?"

"The dogs," said the soldier stubbornly.

"Ah, yes. Well, the dogs can interrogate them after the major, I suppose. We like to keep a sense of order around here."

The crowd broke into laughter.

"This way," said the policeman to Armand.

Lora was staring into the distance, pale and frowning. She gave a slight, nearly imperceptible shake of her head.

She couldn't Turn yet. Mandy wasn't even certain *he* could. He felt jittery and oddly unfocused. When he thought about smoke, the sensation of dissolving, all that came back to him were the words *don't leave her.*

As if he ever would.

One of the onlookers gave him a sharp thump on the back.

They followed the policeman.

The police headquarters seemed nearly deserted. He wondered over that, until he realized most of the force was probably outside searching for mechanical dragon parts. The officer led them to an office with a frosted glass door, waved at them to sit, then took his own seat behind a desk.

He removed his hat, placing it gently upon a corner of the desk. Light from the open balcony doors behind him gleamed off the oil in his hair.

"Your names, please?"

"Karl Abt. This is my wife, Gitta. We're visiting from Bonn."

The man smiled at Eleanore. It seemed warm and friendly enough, but something about it struck a chill down Armand's spine. Something both curdling and familiar.

I know you, he thought, unsettled.

"Your occupation?"

"Bookseller."

"Bonn is a fair city. Why did you decide to visit us here?"

"We're on our way to Königsberg. We have family there."

There was a notepad and pencil in front of him, but the man wasn't taking notes. He was watching Lora, watching her as a cat would watch a moth trapped against a windowpane.

Like he wanted to creep closer. Lick his lips.

"Your hotel?"

"The Crown Prince." He'd glimpsed it on the walk here.

"Ah! Then you've met my friend Magnus. He works there."

"I'm afraid we haven't had an opportunity to mingle with the staff," Armand said stiffly.

The policeman had eyes the color of gunmetal. Hunting eyes, focused and rapt.

"Mrs. Abt, forgive my poor manners. You seem winded, my dear. Would you enjoy a glass of water?"

Right on cue, Lora looked at Mandy. He returned her gaze, allowed himself a trace of a self-satisfied smile, and answered for her.

"My wife is with child. You know how it goes, she's always needing this or that. Water would be welcome."

"Vogler," said the policeman, not even raising his voice.

"Yes, sir?" Another man appeared at the doorway, standing at attention.

"Escort Mr. Abt to the facilities. Let him fetch a glass of water for his wife."

"Yes, sir."

Shit.

Armand remained in the chair, unable to move.

"It's not far," said the police officer to him. "Go on."

He'd left the pistol with the knapsack, because his coat wasn't long enough to conceal it. There was only the knife in his boot. He'd been trained to fence and shoot and even box, and he did all those things well, but right now, as his mind sped up and time slowed down, all he could think about was how long it was going to take him to free the knife.

He looked at Eleanore. She sat frozen, too, her face a mask, her hair coming loose from its braid to fan along her forearm, satiny sand and gold draped to her waist. He saw her then as he knew the policeman would: slight and milky pale, the full lips of a grown woman and the vulnerable, clouded eyes of a girl who wasn't quite certain of where she was or what was going on around her.

And worse, much worse: the *drákon* beauty gleaming just beneath her skin, provocative and incandescent.

don't leave her.

It was then that he realized who this man was. Whom he reminded Armand of.

Soder had been a fellow student from school, an older boy remarkably welcoming to the younger pupils coming in. He'd had a narrow face and an affected drawl. The same hunting eyes. He was known for hosting clandestine parties in his room late at night, offering sweetmeats and wine to his special chosen few. Armand had been one of those special boys once, uncertain of his place, eager to fit in.

It was only after he'd pulled his father's rank and given Soder a nosebleed besides that he'd been allowed to escape that room.

"Never mind about the water. We've no desire to be a bother to you, sir, especially on a busy day like this. I've promised my wife a fine breakfast as soon as we return to the hotel. And so, if we're finished here . . . ?"

"No," answered the officer, almost apologetic. "We are not. Vogler, escort Mr. Abt from my office. Confine him to a cell if necessary."

"Yes, sir!"

The man at the door took a step toward them.

Mandy locked eyes with the officer behind the desk, and the sky beyond the balcony was stippled with clouds, and the walls were shadowed umber, and the air smelled of papers and anticipation and lust and Armand knew, as surely as he knew anything, that the officer had realized that a line had been crossed, that scales had been tipped, and was going to come to his feet exactly as Mandy did. And the knife was going to end up in that broad, flat belly before the other bloke, the one behind them still, could get another step in. Because he wasn't going to leave her and he wasn't going to surrender and he wasn't going to do anything but fight like hell to get Eleanore out of here.

His fingers grazed the edge of his boot. The officer's lips drew back over his teeth.

"No," said Eleanore suddenly. In English.

Everyone paused, looking at her.

"Don't do it," she said to Armand.

"What is this?" began the officer. "Your wife—"

"I'm feeling better now," Lora said. "You?"

Armand smiled at her, then at the policeman. "After you," he replied, also in English, and she Turned to smoke, then he did, and both men were left staring openmouthed at the two chairs littered with empty clothing.

Eleanore curled out to the sky. Armand waited until the officer had circled the desk, had knocked over Lora's chair in frustration and screamed instructions at the other man, who'd dashed from the chamber.

Then Mandy Turned in front of him.

He said in German, "You'd found your daredevil pilots, after all," and walloped the bastard across the jaw before Turning back into smoke.

It felt even more satisfying than it had with Soder.

It felt, in fact, damned fine.

Chapter 29

We watched the people swarming about from the safety of a bell tower topping a church, one I sincerely hoped no one used. We knelt side by side beneath the cavernous yawn of the bell and peered over the edge of the cupola, which offered an excellent prospect of not only the chaos in the streets below but also the door to the warehouse.

The one holding the last of our things.

And the men walking in and out of it.

"Go away, go away," I chanted under my breath. "Go away, go away."

"It'll be fine," Armand whispered, but, like me, he didn't take his eyes off the comings and goings by the door. "The place was a mess to begin with. Piles of junk everywhere. They won't find the knapsack."

"What if they smell the smoke from the maps?"

"They're only humans, Eleanore. They might discover the ashes, but they won't know what was burned there, or when. They won't smell the smoke."

"Are you positive?"

"No," he said, and I silently resumed my chant.

In daylight the town was sprawling and pretty, nestled up against a giant's backbone of green craggy hills. I wondered where we were, if we'd reached East Prussia yet. I couldn't tell. But for the soldiers everywhere, we might have been in any idyllic, secluded part of Europe, isolated from the war's grisly tendrils.

A breeze wound by, warm enough but still brushing goose bumps over most of my body. Despite my aching head, despite everything that had happened in the past few hours, it had not escaped me that I was fully unclothed, in close proximity to an equally unclothed Lord Armand.

This was the third time we'd been in this fix, and it seemed to me it was getting worse and worse. My reaction to it, I mean.

I'd always thought him handsome. Not in the besotted, drippy way that Belgian girl had—or any of the girls from Iverson, frankly—but purely as an acceptance of fact. Armand was handsome because he was. Armand was wealthy because he was. Armand was *drákon* because he was.

So, handsome hardly mattered. Far more interesting to me, far more intriguing, was the part of himself he kept veiled. The secret animal part that seemed a tantalizing near-reflection of . . . well, of me. I couldn't help but wonder what this marble-skinned, keen-eyed boy was going to look like as a dragon.

I wanted so, so badly to live long enough to see that.

Is there a more powerful tool of seduction for the lonely than that of common ground?

I kept imagining what Mrs. Westcliffe would say if she could see us now.

Proper young ladies do not go into hiding with unclad men, no matter the circumstances.

Ladies do not think about what it would be like to move a mere inch over, so that bare skin may touch.

Ladies do not envisage wildly indecent things, such as kissing or embracing or rolling about beneath a bronze bell.

I concentrated vehemently upon the people below.

I couldn't tell if he was doing the same.

"Mandy," I said.

"Yes?"

"Can you finish things without me?"

His head turned. *Now* he was looking at me. "What? What do you mean?"

"If something were to happen," I said cautiously. "If I get killed." *Or vanish.* "Can you carry on without me? Complete the rescue and get back to England?"

"That is not going to happen."

"Answer the question, if you please."

"I'm not answering the ruddy question because it's not going to happen. You're not going to die."

I risked a glance at him; he was scowling. Unkempt as a pirate.

"I *will* die someday. Maybe in a year, or ten years. Maybe tonight. Pretending doesn't change things."

"I'm not pretending."

"I don't know if you've noticed," I said, "but there are quite a few people out there who'd love to take a shot at us. Again. Therefore I think the question's fair. The maps are gone and likely everything else, but you can go to smoke now. So I need to know—can you carry on without me?"

"No," he said.

I sat up, and so did he. My hair became a curtain that swayed between us, strands lifting free to caress his skin exactly as I'd been trying not to picture them doing.

"You can, though. Don't lie."

"It wasn't a lie. I can't do it."

My temper entangled with my intent; my voice sharpened. "Well, you may have to. You may end up being all that Aubrey has. So think about *that*. Plan for it. Or else be stuck out here with him for all the rest of the damned war. It's up to you."

Just like the grotto back home, the bell swallowed my words and sent them back.

. . . *you-you-you* . . .

"Eleanore." Armand placed his hand upon my forearm. "Aubrey is my brother. He matters to me more than I can say, and I'll do what I can for him. But I've given you the honest answer to your question. I'm not going to be able to carry on without you. Haven't you figured it out yet?"

His fingers felt cool against me. The breeze whispered between us, an invisible barrier that would be so easy to defeat.

"I love you," he said, almost hopeless. "I can't stop it. I can't change it. I've certainly tried. So this is how it is. I don't ask that you love me back. No one could ask that. But do me a favor and don't die, all right? Because I can't . . . *be* here without you."

The breeze. Goose bumps. I was holding my breath, or it had been stolen from me. I was gazing into his eyes and falling and falling into a place I did not know. Into cobalt oceans. Into deep blue nights that held the promise of everything lush and silken and wonderful, dreams and desires. I knew I'd just been given a gift I'd never anticipated: Armand without the veil. A gift so raw and powerful I could barely comprehend it. I was too small, and he was so lovely and bright.

He couldn't be without me. Yet I would be leaving so that he could stay.

All I could think was, *What am I going to do?*

Men began to shout below us. We both flattened at once, then crept to the belfry's edge.

They hadn't seen us; they were reacting to something else. People choked the warehouse doorway, soldiers mostly. They were pushing at each other, and then one in a helmet topped with a silver spike emerged carrying our knapsack in his arms.

My clothing. Armand's. Our pistol and food and medical supplies.

I dropped my head into my arms and made a sound between a sigh and a groan.

"Do you believe in fate?" Armand whispered.

"No," I mumbled into my arms, because of course I did, and what I knew of bloody fate was that it was cold and capricious and could turn on you in a heartbeat. And then you were naked and hungry in a bell tower, wondering if this was going to be the last day of your life.

"Lora. Look."

I raised my head. He was staring at a point in the distance, at one of those outlying hills. I followed his gaze, seeing only woods and rocks.

"What?" I said.

"Look," he repeated, patient, and this time pointed, keeping his hand close to his chest.

I squinted at the hill. At the faraway rocks, which were almost uniform in a way, structured, gray and brown like . . . like a fortress, almost. Like the ruins of one.

All the soldiers in town, so far from the front. The major, who had been going to want to question us—

"It's Schloss des Mondes, I'm sure of it," Mandy said.

I lifted up a bit to make it out more clearly. "Really? It might well be any old ruin."

"No. That's it."

I tried to remember the etching from the travel journal. Mostly what I recalled was that it'd struck me as a pen-and-ink version of romantic drivel: picturesque towers collapsing into piles, wild roses rambling this way and that, a moon as round and blank as a wheel of cheese behind it all.

I tipped my head, searching for a resemblance.

"How do you know?" I asked.

He was taut and eager, a weapon primed. "I feel it. Even from here, I feel it. It's like a blood clot in a vein, isn't it? Like a blemish across the sun. Dark and viscous and awful. And this place. This town, *living* off it, *feeding* from it."

"Mandy . . ."

"Aubrey's in there. I feel it in my bones." He rose to his knees. I grabbed him by the wrist before he did something foolish, and when he glanced down at me, I didn't see oceans any longer.

I saw the dragon. I saw wrath.

"Tonight," I said, and didn't let go until he nodded.

Chapter 30

Schloss des Mondes, in case you didn't know, means "Castle of the Moon." I suppose that's why the artist of the etching had made the full moon so prominent.

On the night we went in for Aubrey, we had nothing like that. We had a sickle moon still, an eerie smile in the sky.

And Star-of-Jesse, above it and to the left.

I'd wanted to survey the prison before nightfall, but the truth was, I needed sleep more. I'd spent nearly all of the previous night flying, and I refused to count the time I'd been knocked unconscious as useful rest.

Up in that bell tower I'd had no mirror, but I daresay I looked a lot like Armand, red-eyed, pallid with strain. Two beggars without a home.

We smoked to a house at the edge of town that smelled only of empty rooms and sadness. Like the lodge, there was dust everywhere and very little food, but we carried all the quilts we could find up into the attic and made a bed there. I fell in first and Mandy right after, and I didn't even protest when he drew me into his arms.

At least I'll know he's still here, I thought. I was a husk of a girl, hollow and drained. *If I can feel him, I'll know he's still beside me.*

I slept.

When I was finally able to climb back up out of that deep, soft oblivion, I found Armand seated at my side, watching me by the light of the oriel window high in the eaves. He was bathed in silvery blue.

Starlight. The day had come and gone, and I was still around.

"I realized that I hadn't thanked you yet," he said. "For doing this. For freeing my brother."

I scrubbed the sleep from my face. "Criminy, don't jinx it! Thank me after."

"No. I needed to do it now."

I lowered my hands. He smiled at me, but it was slight. Almost grave.

"Just in case."

"In case of what?" I asked, but straightaway wished I hadn't, because of course I knew what he'd meant.

He seemed so calm, practically serene, painted with the distant light of the heavens. And even though he must have seen the regret on my face, he answered me anyway.

"In case it's you instead of me who's left behind. You who's meant to go on and rescue Aubrey alone."

What I remembered then was my final goodbye to Jesse, also by starlight. How I'd felt so desperate, looking into his eyes. So bloody stupid terrified, it was as if all my bones had gone to jelly.

How he hadn't bothered to lie to me by saying that all would be well, but only told me—calm, so calm and grave, just like Armand— to leave him. He hadn't even told me that he loved me, although I knew that he did.

After that night, my world had tilted. Jesse was gone from the earth. For such a long while I'd felt as if I was, too.

But it's not going to be like that with Mandy, I reassured myself. *I've made a deal. I will never, never feel pain like that again.*

Because I really would rather be dead than suffer the loss of this boy, too.

I sat up, surrounded by my nest of quilts. "That's rather enough of that sort of talk. You're not going anywhere, lordling. Well, except to that ruin, and then home to Tranquility with your brother."

The smile faded. "And with you, waif. Home with my brother and with you."

"That's the plan," I agreed. I didn't consider it a lie, since it was what I wanted to be true.

I stood, as did he. He took my hand. We descended the stairs in silence together; he opened the front door to the house we'd borrowed; we both smoked away.

Perhaps there was more to have been said, but I had no more words, truthful ones or falsehoods or anything. Sometimes silence illumes more than words, anyway. I'd been by Armand's side for what had amounted only to days, but already it felt as if years had passed between us. As if we'd been doing this together for years, flying and hiding and hurting and hunting, and now, together, we were traveling into whatever came next. I think it was clear to us both that our final few moments of peace were done. It was either finish the job now or perish in the attempt.

So, again: Sickle moon. Jesse above us, along with all the other stars. They were singing without verses, marking our flight with arias and harmonies too complex to follow. Armand and I soared and floated, joined in our unique dance again, moving as one away from the town and toward the hills that cradled the prison Schloss des Mondes.

That's definitely what it was. Once we were near enough, I recognized all the telltale signs. One long wall and three decrepit towers still endured, but were shored up now with freshly cut timbers and brick. The wild roses still bloomed, but between strands of shiny barbed wire. Even the moon had done its bit: It was hanging nearly where it'd been in that etching, but it was spooky now, a grinning warning that slid through me in a whispered chill.

where is he? hissed the whisper. I realized it wasn't from the moon but from the stars. *where does he fall?*

What?

I glimpsed a flash of pale flesh, arms flung out. I swooped after him, but it was too late. Armand hadn't been able to hold his shape, and I wasn't near enough this time to save him.

He saw me. He was facing upward, looking right at me, his brown hair thrashing, a strange almost-smile on his lips, and *I wasn't near enough*. Right before he hit the ground, he brought both hands to his mouth, then flung them back at me.

He landed in a tangle of roses and barbed wire, just outside the perimeter of the prison. It was over in seconds—there hadn't even been time for me to Turn to dragon—and from start to finish it had happened without a sound but for the muffled thud of his body meeting dirt, because he'd kept our precious silence and hadn't shouted or called out for me.

Instead, dear God, he'd blown me a kiss.

Dogs began to yowl. Lights flared on. There was nothing to see, though, not yet. Only a streak of gray vapor and a boy covered in gashes and brambles, unmoving in the brush.

I blanketed him in smoke. I smoothed his face, his eyelids, waited until I was drawn in past his lips and became a part of his lungs, his very breath, and his heart beat for both of us, and his blood whooshed by and I flowed with it and I knew that he lived.

I became a girl crouched over him, ignoring the sting of the thorns. I brought my lips to his ear.

"Mandy. Mandy."

His lashes fluttered. His lids did not open.

You can't take him. You said you wouldn't!

fireheart, whose time is ours: this act is not of us.

A searchlight passed over me, carving the dark into pieces. I ducked lower.

"Mandy." I swallowed. "Sweetheart. Wake up."

His respiration puffed fragile against my cheek. He'd missed the barbed wire but the brambles had slashed into him anyway; some of the cuts were deep. I ran my hands all along him, smearing rose petals and blood.

His right leg. It lay crooked, all wrong. I stared down at it with fright a stone in my chest, certain his leg was broken. It was the one I'd bit, too.

One broken leg. It might not be so bad. He could survive that, couldn't he? He'd be all right once it was set. Once we were home and it was set.

"Wake up, Armand. Damn it, wake up!"

The sugar-ripe perfume of the flowers began to suffocate me. The moon grinned and the dogs howled and the stars began to toll, solemn as a knell, *go, go, go—*

I estimated the tower ruins to be around a hundred yards off. The dogs sounded even farther than that but were getting closer. A series of large tents covered the grounds between here and there;

they were filled with soldiers and maybe prisoners, too, a harsh gabble of voices rising through the night.

go, go, go—

So far none of the guards had figured out exactly where we were. Chances were they didn't really know what had happened, just that the dogs were barking like mad and something might have fallen from the sky. Most of the searchlights were spearing the heavens instead of the hillsides. Perhaps they were hunting for a mechanical dragon.

A dragon . . .

"Stay here," I murmured, my hand over Mandy's heart. "If you can hear me, don't move."

I glanced upward. *Tell him,* I entreated the stars. *When he comes to, tell him what I've done, that I need him to stay hidden.*

go! they insisted.

I lifted as smoke, found a pair of good, strong searchlights crossed against the black like swords, and Turned to dragon within their doubled brilliance.

Not mechanical, but amazing nonetheless. My body reflected the light in scintillating gold. My wings brushed it into shadows, lifting me, allowing me to weave in and out of their beams, to enjoy the din that arose from the ground in a great surge that drowned out even the dogs.

Shots pinged past. I went to smoke, waited, Turned again, farther from Armand this time, drawing the men and their fire after me.

The tent city spread below me. I dipped down, extended a talon, and sliced open the roof of the nearest one. Faces gaped skyward, raggedy men with open mouths. And then—

The men began to shout. To *cheer.* They were lifting their fists to the air, jumping up and down, exuberant.

"Huzzah!"

The prisoners! They must have heard about the new British weapon from their guards, or the papers, or the contagion of underground gossip. But now they saw that I was real, not gossip.

They thought I was here to save them.

Hope lit from face to face, joyous disbelief. I saw the panic of the guards, and it fed me like nectar. My animal heart expanded, seeing them so afraid; I wanted more of that. Much more.

I wanted, suddenly, not just to save one man. I wanted to tear this entire camp apart. I was savage with want.

"Huzzah! Huzzah!"

After all, I *was* a weapon, wasn't I? I was a weapon of fangs and claws, of fantasy and fury. I was the accumulation of all that men feared, and despite the fact that I couldn't breathe fire, I could still render this prison to ash. Turn it to dust, into a ruin again, instead of a place where people suffered and died, because I was sick of hiding, and I was sick of war, and I was sick of death stalking me and threatening me and filling me with dread.

Let it come. I was ready.

I wove higher, waited for a searchlight, dove down again. I pulled free a long span of fencing, until the barbed wire sliced apart in my claws.

Another tent ripped open, more men spilling out, roaring encouragement. The guards around them yelling and pushing, trying to regain control.

Another tent. Another.

We played that game until I had all the soldiers in sight beneath me, pointing their guns at me. Little bursts of light popped from their barrels like embers in a fireplace, but *tat-tat-tat* fast, because they were no longer using their rifles, but machine guns.

go, go, go, go!

Heat punctured my wing—my *good* wing—ripping swiftly into pain.

All my bravado evaporated. Instantly I was me again, only Eleanore, in trouble far over her head. I Turned to smoke and the pain dulled, but I'd been shot. Again.

I retreated through an unglazed window atop the nearest tower, slinking into darkness. I Turned to girl against the wall and mashed my hands against my mouth, because even though I no longer had wings, the wound was crippling, bowing me in half, and there was a scream in my throat that I knew I could not afford to release.

Tears filled my eyes. I bent my head into my palms and pressed them away.

My face prickled hot, but the rest of me was cold as the rock wall at my back; my skin began to creep. The scent of meat and decay filled my nose.

It was only then that I knew that I wasn't alone.

I lifted my head.

There was a man in here, flat on a cot. Just one man; the rest of the chamber was barren. He was swathed in bandages that had seeped through with gore, holding himself very stiff and still, just like the mummy soldiers back at Tranquility who only moved once they recognized that no matter how immobile they tried to be, the agony was still going to come.

I looked at the man. The faint gleam of his eyes confirmed that he was looking back at me. Neither of us spoke.

Beyond the slit of the window, the stars sparked. The moon threw us light the color of bone.

It was Aubrey. Exactly like Armand back in that bell tower, I *felt* him, the dragon locked inside him, faded as an echo. Somewhere beneath this mess of blood and linen was Lord Aubrey Louis, Marquess of Sherborne, ace fighter pilot, his father's obsession and his brother's salvation.

Sssss. Sssss.

His breath wheezed in and out like he was struggling to breathe through a tube, a horrible, scratchy thin sound. The bandaged chest jerked up and down. The fingers of his left hand were curled against the blanket at his waist, and all his nails were black.

I lost myself then. Only for a moment. An awful mixture of rage and bitterness rose up inside me in a blind wave, obliterating all of my careful control, all at once, and I began to tremble.

We'd come all this way. We'd risked so much.

For nothing.

There was no way in hell this man was going to be able to ride my back home. I'd be surprised if he could even sit up.

Jesse, goddamn you, why? Why?

I clenched my jaw and closed my eyes, digging my nails into my palms to stop the shaking. I waited for the wave to recede. When I was able to open my eyes again, Aubrey attempted to speak.

"El . . ."

He ran out of air. Moonlight made a slick, cool sheen over the wreck of his face. He drew in a slower breath.

" . . . leanore," he finished. "At last."

And he *smiled* at me.

Chapter 31

The night had shattered. A clamor shuddered up through the stone walls sheltering us, fed by gunfire and cries far below. I gave a final glance to the moon, then went to my knees beside Aubrey, combing my hair over my chest.

"You knew I was coming," I said.

"Yes." A small rush of a word, imbued with every sort of meaning: faith, trust, wholehearted relief.

"The stars," I said.

"The . . . boy."

"The boy in the stars. Jesse. He sings to you."

A bare nod.

I cocked my head, genuinely curious. "And you didn't think you were going barmy? Or maybe trapped in a nightmare?"

The sound he made this time was more like a laugh. The fingers with the blackened nails twitched.

"Worse . . . than this?"

Good point.

"Is Jesse, perchance, singing to you now? Telling you what we should do next?"

His brows drew together, his lips pulled into a grimace. I took that as a no.

I sighed. "Listen. Here's the rub. I can't hear him. I've come here with Armand—yes, he's below. Don't try to move yet. I've come with Armand, and he's alive but injured, and you're alive but injured, and"—I tugged at my hair, frustrated—"damn it all, so am I. So I don't know what we're supposed to do now. This place is crawling with soldiers, and I stirred up something out there, but I'm not sure what, if it's enough to sneak you out or not, and now . . . now . . . "

I ran out of things to say. The bleak cold of the floor was seeping into me, congealing me, skin to muscle to joints.

"Heard . . . you're something."

I looked at Aubrey. The grimace had relaxed back into a smile. His hair was blond; his eyes were gray. His lashes were long and thick, just like his brother's.

"Scales," he said. "Wings. Helen of the skies. Like to . . . see that."

A Helen of the skies. Like Helen of Troy, whose beauty had moved armies. But all I could move was me.

I shook my head, forcing myself to return his smile. What I really wanted to do was curl up and cry because I was chilled and leaden and at a loss for any clever way to go on. I might try to drag him down the stairs to the bottom of the tower, but there were probably more guards between here and there. I could try to Turn to dragon to get him out, but the window was too small for anything but smoke to fit through. And even if I did succeed at any of that, there was still the matter of maneuvering Aubrey onto my back and getting both of us safely out of range of the gunfire. And the aeroplanes. And maybe even zeppelins; nothing would surprise me at this point. For all I knew, the Germans had already constructed their own mechanical dragon and we'd have to dodge that as well.

The riot sounds outside were growing louder and louder, and I was worried about Armand, even though he wasn't technically inside the prison, because what if the dogs or the guards found him anyway, while he was still unconscious? What if—

"I'm a pilot, you know," Aubrey rasped.

"I know," I answered, distracted.

"Know the hazards. Good hands."

I studied him, trying to understand.

"I can hold on," he said. "Let's . . . clear out."

And all at once, I understood that there was only one way out. There had really only ever been one way.

I leaned very near to him, letting him look square into my eyes.

"Our circumstances are about to become much more precarious. Don't let go of me no matter what, understand?"

"Yes."

I came to my feet, turned a circle to measure the chamber, then Turned into a dragon crouching over him, pressing him down into the cot but not—please, please—squashing him.

The tower was too small for me. I'd been counting on that.

I arched my back against the ceiling. I felt the stones shift. I heard the mortar grinding, and the tower resisted me like a monster holding in its last meal.

Yet I was monster, too.

I arched higher, pushing, pushing. My face was smashed against one wall and my tail against its opposite; I pushed harder, squeezing my eyes closed, holding my breath against the powdery grit of the air.

The ceiling began to come apart. Little fissures at first and then—with a mighty *crack!*—the entire roof exploded, and I was standing up into the night, still arched like a cat, my head free, my tail thrashing away at the walls. Stones began to rain the earth below us, provoking fresh shouts.

My wings opened before I remembered my wound, but I couldn't let it control me now. I'd give in to the pain later. Right now I needed to fly.

I'd been seen, of course. I was difficult to miss. The machine guns were aimed at me once more, and I swiftly flattened, covering Aubrey again.

I twisted my neck around to find him. He was cradled against my belly, staring up at me, eyes wide. But he met my gaze and nodded.

Gently, gently, as gently as I could, I wrapped my front talons around his body. Without lifting him yet from the cot I held him in place and stretched my head upward, peering out over the rim of the wall. I was going to have to do this next part exceptionally quickly.

A few more bullets whizzed by, pocking the stones to my right. It was a mess down there, exactly as chaotic as I'd hoped, with soldiers in all manner of uniforms running in all directions, tackling each other, fighting. The strict order of the camp had disintegrated. I saw bodies motionless on the ground, raggedy men with arms and legs askew. I saw severed loops of barbed wire stabbing the air, figures vanishing into the darkness of the hills.

And, just beneath my tower, standing on one leg near the brambles: a man without a uniform. Without clothing at all. He looked up at me and my own joy pulsed through me (*he's alive, he's here, he's alive!*) and then Armand lowered his head and touched his hand to his mouth, rather like when he'd blown me that kiss as he'd fallen.

But as his hand dropped away, a dab of yellow light followed. A dab of what looked like, I swear, fire.

It landed in the rosebushes, and before I could blink, they were aflame.

He blended with their smoke, moved around the corner, and did the same thing.

More flames. Fire licking the walls, spreading from plant to plant. Billowing thick smoke twisting up at me, obscuring the ground so completely that all I could see now was the patch of stars and sky straight above.

Armand had provided us cover.

I lifted Aubrey, clutching him like a doll to my chest. Then I took off, heading up into the cool blue starlight.

I flapped away from the camp, away from the town, away from all those prisoners snatching back their fortunes and their lives to become part of the Prussian woods. They were far from home, all of them, and as I struggled to leave them behind us my heart echoed the knell of the stars. I thought for all those men, *Go, go, go.*

Go forward and never look back. Find a better fate.

Aubrey dangled from my dragon fists. Armand was smoke at my side. We couldn't continue long like this. It was too hard on Aubrey, and I didn't trust that I wouldn't lose Armand again, and anyway, my wing was killing me.

I found a meadow far from any lights. I set us down in sweet tall grasses. Armand Turned as soon as his brother was on the ground, leaning over him with his broken leg stretched out.

"Hello," said Armand in a happy voice. "You look wretched."

"Have you seen . . . yourself?"

I sat in the grass with my knees tucked under my chin, watching them.

I'd never really been ashamed before about my nudity from the Turns. Discomfited, yes. Ill at ease. But practically the only people who'd ever seen me like this were Jesse and Armand, and somehow, with them, it was almost as if it didn't matter. As if the magic we shared made it nearly normal.

But now there was Aubrey in our mix, and I felt—*aware*. I wished for a dress, and settled for blades of grass.

At least it was still dark. The moon had set; the stars had gathered into different constellations.

Jesse was gone.

"How long have you been able to do that?" I asked, and both of them turned their heads.

I gestured to Armand. "Blow fire like that?"

"Oh." He ruffled a hand through his hair. "When you spotted me? About ten minutes, I'd guess."

"You did . . . what?"

"He blew fire," I explained. "He breathed it, like in fairy tales. It was bloody amazing."

"Well . . ." Mandy looked embarrassed. "I found out by accident. I woke up and you were gone, and I wanted to call for you and knew I couldn't, and it just—it burned in me. Don't know how else to describe it. I felt a burn in my chest, and then my throat, and I meant to cough. But instead . . ."

He began to laugh. I did, too. Right then, in that quiet meadow where everything smelled of grass and smoke and fresh blood, it seemed very, very funny. I laughed so hard I started to cry, so I pushed my face into my knees and let the tears come, dripping down my legs.

Armand limped to sit beside me. I felt his hand stroking my hair. He didn't say anything, just kept stroking.

A bird began to sing far out in the coppices. It sounded like a nightingale. It paused, waiting, until it was answered by another. They caroled like that, back and forth, as piercing and passionate as the emotions careening through me.

Eventually my tears transformed into hiccoughs. My nose was running. My knees were sticky and wet.

"Don't worry," Mandy whispered. "I'm sure you can breathe fire, too."

"Oh, God, I hope not," I said around my hiccoughs. My life was abnormal enough as it was.

I looked up, wiping my nose along my arm.

"Doesn't that hurt? Your leg?"

He glanced down at it with an air of surprise, as if he'd forgotten all about it.

"Er . . . rather."

"I think we should return to the hunting lodge. We can do something about it there. We'll wrap Aubrey in that blanket." It had made the journey with him, caught in my claws. "Both of you ride my back."

"Hunting . . . lodge?" Aubrey asked.

"There are beds there, and clothing. Food in the village close by."

"Sounds like . . . paradise."

I had to agree. It did.

Chapter 32

Three dragons survived this world, not merely two.

It was driven home to me as I helped Aubrey into the bed I had slept in not four nights before, into sheets that were still marked with the mud of Mandy's transformation.

Three of us. Perhaps the last three, so damaged and undone that if you were to combine us all together, we scarcely made up one sound creature. But here we were, back in the early dawn solitude of this cabin in the woods, and as I bent over to stuff the pillow beneath his head, Aubrey's gaze slipped downward—so very briefly—to my bare chest, and my skin began to burn.

That dragon echo in him from before. It was louder now. More difficult to ignore.

I backed away and went to find the trunk of clothing in the other chamber. I discovered Armand already there, lifting up garments. Like me, he was crisscrossed with rose-thorn scratches. Unlike me, the shin of his broken leg was swelling into a gruesome, livid blue.

I took the sweater dangling from his fingers without bothering to examine it. It was large and loose and fell to my thighs.

"You need to get off that leg," I said.

"I know. I will. It's just . . ." He was gazing at the wall, then at me. "We did it, waif. We did."

I smiled. "Cursed near thing, though. And we're not done yet."

"But—"

"But you're right. Bully for us. We did it."

I moved to him, or he moved to me, I wasn't certain. We were in each other's arms, holding tight as the shadows shifted into violet and the morning's first rays lit pearl through the foggy green forest. It was going to be a fair day somewhere, perhaps even here. Yet I longed for the fog to linger, for the mist shrouding the lake to roll closer and erase us from the sun. I wasn't ready for daylight.

I lowered my head and let my hair cover my face. I ached for sleep and for poise and for the bandaged and broken man in the other room. For Armand and his leg, and the soldiers we'd left dead on the ground behind us. I knew I wasn't going to be able to wipe them from my conscience anytime soon.

I also knew I was at the edge of my limits, because everything had taken on a flickery, unreal cast. Even the heat of Armand's body felt like something I'd dreamed. If I lifted my head, I wouldn't be in the hunting lodge. I'd be in my dormitory at Blisshaven. My cell at Moor Gate. I was a gifted dreamer and had conjured a daydream beyond all others, but in the end I'd wake and still be a nameless girl trapped behind locked doors. Ordinary and alone.

"Eleanore."

I looked up. Armand was still there. All of it was.

"Go to sleep," he said kindly. "Take this bed in here. I'll bunk with Aubrey."

"Someone should . . . someone needs to keep watch."

"Yes. I will."

I glanced at the bed, a bare mattress bumped against a head-board, a heap of blankets at its foot.

"Go on," he said, and gave me a gentle push.

"Wake me when you need to rest," I said, dropping to the mat-tress, dragging the blankets over me.

"Right."

"Don't . . ." My thoughts were drifting into soft, muddled clouds.

"Don't what?" he murmured.

"Don't burn the place down."

My eyes were closed; the clouds had won. But I thought I heard him laugh a little.

"I'll hold my breath," Mandy said.

I *was* a dreamer, though. So, even though I fell into those clouds, I dreamed I heard Armand and Aubrey talking. Armand's voice low and soothing. Aubrey's weak at first, growing stronger and stronger.

" . . . landed in a field. Engine on fire. Nothing . . . I could do. Crawled out. Hid in a . . . ditch. Three days. Farmer turned me in. Didn't blame him. Children . . . needed to eat."

"Reginald took it hard. Very hard. You should know that he's changed."

"Heard. Asylum."

"That's not the half of it."

"The . . . girl."

"Yes, her. And us. You and me, too, mate. All three of us the same."

"Bespelled . . . by stars."

Silence for a while; I nearly floated away. Then Mandy spoke again. "You never thought—it might not be real? That you were going mad?"

Aubrey chuckled. "She asked . . . the same thing."

"She has good reason. It's been hardest on her, I think. She was the first, and she was alone."

"She's . . . "

Mandy and I both waited.

"Miraculous," Aubrey said.

"You've no notion."

"But I will, Mandy. Swear to you I will."

I stole food from the village, a loaf of bread here, a mutton pie there. Small things from different houses, so we'd not be easily tracked.

I took the sword from the hearth and hacked free two fine straight branches from a pine, and made a brace for Armand's leg.

I stood as a dragon by the lake at night and mourned without words the gaping tear in my wing. It could have used some stitches, but I'd have to stay in this shape too long for it to mend. So I would endure it.

There were, after all, many others enduring much worse.

On our second morning there, I sat with Armand and Aubrey upon the big bed, offering hunks of bread and cheese as Armand smoothed out the newspaper I'd used to wrap it all in for my hike back to the lodge.

There I was again, right on the front page. I looked even more fiendish than the last drawing. This time I'd been given horns.

"Stylish," I decided, analyzing the illustration. "Elegant but deadly. Perhaps I'll grow some for real."

"Perfect as you are," Aubrey assured me.

"Even better than perfect." Armand had to top him.

I eyed them both. I'd been hoping, now that the flickering had stopped and the sun had firmly shoved its way inside the cabin, that Aubrey's condition wouldn't look so dire, that Armand's leg wouldn't be a true break but a sprain or a very bad bruise. But there was no denying that the situation was quite as critical as I'd feared. Aubrey was propped against the pillows; he was sitting up on his own, but that was about all he could do. Armand rested beside him, his bad leg stretched atop the covers, because otherwise the bark from my brace flaked off into the sheets. His toes were turning puce.

"I've been thinking," I said. "Trying to work matters through. Obviously we need to leave here as soon as we can. Tonight. I believe if we start early enough I can get us across the Channel from here in one stretch, but we should consider what's going to happen after that. We can land in Dover, and Mandy can say he's been in an accident or something. But Aubrey, you're inexplicable. You're a peer. It's been widely reported in the papers that you've been captured. You'll have to have either a new name or a new face or a damned credible reason for being in England instead of a German prison camp, and I swear I can't think of a single one."

"No, I can't go . . . to England. I'm no . . . deserter. France. Get me there. I'll get myself home."

My gaze fell to his hands, the blackened nails, the fingers and knuckles scabbed over so severely there wasn't any skin left. *Good hands,* he'd told me, but I'd seen enough burns at Tranquility to know he'd likely never open his fingers again.

Tears pricked behind my lids, which irritated me. Neither of *them* was acting overly emotional, and they frankly looked as if they might breathe their last at any moment. I had to be stronger than they.

"Where in France?" I asked.

"Casualty clearing station. Army. They'll take me in."

I pressed, reluctant, "But I think I'm supposed to get you home."

"Eleanore. You already have."

I looked up, took in his ravaged face, the tender smile. The tears pricked hotter.

"Thank you," he said. "Thank you, miracle Eleanore."

"What is it with you two?" I snarled. "Don't thank me until it's all done."

I got up and stalked to the window. The lake outside gleamed green and slate, smooth as a looking glass, unbroken as far as I could see. The forest surrounding it seemed a lot less like the safe haven I'd first thought it. More full of holes.

"You'd better live," I said without turning around. "Both of you."

"I shall," answered Aubrey.

"To my dying day," topped Armand.

Boys.

Chapter 33

A casualty clearing station was like a field hospital near the front. Which meant, logically, having to venture near the front. I promise you, it's even more harrowing than it sounds. I attempted to keep us high enough to avoid the gunfire, the terrible strands of poisonous gas that slithered along the ground and ate like acid into everything they touched. Chlorine gas, phosgene. I'd seen firsthand what harm chemicals and sinister minds could do, and none of us had masks.

Trenches were laid out below us very much as they'd been on the maps, long, winding lines scarring the earth, hiding desperate men. Protecting them from the mortars that arced white and yellow fire above their heads. Smothering them with dirt and desolation.

I was glad that I knew no one down there. Glad that the only two beings I cared about were being carried safely over this crisis, at least.

As safe as I could make it, that is. The sickle moon had finally waned from the sky, and this would be the night the airships took flight. I kept a wary eye out but didn't see any. Perhaps they were already across the Channel.

Stars of the heavens, who own my time: guide us safely only just a bit farther.

a bit farther, a bit, they sang in reply.

We were renegade magic, temporarily liberated from gravity and bloodshed. We were stars falling to the earth, to the shelled remains of a French village. To a pasture with very little cover because the grass was stunted and all the trees had burned away.

To a cathedral that had been converted into a hospital for damaged men.

I left Aubrey and Armand behind in the grass. I smoked into the nurses' tent, where there were women sleeping fitfully and uniforms lay folded at the base of their cots, begging to be borrowed.

Then I ran outside to find a doctor and pulled him from his breakfast, protesting all the way, to my men.

That was how my rescue of Aubrey ended. Where my part in it ended, in any case. He was taken in, absorbed by the frantic yet diligent inner workings of the hospital, and I lingered long enough to see that he was cleaned and rebandaged and given back his name and rank.

Yes, he'd been shot down and captured last spring.

No, he'd never been taken so far as East Prussia. That must have been an error in the paperwork.

He'd been taken to Belgium instead. He'd been lucky enough to escape during transport, and subsequently hidden by a sympathetic farmer's widow who had tended to him as best she could.

And, yes, somehow he'd made it back here to France after that.

And even though it was perfectly clear that he was in no shape to have traveled any distance on his own, the Marquess of Sherborne's story was scribbled down and accepted because by then it was two hours past daybreak, and the next batch of wounded men was already crowding the cathedral floors, ready to take his place.

Armand had his leg set and cast. He hadn't been too pleased about it, but had resigned himself to the fact that I wasn't going to carry him back to England unless it was done. He had become Lieutenant Laurence Clayworth, injured in action. Had I been in his position, I would have made more of an ado. After all, the actual Laurence Clayworth was a selfish blighter, and I had no doubt he'd be whining for drugs and attention the instant a pretty nurse hurried by. *This* Lieutenant Clayworth refused the shot of heroin the nurse attempted to give him. He only glued his eyes on me and clenched his teeth and broke into a white, cold sweat as the bones of his leg were pulled and stretched and snapped back into place.

He did not cry out. He did not faint.

I fared worse than he did. I held his hand and knew it'd be a mistake to look back, but I did it anyway, and then I had to plunk down to the floor and put my head between my knees.

Armand's hand released mine to pat me on the head.

"Sorry case of nerves, that," I heard one of the real nurses mutter. "How'd she get in?"

"Now, now," muttered back her companion. "Some of us are more durable than others."

I could not agree more.

We said our farewells to Aubrey that evening. I was relieved to see that he, at least, had accepted his measure of heroin. His eyes were huge and dark in his face. But his smile was just as tender as ever.

"See you soon, old man," murmured Armand, on crutches at my side.

"Soon enough," his brother replied.

"By the by, did I mention I turned Tranquility into a convalescent hospital?"

That seemed to rouse Aubrey some. "Did you? I say, don't send me there. Loathe that place."

"Sorry. I plan to shamelessly exploit Reginald's connections as soon as I get back."

"Bollocks." Those dark gray eyes shifted to find mine. "Will you be there?"

"I'll be at school. At Iverson. I hope," I added.

He gave a nod, relaxing back. "That's something, then."

Mandy touched a hand to his shoulder. "See you soon," he said again.

"Right."

I leaned down and brushed my lips to Aubrey's cheek. "Goodbye."

His face angled toward mine; he returned my kiss. "Soon."

Armand seemed to stop breathing. As we moved off, he stared down at the limestone pavers of the floor, scrupulously following the front-back-front swing of his crutches.

After that, flying back to England seemed very nearly easy. We crossed the Channel with the aid of a checkered layer of clouds, and it was curious now, but I didn't really need Armand or the stars pointing me the way. I could feel England calling me, pulling at me. Tugging at my heartstrings, drawing me onward.

Toward my home.

We landed on the beach at Bournemouth a scant twenty minutes before first light. I was able to let him down and Turn to smoke in time to flow back to our hotel. I found our room exactly as we'd left it. Even the unfinished champagne was still in its bottle on the table.

I dressed. Then, as furtively as possible, I slipped out of the suite and back to the beach.

The sky to the east had become streaked with cherry. To the west, the first of the fishing boats were departing for the day, heading out into the blue with bells clanging.

A constable was patrolling the boardwalk with rhythmic, deliberate footfalls. At the very end of the pier a man and two little boys were casting their lines, hoping for fresh fish to begin their day.

Armand and I made our way to the entrance of the Sea Vista, only to encounter the innkeeper right as we cracked opened the front door.

His eyes widened, taking us in.

"Why, Mr. Pendragon! Mrs. Pendragon! Look at you! Whatever has happened?"

I exchanged a glance with Mandy, impaired by his cast, marked by roses, and remembered all my own scratches.

À la Chloe, I gave a trilling laugh. "Oh, dear. I'm afraid there was something of a disagreement between our auto and an unfortunate tree by the road. But it's nothing too awful. His leg's in something of a fix, but Mr. Pendragon and I will be fine."

"I should not have allowed you to drive," Armand said. "Next time I'll not be so pleasantly persuaded."

I directed my smile at him, fierce and glittering. "At least we came out at the better end of things this time! Not at all like the time you demolished that hansom cab, was it, my darling?"

"Tsk!" said the innkeeper, still staring at us, back and forth. "Modern days! I've always said these motorcars are treacherous devices. I've always said!"

I softened my smile. "I wonder if you wouldn't mind sending up some food for us?"

He brightened; breakfast was plainly more acceptable than modern days. "Certainly! What would you like? The wife's beefsteak and eggs is always lovely, if I do say so, but the eldest went out yesterday and came back to us with a tidy haul of oysters and crabs that we thought—"

"Yes, that, all of that."

"Er—pardon?"

"All of it," I said.

"Ah," said the innkeeper, even wider-eyed than before.

"Everything you've got." Armand swung past him with the crutches, front-back-front. "It's been an arduous trip from there to here, my good sir, and we're really quite famished."

And we ate it all, too. Beefsteak and eggs, fried oysters with red sauce, omelets stuffed with crab. We ate until we were both sated and heavy-eyed, and the sound of the surf beyond our balcony rolled over us like a lullaby.

Children shrieked and laughed, playing in the sand. Out on the boardwalk people tottered about in heels and hats and talked about the weather and listened to an organ grinder playing song after song for copper pennies.

I stood upon the balcony and shielded my eyes from the sun with one hand, letting the sea breeze push cool and welcome through my hair.

"Wife," said Armand from behind me, very quiet. "Will you come to sleep with me?"

I turned around. He was resting atop the covers, propped up by pillows with his broken leg out, just as he'd been at the hunting lodge, except now with a proper cast. The wallpaper behind him nearly made me smile: giant pink and lavender lilacs entwined with pale green vines. He was dark and scruffy against it, a pirate again, stranded in a room of pastel blossoms.

Since we'd been sleeping in each other's arms for days now, I knew he wasn't truly asking about sleep.

"Yes," I said. "After."

"After what?"

"There's one last thing I must do. I'm going to see your father."

His hands clenched. "I'll come with you."

"And undo all that good work on your leg by Turning to smoke? I think not." I abandoned the balcony and its uncluttered sky, plunging back into the shadows with him. "Besides, I imagine one *drákon* materializing in the middle of an insane asylum will be plenty. Let's ease him into the story of you, shall we?"

He was silent, studying me. I could practically feel him weighing my words, his options. How much of a fuss I was going to make.

"I'll be back soon," I promised.

"Then I'll be waiting." He watched me with those blue, blue eyes. "Fireheart. I'll always wait."

Chapter 34

Mental asylums are solid places. Everything locked up all right and tight, all the time. But the architects and doctors, the burly guards with batons, were thinking only of the delusional. The shackled. The helpless.

They never anticipated *me*.

The duke had iron bars on his windows (which probably didn't open anyway) but also his very own fireplace. Which meant a chimney.

I emerged as smoke in his cell. His Grace was seated in the same chair before the hearth as he'd been the first time I'd visited him. He was staring blankly into the distance, perhaps to a place that did not have barred windows and locked doors and the scent of human misery lingering beneath that of bleach.

A cup of tea had gone cold on a table, next to an ashtray overflowing with crumpled cigarettes. A pair of electric lamps burned upon the writing desk, tiny dots of heat. There was no crackling fire to warm him today.

I took my shape behind the wing chair facing his, my fingers curled atop its back.

"Reginald," I said.

"Rose?" His eyes regained their focus, surrendering whatever private realm had held him.

"No." My lips curved. "Eleanore."

"This isn't a dream, is it?"

"It is, if that's what you wish."

"No." His face hardened. "I've done enough dreaming, I think. Is he safe?"

"He is alive."

"I know that!"

"He is no longer a prisoner. He's in France now, being cared for. He'll be home again."

"Tranquility," he whispered.

"Yes."

The duke became old and small in his chair. "Good," he sighed, gazing at his lap. "Good."

Past his door sounded footsteps, masculine voices too hushed to make out. Beyond all that was a woman crying, the heartbroken sobs of the forgotten, muffled and endless, as if she'd never draw steady breath again.

"Perhaps you might renew my scholarship to Iverson, Your Grace."

"What's that? Oh." He looked back up at me, puzzled but calm. "Is that your price?"

"My price? No. Merely a request."

"You desire to be a schoolgirl again? A beast such as yourself, bound to classroom schedules and lectures about etiquette?"

I dug my toes into the rug beneath me, all the way down to the nubby base.

"Yes," I said.

"Very well. I shall inform Irene you're to be readmitted for the fall."

I smiled again, performing a mock curtsy behind the chair. The duke did not return my smile.

"One last thing, Your Grace. If you *do* dream again—if you share dreams with that boy in the stars again, tell him this. I'm ready any time he is for the bargain to be concluded. I'm ready to hold up my end of the pact."

"As you say," he agreed, unruffled.

I nodded, he nodded, and I left.

Chapter 35

The next four nights were amethyst, but I resisted them. I would not go outside to bathe in purple light; I would not listen to the stars. Despite what I'd told Armand, we were only sleeping in the bed at the inn, sleeping with the balcony doors open and the surf and the gulls and the salty breeze that flitted in and out of the suite like a suitor who could not make up his mind. And it was all that I required.

Armand would need to travel to London soon. I would need to return to Tranquility, and then to Iverson.

Yet neither of us spoke of what we needed to do, allowing instead the mild lazy hours to waft by.

During the day, I counted out the planks of the boardwalk. I walked to the end of the pier and back, and gave the organ grinder pounds instead of pennies, and carried seashells and toffees to Mandy, who was gradually looking less like a pirate and more like a nobleman, albeit one itching to shed his cast.

It was quite a honeymoon. At least, that's what the innkeeper thought.

"Mrs. Pendragon! How about some nice scallops for tonight, eh? Or fresh clams in chowder, or lemon sole. We've got—"

"All of it," I'd say.

"Righto." He winked at me, merry as a child at Christmas.

We were rather dear guests, I presumed.

But on the fifth evening the feeling of dreamy suspension I'd nurtured so carefully would not come. I could not ignore the summoning of the stars any longer. I could not ignore the color of the heavens suspended over the sea, that dark purple velvet dotted with fire, the deepest night beckoning.

We'd spent the afternoon on the sand, getting crusty and sunburned, watching the white lip of the tide rolling and reaching and retreating once more. We'd brushed the sand from our clothes and eaten our dinner and sipped our wine. I'd cleared the dishes and gone out to the balcony and at last given in, breathing in deep, allowing the stars to garland me with songs once more.

fireheart! fireheart! fireheart! Beneath the drumbeat of the surf, it was all I could hear.

Then, a counterpoint:

lora. low and lovely, sad and far.

I swallowed, searching until I found him, golden green, more beautiful than the moon.

Jesse.

miss you.

I couldn't think of a reply. I could only smile and close my eyes so I wouldn't cry.

above you, inside you, within and without, he sang. *forever and always. remember?*

Yes.

*so we can wait. we can wait awhile longer. love the earth while you
can. love this last gift of time. love the dragon i've given you, who already
loves you.*

I did not need to see him to know that Armand had come to
stand beside me on the balcony, leaning against the railing. But I
opened my eyes anyway. He was watching me, somber, purple in
his hair. The wind slipped between us, separating, then shifted and
pushed the other way.

Jesse had become a nimbus, a shadow of light behind him.

"Thank you," Mandy said to me. "It's all right to say it now, isn't
it? Now that it's over?"

I nodded. There were too many words crowding inside me to
speak, words like *I suppose so* and *You're welcome* and *Don't stand so
near* and *Please come nearer.*

"Thank you," he said again. "Thank you, Eleanore, for saving
me."

He bent his head, slowly, slowly, never taking his eyes from
mine. So when our lips met I was ready and not, because his kiss
was more fiery than I'd thought it'd be, and sweeter, and spread like
a wild and unknown fever right into my blood. I was alight.

He tasted of wine and magic. He tasted of hope.

I lifted my arms and wound them around his neck. We were
pressed together at the rim of the world, water and sand, enchant-
ment and flesh. Two beings fleetingly, lusciously exploring how it
felt to become one.

Beneath the silver netting of the stars, I reveled in Armand's
kiss, and offered it back to him.

Epilogue

Who would hold a dragon in his hand?

Who would hold back love?

I, it seems, cannot do either. It's just as well.

My love is a tether, but I never wanted it to be a bridle. She lives on borrowed time, and because I love her, because I did not lie when I told her forever and always, my sorrow is tempered by her joy. I want her still for my own, but he can give her now what I cannot, so I wish them both well.

I'm trying to.

I slide along the indigo vault of the ether. I sing with my brothers and sisters, peering into universes unseen. I descend into dreams, but I'm pale to them now, a memory, yet one that will never fully fade.

When I can, I tie knots in her path. I mean them to strengthen her, to better knit the thread of her destiny into something thicker and more sound than what has come before.

Because in the end, she's still a girl. My dragon-girl. And soon another dragon will step across the open threshold of her life, and

Lora-of-the-moon will have to look upon the face of her past without flinching.

It won't be easy. Not for any of them.

I am the shooting star that lights their way.

I am the answer to the questions they have not yet asked.

I am patient.

I blaze above them, ready to be needed.

Acknowledgments

No matter how sweetly flowing the idea, a book takes hard work and a team of clever people willing to help and inspire. I owe so much to Shauna Summers, Annelise Robey, Andrea Cirillo, Ania Markiewicz, Sonya Safro, Sarah Christensen Fu, and Sarah Murphy—really, everyone at Jane Rotrosen and everyone at Bantam/Ballantine/Random House, because the series would not have happened without them. Thank you forever.

Many hours of creative musing were aided by N.R., Monsieur Le Roi, B. Tigress, Gracelope, Hippy, Happy, and Pahroo (and all those before, and all those to come).

Thank you to my fans! I love you, too.

And, finally, *mahalo* to Sean, who bought me a ukulele because I said out loud I thought it'd be fun to play. (It is.)

About the Author

SHANA ABÉ is the bestselling author of fourteen novels, including the acclaimed Drákon Series and The Sweetest Dark Series. She lives in Colorado in a happy home with a good many pets.

www.shanaabe.com

About the Type

This book was set in Stone, a typeface designed by the teacher, lecturer, and author Sumner Stone in 1988. This typeface was designed to satisfy the requirements of low-resolution laser printing. Its traditional design blends harmoniously with many typefaces, making it appropriate for a variety of applications.